Bog Child
SIOBHAN DOWD

David Fickling Books

OXFORD · NEW YORK

31 Beaumont Street
Oxford OX1 2NP, UK

BOG CHILD
A DAVID FICKLING BOOK 978 1 849 92042 1

First published in Great Britain by David Fickling Books,
a division of Random House Children's Publishers UK
A Random House Group Company

Hardback edition published 2008
Definitions edition published 2009
This edition published 2010

5 7 9 10 8 6

Set in New Baskerville

DAVID FICKLING BOOKS
31 Beaumont Street, Oxford, OX1 2NP

www.randomhousechildrens.co.uk
www.randomhouse.co.uk

Addresses for companies within The Random House Group Limited can be found at:
www.randomhouse.co.uk/offices.htm

THE RANDOM HOUSE GROUP Limited Reg. No. 954009

A CIP catalogue record for this book is available from the British Library.

The Random House Group Limited supports The Forest Stewardship
Council® (FSC®), the leading international forest-certification organisation.
Our books carrying the FSC label are printed on FSC®-certified paper.
FSC is the only forest-certification scheme supported by the leading
environmental organisations, including Greenpeace. Our
paper procurement policy can be found at
www.randomhouse.co.uk/environment

MIX
Paper from
responsible sources
FSC® C016897

Printed and bound in Great Britain by Clays Ltd, St Ives plc

Praise for *Bog Child*

'A harrowing story of choice and obligation, peace and politics'
Independent

'Dowd's lightness of touch allows humour and poignancy to shine through'
Telegraph

'Telling two tales of sacrifice for peace, and offering an insight into Irish history, this book is sometimes funny, despite the seriousness of its subject. It is also psychologically and historically convincing, showing the impact of politics on domestic life. The work of an outstanding writer'
Sunday Times

'A captivating first love affair, a hilarious red herring and profound truths about politics and family add up to a novel set to win awards'
Observer

'Despite its heavy themes it's a book brimming with passion, humour and hope'
Scotsman

'One of the joys of this book is its willingness to confront big themes . . . *Bog Child* explores political conflict, personal heroism, human frailty, love, and death. As a writer, Dowd appears to be incapable of a jarring phrase or a lazy metaphor. Her sentences sing, each note resonates with an urgent humanity of the sort that cannot be faked. *Bog Child* sparkles with optimism and a deep passion for living. Love falls from it in particles, like snow'
MEG ROSOFF, *Guardian*

'An unflinchingly honest and brave novel . . . this important, challenging and powerful book will grip any mature teenage or adult reader'
Irish Independent

'The story grips you straight away, and it is beautifully told,
with lots of humour and sensitivity'
Sunday Express

'*Bog Child* is a beautiful novel offering
a unique insight into Irish history'
Irish Post

'Fergus is an appealing hero, and the entwined secrecy of borders,
soldiers, volunteers, smugglers, and families are interestingly used'
Dublin Evening Herald

'How to find peace? What sacrifices are justified? Will we ever
learn the lessons of the past? Dowd explores all these questions and
more, in words of lyricism and beauty, balancing the harshness and
the tough realities with a little magic realism. It's a perfect blend'
JILL MURPHY, *The Book Bag*

'With plenty of humour, surprising twists and almost audible dialogue,
Dowd juggles expertly and sensitively with this compelling, entertaining
book, which is a recommended read for teenage and adult readers'
Irish Examiner

'Dowd creates a complex world of death, morality, fear,
the longing for a united republic, for freedom'
Oxford Times

'Siobhan Dowd's *Bog Child* is an astonishing read
and the kind of book that holds you in a trance'
The Bookseller

'*Bog Child* is a beautiful novel'
www.chicklish.co.uk

www.davidficklingbooks.co.uk

For my three sisters,
Oona, Denise, Enda –
my love as ever.

The bog lay in the bright, slanting morning light, the dew-drops sparkling like millions of diamonds. A large crowd of the local inhabitants had already gathered . . . They were tightly grouped in a ring around a dark-coloured human head, with a tuft of short-cropped hair, which stuck up clear of the dark brown peat. Part of the neck and shoulders was also exposed. We were clearly face to face once again with one of the bog people.

P. V. Glob, *The Bog People*

*Ireland, near the north-south border
1981*

Part I
FIRST LIGHT

One

They'd stolen a march on the day. The sky was like dark glass, reluctant to let the light through. The only sound was the chudder of the van skirting the lough. The surface of the water was colourless. The hills slumped down on the far side like silhouettes of snoozing giants.

Fergus yawned. It was still before five as they turned off up the mountain road. Uncle Tally chewed on nothing as the tyres lumbered over the ruts. Fergus cradled the flask of sweet black tea. There'd been no milk in the fridge that morning.

'Too early for you, huh?' mocked Uncle Tally, changing gear.

'Too right,' said Fergus. 'When I go running, it's not dark like this.' His throat was furred up. The words came out stretched by a yawn. 'It's unnatural being up before the birds.'

They approached the border checkpoint and the van slowed. The soldier by the hut stood with a rifle but did not move. He was young-looking and pale, with freckles. He waved them on, tipping the butt of the gun, and they drove past without having to stop. Uncle Tally laughed. 'I could have a truckload of Semtex for all that wee squaddie cares,' he said.

Fergus grunted. 'Yeah,' he said. 'Deus would be delighted.'

Deus, Latin for 'God', was the local nickname for a rumoured bomb-maker, said to be active thereabouts.

'So he would.'

'Only you'd be going in the wrong direction. We're *leaving* the Troubles, Unk, not joining them.'

Uncle Tally thumped the wheel. 'So we are. We're in the free state now. Free as a bloody bog-frog.' They both laughed like clowns. Going over the border always had that effect. Without your knowing it, your jaw-bone would stiffen and adrenalin pump through your veins as the checkpoint approached. Then, when you were through, hilarity would erupt at the relief.

The van turned up onto a steep road with grass growing up the middle. The gorse got yellower as they climbed, the sky brighter. 'The border. Even a nun would be nervous crossing it,' suggested Fergus.

'And we'll be crossing back over it at the top.'

'Will we?'

'If you look at the map. You can see.'

Fergus opened the map and saw the dotted grey line, almost invisible, meandering across Ireland's north, but leaving a thin tract of land to the west that was Donegal. '*The most northern bit of Ireland's in the south,*' he quoted.

'One day, one day . . .' Uncle Tally muttered like a mantra.

'One day what?'

'One day the only border will be the sea and the only thing guarding it the dunes and the only people living in it Republicans. One day, Fergus.'

'Where will the Unionists go, so?'

'They'll be beamed to outer space, warp factor five.' Uncle Tally drove round a loop of road, heading back to where the light was growing on the horizon. 'Lucky them. Now, here's the spot to park, Fergus. Get cracking. The JCB crew will be down on us before you know.' He pulled up and they got out the shovels and bags from the back and walked over a track for a hundred yards. On either side, brown grass sprouted out of black, wet earth, and bright green weeds spread like mildew over the soggier areas. The first skylark of the day darted from cover. Fergus approached the JCB, which was still, abandoned. Earth was churned up all around it, the leftover diggings from the day before. But 'earth' was the wrong word. It was turf, rich foaming peat, made from the things that had lived here in millennia gone by and pressed by time into a magic frieze of the past. You could dig up wood from primeval forests, find resin with insects of another age frozen in it. And what you dug up you could burn as fuel.

And, as his da said, there was nothing like the smell of the turf on a hearth to bring comfort in a dark world.

A pink tint grew on the horizon as they dug and

filled the bags with uncut clumps. Dawn intensified. The sky was clear and close up here, the mind uncluttered. Uncle Tally grunted as he shovelled, his taut, fit frame enjoying the work. Fergus held the bags open for him and then they swapped over. They'd sell the bags for ninety pence and Fergus was promised a cut of thirty per cent. But the JCB crew would be arriving soon and they'd have to be well gone by then.

A cry made Fergus swivel round. It was only a wild kid with a creamy coat, bleating at its mother fifty yards away or more.

'Get the flask, Fergus,' Uncle Tally said. 'I'm parched. I'd a skinful last night.'

'Did you?'

'Yes. Your da and Pad McGuire. They came down to Finicule's for one. And you know how it is.'

'Were you singing, Unk?'

'We were so far gone we were singing *Three Blind Mice*. I ask you. And your da couldn't get beyond *See how they run*. And it was only ten o'clock.'

'I don't believe you.'

'OK. Maybe not *quite* so wild.'

Fergus went to the van and found the flask of tea. He brought it over and they strolled down to an outcrop of rock and shared a capful. The rim of the sun came over the mountain. A wind picked up.

'Christ, it's quiet up here,' said Uncle Tally.

'It'd be a strange place to live.'

'You'd have to be a hermit.'

'There'd be nothing to do but pray,' said Fergus.

'Aye. You'd have plenary indulgences made for

every last sinner by the time you died yourself. And then you'd be whisked up straight to heaven.'

'You should move up here.'

'I would too. Only it's a bit far.'

'Far from where?'

'The nearest bar.'

'You could make your own distillery, Unk.'

'But what would you distil?'

'The prayers. What else?'

Uncle Tally clipped his ear. 'You're too sharp, Fergus McCann. Pass me the flask.'

After tea, they filled another ten bags. When there was no loosened turf left, Uncle Tally left the shovel prodded into the earth and they began to load the bags into the van.

'Not a bad haul.'

Fergus wandered off to the other side of the JCB. He watched the skyline and listened to morning getting under way. There was a hum of insects now, small movements of birds and, far off from the floor of the valley, the sound of the odd truck. The sun was up, white and smooth behind a whisper of cloud. The track led back to the road, and the road truncated the bog-land and headed straight to the horizon. Up here was borderland too. He was looking back into the North, but behind him was the Republic.

'Ferg, shake a leg,' called Uncle Tally.

'Will we do another few bags?'

'What time is it?'

Fergus looked at the watch he was minding for his older brother, Joe. 'Not seven yet.'

'OK. But we've to make a fresh cut of it.'

A shovel apiece, they scrambled into the cut the JCB had made last thing the day before.

'You work that end, I'll work this. You've to ram the sharp side in straight and up in a line.' Uncle Tally showed him how. 'Then down along.'

'Like a grid?'

'That's it. Once you've the first line out, it's easier.'

It was slower going than working with the JCB's leavings. But the smell of the fresh peat was clean and the springy consistency strangely satisfying to cut into.

Fergus finished a good-sized grid and worked down along the cut, away from his uncle.

'Hiyack!' he shouted as he brought the shovel hard down at a fresh angle. One inch from the wall of brown turf, he froze. A foreign colour stopped him, a dull, tawny glint. He let the shovel topple at his side and his eyes blinked. Then he stretched out a hand to touch the surface. Maybe it was a trick of the light. Or a stone. Or—

Whatever it was was hard.

He spat on his forefinger and wiped it. It gleamed a little, like a smile.

A coin's edge. That was it.

Excited, he spat on his fingertips and rubbed it again.

No. It was bigger. A coil of metal, fashioned like a plait, chased itself round.

And as he stared, fingers, four of them, appeared below it. They were brown and lined and tiny. The skin on them was too big for the bones, drooping

8

slightly. They reminded him of his mother's, when she wore the extra-large Marigold rubber gloves.

They were beautiful, poised like a pianist's getting ready to play, but only half the size of his own.

'Jesus.'

Uncle Tally, hard at work down his end of the cut, didn't hear.

'Unk. Jesus, Unk. Come here.'

'What?'

'There's something here. In the earth. A hand.'

'What d'you mean *a hand*?'

'A tiny hand. And a bangle on it. And some cloth stuff.'

Uncle Tally hee-hawed. 'Hey, Ferg. It's June. Not the first of bloody April.'

But he came and looked where Fergus pointed.

They stood in silence, staring at the wall of turf.

'Shit,' said Uncle Tally.

It was like a mural.

The legs were missing.

The side of a twisted torso covered in brown-stained cloth was visible above the hand. The shoulders, neck and head disappeared into the earth behind.

'It's a body,' said Uncle Tally.

'Dead right it's a body,' said Fergus.

'You could say dead again.'

'Is it the Provos, Unk?'

'The Provos?'

'Is it somebody they killed?'

'Why would they bother burying a child like that?'

9

Fergus realized. Of course. The tiny hand: the body of a child. 'Maybe it was an execution. A child of a traitor. Somebody who'd done the Cause a bad turn.'

'Nah. That's not the Provos' style.' Uncle Tally put his shovel so it matched up against the torso's length.

'It's a girl, Unk,' Fergus gasped. 'A poor wee girl. Look at the bangle and the dress on her.'

'Mother of mercy. Let's get out of here.'

'But Unk—'

'Look, she's dead, right?'

'I know she's dead, but—'

'Yeah. And probably murdered, right?'

'Murdered?'

'So if we report it, we're done for the turf-cutting.'

'But, Unk, if the JCB crew arrive, they'll just cut her up. Into ribbons. It's a miracle they stopped when they did. And that I saw her.'

'Fergus, nobody's going to bring that child back to life.'

A clod of earth fell from the cut as he said that and an elbow appeared, small and leathered.

'Jesus Mary.'

'Oh, Unk. Please.'

'What d'you want me to do, Fergus?'

'Dunno.'

They stood still in the cut. The kid bleated from far away like it was lost. Fergus felt a tear forming. Furious, he bit his lip.

'It's a girl like our Theresa or Cath, Unk. We can't just leave her to get mashed up by the JCB. It's easy to

10

miss her. She's gone all brown with being in the bog.'

Uncle Tally sighed. 'We're in the Republic, I suppose. It'd be the Gardai I'd tell. Not the RUC.' He picked up Fergus's shovel. 'I'm heading away back along the road and over to Inchquin. If the JCB comes, you were up here bird-watching.'

'Bird-watching?'

'And you made a covert of the cut and just happened to spot this. Got it?'

'Yes, Unk.'

'I'm away to get the guards.'

'OK.'

They loaded the shovels and last two bags of peat into the back of the van. Uncle Tally got in and wound down the window.

'And Fergus?' he said.

'What?'

'Don't touch her. Don't try to dig her out any more.'

'Why not?'

'Fingerprints. They'll think you're the murderer, stupid.'

'Ha-ha.'

'I'm serious.'

'OK, Unk.'

'And take this.'

'What?'

Uncle Tally rooted in the glove compartment and handed Fergus some binoculars. 'Bird-watching. Right?'

'Right.'

'Stay away from that body.'

The van drove away. Fergus went back to the cut and waited above it, trying out the views through the binoculars. Half the time he stared at the magnified brown body in the bog. He could see lines on the finger-pads, as if the small girl had been alive yesterday. They looped and spooled like rivers. Some property of the bog had accentuated them. Then he noticed a grey-white bone, sticking out a fraction. It was where the JCB had cut through her lower leg. His stomach somersaulted. He whisked round and examined the view of the plain below, a great swath of County Fermanagh. But however hard he peered, he could have sworn the child behind him was staring into his back, her eyes needling his shoulder blades. He shrugged and pinched himself and looked through the binoculars to the far horizon. From up here, on the peaceful mountain, it was hard to believe that such unquiet existed amongst the people living on the plain below. Curls of smoke, swaying trees, cars flashing blue and red along the tarmac roads, all moved in silence. A sparrowhawk glided across his field of vision, swimming on a current of air, wavering. Then it swooped to earth and vanished from view. He crawled forward on the springy earth and lay flat on his stomach, spying down on the world. Behind him, the grass sighed with the sound of waiting.

Two

Mam combed my hair every night and said how fine and tidy I was. So I grew, bit by bit like the stone icicles in the caves. She gave me jobs. I ground the grains up for the bread like she showed me and I swept the floor of the house almost as soon as I could walk. Dust from the day before flew out the east door every morning, and the dead in the shadows at the back curve of the house breathed again. In the afternoon, I gathered the berries and the kindling and other things from outdoors, and that was my share in the work, and as well I minded the baby who slept in the knotted shawl, tied over my back. She went where I went.

One winter day, I remember Da looking on as I swept around his chair. He laughed and trapped the broom between his feet and patted my head. He called me the child time forgot. And the joke stuck.

The voice in the dream stopped short. Fergus started awake, with the ground trembling beneath him. He must have nodded off. The binoculars had fallen to one side and the sun had climbed higher. He was flat on his belly in the bracken by the cut. He looked

13

around and saw the JCB men, arrived already. The ground-shudders were from the machine. *Kata-thurra-thurra-kat.*

They hadn't noticed him. The orange vehicle was reversing and the cutter section rose to full height, with its sharp edge poised as if to attack.

'Stop,' Fergus shrieked, springing up. 'Stop!'

The man in the machine didn't hear, but another man walking towards the cut jerked his head round and stared at Fergus.

'Stop! *Please.*'

The second man made an arm signal, as if to say, *You're for the chop,* and the JCB cut out. In the distance came the wail of a siren.

Fergus moved forward so that the man in the JCB could see him.

'Stop,' he called again. His voice carried around the bog-land. 'There's a body in there. My uncle's gone to get the police. That's them now.'

'The police?' said the man in the JCB.

'Body? What body?' said the man on the ground.

A police car came into view, then another. You could tell by their colours that one was from the North and the other from the South. They bounded over the mountain track and pulled up some distance away. Car doors slammed. Uniformed men got out and Fergus recognized Uncle Tally emerging from the back of the Gardai's car. He pointed to Fergus and the JCB men, and the uniforms advanced over the bog-land, picking their way carefully, occasionally stumbling in the spiky grass. Uncle Tally trailed behind, his hands in his denim jacket as if oblivious to the treacherous nature of the ground.

'Feck it,' Fergus heard a guard say. 'My boot's wrecked.'

'Bugger this,' said an RUC man.

'What the hell's going on?' said the JCB man. He'd climbed down from the machine.

Fergus pointed to the body in the bog, the point of elbow, the neat twist of gowned torso, and jutting bone. Against the brown of the earth, and with the way the light fell, it wasn't immediately apparent.

'He's raving,' said the man on the ground. 'There's no body.'

'There is. See.' Fergus dropped down into the cut. His finger traced the body. 'That's a hand. And, look – a bangle. Gold, maybe.'

'Christ. He's right, Mick,' said the JCB man.

The police drew up, panting.

'Uncle Tally and I,' Fergus said. 'We found her. We were up early, bird-watching.'

'Bird-watching? Oh, yeah?' said the man called Mick.

''S true.'

'More like—'

'Bird-watching,' said Fergus. 'And here's her bone. Broken off.'

Nobody spoke.

Uncle Tally approached the cut and got a fag out but didn't light it. 'Somebody's killed her and buried her here,' he suggested. 'And it's thanks to Fergus that she didn't get mashed up by your bloody JCB.'

'OK, OK,' said the man called Mick. He offered Uncle Tally a light for his fag and lit one himself.

'How long d'you think she's been here?' said the Irish guard.

'We can't be sure it's a she,' said the RUC man.

'But the bangle. And that gansey she's wearing. Some kind of woollen nightie.'

'Maybe it's more of a shirt. A long nightshirt.'

'I never saw a nightshirt like that on a boy. Not nowadays. It'd be pyjamas, wouldn't it?'

'And are we north or south of the border? That's what I want to know.'

'According to my OS map, there's a stream hereabouts. And the North is one side and the South the other.' The man who spoke was plainclothes, with an English accent.

Uncle Tally spoke. 'Fergus and I've been up here a few hours. Watching the birds. But we haven't seen a stream. Just bog.'

'It's been a dry spring. The stream's probably dried up,' suggested the Irish guard. 'I'd say the body's yours, though. Going by the map.'

'And I'd say it's yours.'

There was another silence.

'Son, you'd better come up out of there.' It was the English plainclothes, sounding quietly authoritative. He reached a hand down into the cut but Fergus shook his head. He flattened his palms on the top and leapfrogged up.

'The poor wee girl,' said the JCB man. 'She looks about seven or eight. Less than my Mairead.'

'We've a call out for the pathologist. But meantime, we'll seal off the area. Is that OK with you?' The Englishman spoke to the Irish guard.

'We've a call out too. But our pathologist has to come from Galway.'

'Galway?'

The Irish guard shrugged.

'Well, ours will be here before yours. We've brought some tape. Can we seal her off?'

'Seal away. Our tape's the same colour. It makes no odds.'

The police shooed Fergus and the JCB men and Uncle Tally away.

Uncle Tally motioned with his head for Fergus to move off down the track some distance, so they could talk alone.

'It's a detail, Ferg. We're stranded. I'd to leave the van in the town car park before I went into the guards. I didn't want them nosing around our bags of peat. Then they made me escort them here in the police car. With the siren wailing, anybody who saw me would have thought I was off to Long Kesh prison. I ask you. And my van sitting in the middle of Inchquin, with thirty pounds worth of turf.'

'You could walk back, Uncle Tally. Once off the mountain, you could thumb it.'

'You're joking. Who'd pick up a fella like me in a godforsaken place like this? Bandit country!'

Fergus laughed. 'I can hear the drums over the next hill, Unk. The natives are getting restless.'

Uncle Tally grunted. 'We're bloody stranded.'

'We could run down the mountain. Inchquin's only ten miles.'

'Away you go so, Marathon Man.'

'Unk?'

'What?'

'Have you heard of any girl – or child – gone missing lately?'

Uncle Tally thought. 'No. Not lately. Years back, there was a lassie that vanished over Dranmore way. But she was older. Thirteen. And it turned out she'd only run off to go on the game. The scamp. I reckon whoever murdered this wee one drove her body up here from miles away. She's probably not local at all. Maybe not even Irish. Who knows?'

'I'd say she's Irish.'

'Why?'

'Did you see the bangle?'

'No.'

'The metal was twisted into strands. Like something Celtic.'

'Never.'

'It was.'

'Poor wee mite. But tourists buy that tat too.'

The plainclothes policeman approached them. 'We'll need you to make statements,' he said. 'What you were doing, when you found her . . . that kind of thing.'

'There's not a lot to say. We were up here early, bird-watching—' Uncle Tally began.

'And then I spotted her,' interrupted Fergus. 'I saw her in the earth. It was like camouflage.'

'Camouflage?'

'You know. Soldiers in combat fatigues. Or birds in the field. Camouflaged so you can't see them.'

The RUC man's eyes flicked heavenwards. 'I get the picture.'

'I saw the bangle first. Then her hand. Then her body. And then . . . the bone. Cut off.'

'And then what? Did you touch her?'

'Maybe. Just on the cloth.'

'And I drove down to Inchquin to alert the guards,' said Uncle Tally.

'Why Inchquin? Why not Roscillin, over?'

'Well, we thought we were south of the border.'

The plainclothes man had a sharp chin and thick dark hair that flapped in the breeze. 'And I'd say you were right. But Paddy over there says that as you crossed over from this bridleway to where you found her, you crossed back over the border, to the North.'

'You don't say?'

'Are you Northerners yourself?'

Uncle Tally nodded. 'We're from Drumleash, Fergus and myself.' He gave the officer their full names and addresses.

'Are you still at school?' the officer asked Fergus.

'I'm on study leave. My A-level exams start soon.'

The officer tapped his pen on his notebook. 'And you, Mr McCann? What do you do?'

'This and that. Bar work. Work's hard to come by these days.'

'A fine fellow like yourself? You should join the RUC.'

19

'I may be Irish,' Uncle Tally said, 'but I'm not a lemming.' He guffawed at his own joke. After a moment the plainclothes joined in.

Another car drove right up to where they were standing. 'It's the pathologist,' the plainclothes said. 'He's driven from Londonderry double-quick.'

A plump man in his fifties got out, carrying a battered holdall.

'That was fast, Jack,' said the plainclothes.

'Hi, Duncan. Where is she?'

The two men walked away over the bog-land towards the body. Uncle Tally put a hand on Fergus's shoulder.

'I don't like this police stuff,' he whispered. 'Let's go.'

'Unk. No. Not yet. I want to hear what the pathologist says.' Before Uncle Tally could stop him, Fergus wriggled free and picked his way to a few yards from the cut. He lay flat to keep out of sight and listened to what the officials were saying.

The doctor slid on some mud and swore. He'd trouble getting down to view the body. Then there was silence.

'So how long do you reckon she's been there, Jack?'

Fergus pushed the grass aside and saw an Irish guard drop to his knees at the side of the cut, as if in prayer. An aeroplane passed high overhead, a silent crucifix truncating the sky.

'Bloody hell.' It was the doctor's voice.

'How long?'

'Poor child. And her skin intact.'

'I know. She's fresh. Is it days? Or weeks?'

'Longer than that, Duncan.'

'Not months?'

'Centuries.'

'*Centuries?* You're having me on, Jack.'

'It's an archaeologist you need here, not the police.'

'An archaeologist?'

'There was another body, I recall. Found in similar terrain, down south. It turned out to be ancient. Iron Age.'

'Never. Look at the state of the skin. The cloth.'

'It's a quality of the bog. It preserves things. Like a mummy in an Egyptian tomb.'

'Christ. You're pulling my leg. You have to be.'

'Christ is right and no joke.' The doctor's voice was breathless as he struggled back up to the higher level. 'Thanks. For all we know, this child might have walked the earth the same time as Your Man Himself.'

'What man himself?'

'Jesus Christ, who else?'

'Jesus?'

'We're talking two thousand-odd years ago, Duncan. Maybe more.'

'Which makes that bangle, the cloth, everything—'

'Priceless. If I'm right, you've a sensation here.'

'I *knew* she was on our side of the border. I knew it.'

Three

More police arrived and more arguments broke out about where the border was, but in reverse. The body of the girl had gone from a serious crime headache to a valuable find. Everyone laid claim to her. Fergus listened in silence; Uncle Tally kept his distance.

It was gone noon when a guard remembered them and gave them a lift down from the mountain. They collected the van from Inchquin and drove back over the border. A different soldier was on duty, a big, bald fellow who looked fit to down ten pints of beer in as many minutes. He asked for Uncle Tally's licence and read it over, holding it at arm's length as if it had fleas.

'God,' said Uncle Tally. 'Someone must have jogged Lloyd George's hand when he drew that bloody border and left Drumleash on the wrong side.'

'What d'you mean?'

'You'd have thought they'd put us Fenians in the Republic to be shot of us.'

They drove into Roscillin with the bags of turf and sold all but three to Uncle Tally's mate Frank, who ran a hardware business. They stopped there for some cans of beer. It was nearly three when they hit the out-skirts of Drumleash.

Da was filling up a posh blue Rover at the petrol station as they went by. Uncle Tally tooted his horn and Da looked up and raised his eyes to heaven. The village was peaceful otherwise. The modern Catholic church with its flying-saucer roof loomed like an abandoned UFO. Two sleeping dogs sprawled on top of each other outside Finicule's Bar, the pub where Uncle Tally rented a room and served as barman.

'I'm wrecked,' said Uncle Tally. 'I'll drop you at your place but I won't come in. Say hello to your mother and give her a bag of turf. Then she won't be cross with me.'

They turned into the close at the far end of the village and drew up at Fergus's family's white bungalow. In the afternoon sunshine the place wore a cheerful aspect. The roses were out. Outside the front gate was a sign saying B & B. APPLY WITHIN. Fergus could barely remember the last time there'd been a taker. They'd had a few Americans visit, looking for their roots, but when the violence escalated, custom had dried up.

Fergus sprang out and heaved out a fat bag of turf. 'Ta-ra, Unk.'

'Fight the fight.' Uncle Tally waved and drove away.

Fergus dragged the turf round the back of the house and found his mother there, peg in mouth, hanging out the washing. The wind whipped her blonde hair across her face as she glanced over to him.

23

'Giv urs a hind with thus shoot,' she said.

'What?'

She took the peg from her mouth. 'Give us a hand with this sheet.'

Fergus grinned. 'Sure.' He grabbed a flapping corner.

'Where've you been all day, Fergus? You smell of beer.'

'It was only the one.'

'It's always only the one.'

'It was really only the one. Uncle Tally and I, we went to get the turf. I've a big bag of it there. But then we got delayed. We found a body, Mam. Up there in the mountain bog. A wee, tiny child.'

Mam stopped and stared open-mouthed, holding small Theresa's dungarees to her chest. 'A child?'

'A child, Mam.'

'God help us. She was dead?'

'Of course, dead. Buried. But the JCB unburied her.'

'Mother of God. Was she murdered?'

'I don't know, Mam. They think she's ancient. Iron Age.'

'What d'you mean?'

'Iron Age. Two thousand years old or more.'

He poured out the story, helping her with the washing between breathless sentences.

'They're waiting for the archaeologists,' he finished. 'What d'you think of that?'

'Remember to shake the shirts before you peg them, Fergus.'

' 'S that all you can say? They think she was alive when Jesus was.'

Mam hung up the last sock and her arms dropped to her sides. She sighed and started to cross herself. 'A small girl like that, ending up on that godforsaken mountain. And her a pagan.'

'She couldn't have been a Christian, Mam, if she was born before Christ.'

'I know. But it's the thought of her, buried without a prayer.'

'Maybe somebody did pray for her.'

Mam sighed. 'And maybe He heard them. Or maybe not.' She pegged up the dungarees. 'I'm glad they think she's been there all this time.'

'Why?'

'It makes it further away. Less to do with us. With now.' She picked up the plastic laundry basket. 'We've enough troubles on our doorstep.'

'S'pose.'

'We do. I'm just back from visiting Joe. So I know.'

'You went to see Joe, Mam?' Fergus put a hand to Joe's watch. 'How was he?'

Mam smiled. 'He's grown.'

'Since last week?'

'Not that way. I mean in his head. The way he speaks.'

'Is he getting hassled in there?'

'No. He's been reading.'

'Reading?'

'Reading about science. About what happens when light hits a mirror.' She smiled. 'It bends, he tells me.'

25

'It's called refraction, Mam.'

'Is that what it is? I didn't understand. He's mad keen to re-sit the science O level.'

'Is he?'

'He is. And look at you, Fergus. Brains to burn and the books unopened all day.'

'I'll do some later. Honest to God.'

'Always later. Never now. You sound just like Joey. He promised me he'd get away to England for a job, if not next week, the week after. And now look. There is no later. Or none to speak of. He's locked away for ten years.' She flung down the empty laundry basket. 'I'm worn out with the pair of you.'

'Mam!'

'You and Joe. Always up to mischief.'

'Mam?'

'I remember the two of youse trying to knock down the house. Banging at the back extension with spades bigger than yourselves.'

Fergus put his arm around her shoulder. 'Hoodlums, the pair of us.'

She grabbed a shirt-tail from the line and dabbed her eyes. 'Now look what you've done. If Theresa and Cath didn't finish me off this morning, monkeying with my nail varnish, and you swanning off without a word and Joey locked away for a decade. I swear to God. I wish I'd stayed in Leitrim where I was born and never married into all this trouble.'

'Oh, Mam. We're a terrible brood. You should have drowned us at birth.'

Her hand was on his hair, moving over the wiry

ends. 'Please don't go the same way as your brother, Fergus. Tell me you won't.'

'I won't. I've no intention.'

'Every last boy in this village wants to be a bloody hero. It's a waste. But you won't, will you?'

'No.'

'You'd know better, wouldn't you?'

'Yes, Mam. I would.'

'Do your revision, then.'

'OK, I will. But Mam?'

'What?'

'Can I go up the mountain tomorrow? With Uncle Tally? To see what they're doing with the body? He says he'll give me another driving lesson while we're at it.'

'You and your Uncle Tally. Like two peas in a pod. OK. Only put up the learner plates I bought for you this time.'

'Do I have to, Mam?'

'It's the law.'

'But it's like telling the whole world in big letters, I'M A PROVO.'

'What?'

'A holder of a provisional licence, Mam.'

She cuffed him and laughed. 'You're a wicked tyke, Fergus. Now scoot and get cracking on those books.'

Four

That evening, Da came home as the table was being
laid for a fry. He slammed the *Roscillin Star* down on
the sofa and cursed, and his thick grey eyebrows
scrunched together.

'Was it a bad day at the garage, Malachy?' Mam
said.

'No. We'd a fair bit of trade.'

'So what's eating you?'

'You've not heard the radio? Two more dead,' he
said. 'After sixty-one days of starving.'

'Mother of God.'

'They're letting them all die. Bobby Sands was
only the start.'

'The Maze is a place accursed.'

'It's not the Maze, woman. It's Long Kesh.' He
plumped down on a chair.

'The Maze, Long Kesh. What's the difference?'

'You might as well call Britain the mainland,
Pat.'

Mam pulled out the table from the wall. 'I've a fry
done.'

'Is that all you can say?'

Mam got the fold-up chairs for the girls and arranged them between the wall and table. 'Where are those two hoodlums?' She went to the back door. 'Th'rese, Cath,' she hollered. Then she arranged the last knife and fork at Da's place. 'No point us starving too.'

'Jesus. Women.'

'OK. So the hunger strike's a tragedy. All over a few old clothes.'

'It's not about clothes.'

'It is about clothes.'

'It's what the clothes *mean*, Pat. If you don't wear prison garb, you're a political prisoner. And if you're a political, you're not a petty criminal. And that's what the Brits make out they are.'

'What matter is it what they think?'

'Next you'll be saying your woman Thatcher over's right to let them die.'

'I'd never say that. She should let them wear what they want, if it would stop the insanity. Now sit and have your tea.'

Da grunted and sat down. Fergus joined him. 'I heard Uncle Tally say "the mainland" the other day, Da.'

'Was he having a rise?'

'Don't think so. He was just saying how he was planning a trip over later this summer.'

Da chuckled. 'You'd be tarred and feathered out of Drumleash if you were anyone else saying that but Tally. How he gets away with it's a mystery.'

29

'Da. Uncle Tally and I, we found a body. In the bog.'

He was just finishing the story of his day on the mountain when the girls burst through the back door.

'I'm famished,' Theresa wailed.

'Where've you been?' Mam got their plates from where they'd been keeping warm under the grill.

Fergus winked at the two of them. 'You're flushed like you've been running, Cath,' he said.

'We were playing "Save All" with the Caseys,' Theresa said. 'And Cath saved Seamus. And then Seamus kissed her. And I saw him at it.'

'You did not.'

'I did.'

'Whisht,' Mam said. 'Eat your eggs before they set solid.'

There was a silence as everyone ate. Da put down his knife and fork and looked over at Fergus. 'That was a strange day you had, Fergus. I wouldn't be surprised if that bog child of yours turned out not so old after all.'

'Why d'you say that?'

'I remember an old story about another body being found up there on the mountain. Forty years back or more. It was the wife of a local man. Up until then, he claimed she'd left him for another man and gone to England.'

'A body?' said Theresa, her eyes wild with excitement. 'Did you find a body, Fergus?'

'I did.' He'd to tell the story all over again.

'I want to go and see it. Mam. Da. Can I? Please?'

'And me,' said Cath.

'You can't, either of you,' Mam said.

'Oh, but—'

'No buts.'

'We saw the Caseys' granda when he was laid out, didn't we, Cath?'

'Yes. He was all waxy.'

Da thumped the table. 'No buts. Like your mother says. This is a child, maimed and murdered. Not a decent body.'

There was silence. Cath's face was an image of tragic loss, while Theresa made a grimace that would curdle cream.

'What d'you make of the hunger strikers, Fergus?' Da said to change the subject.

Fergus speared a sausage. 'They're very committed,' he said. 'I couldn't do it.' He munched on the meat and swallowed. 'I wouldn't last a day without food.'

'Thank God Joe's not part of it,' Mam said.

Da nodded. 'It's an odd thing, when you thank God for your son not having to make a sacrifice like that.'

Mam grunted. 'Sacrifice? Some sacrifice.' She reached over to Cath and forked a grilled tomato from the plate's edge towards the centre. 'Eat up, Cath.'

Fergus chewed on the last bacon rind and listened to the clock on the mantelpiece tick. *Soon*, it seemed to reassure, *you'll have the grades and be away. Over the roads and hills to the ferryboat. Across the sea and to the mainland. Away from this.*

As soon as he put his cutlery down, Mam reached

over to take away his plate. 'Sacrifice is what Jesus did. He saved us all. Who did Bobby Sands save?' she said. 'Who?'

Nobody answered.

Five

After tea, Da went down to the village for a pint. The girls watched TV. Fergus offered to help Mam clear away, but she whisked him out of the kitchen, back to his studying.

He groaned, but returned to the tiny front room and sat at the drop-leaf table. His Nelkon and Parker physics textbook, the size of a doorstop, was open at Young's Modulus. He stared at the formula, doodling spirals in the margin.

$$E = \frac{\text{tensile stress}}{\text{tensile strain}}$$

His mind wouldn't settle. Expansion, temperature, fixed load. The words floated in his head like lazy gulls. He got up and went to the record player, tempted to put something on. He picked through Joe's LPs. The Jam. Stiff Little Fingers. *London Calling* by The Clash, his own favourite. Then Joe's all-time favourite, *Imagine* by John Lennon. He'd the grooves nearly worn away at this stage. The cover was frayed and torn. Lennon's glass lenses staring through the blotched clouds as if he was already a memory in a photograph album when the shot was taken.

'*Oh Yoko,*' Fergus hummed, remembering. '*Oh Yoko.*'

When Lennon was gunned down last December, Joe had spent the night in a vigil in this room with the candles burning and tracks blaring. Two days later, the police had come for him.

'That doesn't look like studying to me.'

Fergus started. Mam was standing in the doorway, a glass jug of water in hand. He put the record away.

'Mam – that water.'

'What about it?'

'Bring it over.'

'It's for watering the geraniums. Not for you.'

'I want to show you something.'

She sighed and put the jug down by his side. Fergus picked up his pencil and plunged it halfway in.

'What d'you see?'

'I see a pencil, half in, half out. It'll drip over the polished wood when you take it out.'

He lifted the jug to her eye-level. 'Look at it harder, Mam.'

'Red. HB?' she suggested.

'No, Mam. See. It's bent. Where it goes in the water.'

'So it is.'

'That's refraction for you.'

'It's not really bent. It's an illusion.'

34

'Illusion or not, Mam, it's how the light behaves, going from one medium to another. Air then water.'

Mam's face brightened. 'Clever clogs.' She took the pencil from him, wiped it on her jeans and handed it back to him. 'Carry on with that studying.'

He groaned and turned back to his physics book, while Mam went out to the porch with the jug. He slammed the tome shut. 'Force equals mass times acceleration,' he said, as if that explained everything. He shut his eyes and thought of an arrow speeding through the air, then a hand, dealing a heavy blow on the head of a kneeling, terrified girl.

The girl in the bog. Somebody murdering her.

He bit his lip. He couldn't get those little hands, the spools on the finger-pads, the coiled metal of the bangle out of his mind. In his head there was a strange explosion, as if his brain had collapsed like a clapped-out star. He threw down his pencil and shut his eyes.

He heard his teacher at school, Mr Dwyer, tut-tutting. *Three Bs and you've a place for medicine in Aberdeen, Fergus McCann. A whole new life. A whole new world.* He opened his eyes and the curtain fluttered in the darkening evening breeze. He switched on the desk light, picked up his pencil and reopened Nelkon and Parker back at the beginning of the chapter. He pressed his hands into his eyeballs and began to read.

Six

In the dark, we slept in a line. Mam at the wall, then Da.
Then the pale wool curtain that floated in the night breeze.
Then my own self and a gap and my brother Brennor and a
gap and then the small ones. Wherever a gap was, it stood for
a child that had died. And we dreamed as a family. Brennor
would wake up and say how the moon had fallen down in the
night and he'd caught it and climbed up a tree to put it back.
And Mam would say she dreamed the baby in her belly came out
a fat white goose. And I'd tell my dream, which was of a crooked
wheel rolling down the mountain and it growing bigger like a
ball of snow and flattening every last living thing. And Da'd
say we were all deranged, except maybe the small ones, because
they'd slept soundly, like the good wee ones they were.

'Didn't you dream anything, Da?' I asked.

He put on his jacket and smiled. 'Maybe I did. But not of
wheels or moons or geese.' He put his hand on Mam's round
front. 'Honk, honk,' he went. Mam cuffed him.

'What then?' I asked.

'I dreamed of you, Mel. Walking round the hut in a
circle, chattering, and time forgetting you. And your hands
dancing like birds but nothing in them.'

36

'And what did the dream mean, Da?'

Da winked. 'It meant you've a floor to sweep and wheat to chaff. Remember?'

Fergus awoke in the morning silence. A girl in a white shift was laughing, her hands fluttering, a dream of a dream. The image faded. Cath must have cried out in her sleep again. The walls were paper-thin. He sat up and listened. All seemed quiet.

It was a Saturday, he remembered. The clock said 6:10. Between the curtains, sun crept in. He smelled crispness in the air.

It was a running day, definitely.

He got up, stripping out of his pyjamas. Within seconds he was in his shorts and sweatshirt. The sweatshirt was bright red, with a black puma running across it hell for leather, slinky and fast. It had been a birthday present from Mam and was now well-worn.

He brushed his teeth in thirty seconds. On the bath's ledge was Joe's watch. He picked it up and put it on.

Once out of the house he pattered softly from the close and down the street. He turned off, past the primary school, and headed down along the last bungalows to where the road turned rural. Here he stopped.

He could see his breath. The birds were deafening.

He bent and stretched, feeling his hamstrings tug and his heels tingle. His back felt like he'd been lying like a corkscrew all night.

He started to run. It was a slow ascent. The mountain drew him like a magnet.

God. Why did I do this? His legs were heavy. Every breath felt like his last. When people asked him what was the worst bit of a run, the answer was always the same: the first mile.

The road wound up a hill and then turned into track. He'd to vault a gate and then zigzag along the path through the Forestry Commission. Even after a dry spring, it was a place of pine cones, moist earth and secrets trembling among the evergreens.

His breathing became more assured. *Sharp-IN-huh-huh-and-OUT-huh-huh* . . . His legs gave under the soft ground. An affronted blackbird clucked a warning. Pieces of the last twenty-four hours hovered in his head. Uncle Tally and the flask of sweet black tea. Mam and the bent pencil in the water. Da coming in and flinging down the *Roscillin Star*. The girls and their flushed faces. And again, the clods of turf, the cut, the white, jutting bone, the gleam of gold. And the spools on the finger-pads.

You're fine and dandy as you are. That's what my mam said.

The childlike voice of his dreams came back to him as he broke from the forest cover, up onto the high ground.

Running on the spot, he turned round. Drumleash was way below. An arm of the lough curled away into haze. He whooped out loud at the joy of being above it all.

Freedom. This is what it feels like.

He could pick up a minor, dead-end road if he circled the hill, or he could head straight up and over, but this meant scrambling rather than running over rocks and gorse. He wanted to keep the steady rhythm, so he made for the road. It involved passing a border checkpoint, but it was seldom attended.

He hopped over a stream to get to the tarmac. The watercourse had dwindled to the size of a pipeline. He splashed his face and drank some scoops. Once on the road, he picked up pace. He could hear the wind whistle past his ears, mixed up with faint baas of sheep. Above, a flock of birds drifted like bits of ash. He smiled. He was five miles into the run. This was the magic middle of things, where moving felt the same as staying still.

He approached the border checkpoint, a tiny wooden hut. He was so used to passing it with nobody challenging him, he got a shock to see a silhouette, rifle in hand.

He slowed as he drew near. It was the pale, freckly young man he'd seen on duty the day before on the main road.

'Hi, there,' the soldier called.

'Hi,' he said. He stopped, but kept his running legs going.

'D'you have ID?' the soldier said.

Fergus panted. 'No. I've nothing on me, just the door key. I'm out running.'

The soldier smiled, his blue eyes crinkling. 'You're not the kind of traffic I was expecting.'

'I'm not exactly gun-running,' he said, putting his hands in the air. 'Honest to God.'

'I can see that.' The soldier slung the rifle over his back. 'Not a petrol bomb in sight.'

Fergus let his arms drop.

'You a Catholic or a Prod?' the soldier asked.

'What difference does it make?'

'No difference. Just curious.' His accent was hard to place, flat but with a catch at the end of each phrase.

'I'm Irish. And Catholic. Only I don't believe a bloody word.'

The soldier grinned. 'I'm a Pentecostalist. Which means you'll burn in hell.'

'Thanks.'

'Don't worry. 'S nothing personal. The Queen will too by our reckoning.' The lad shrugged. 'Anyway, I'm a *fallen* Pentecostalist. I'm off to hell too.'

'That's religion for you,' said Fergus.

'Yep. Bollocks.'

'Crapology.'

Fergus remembered that by Drumleash standards he was fraternizing with the enemy. But up here in the open, wild space it didn't seem to matter. 'You're one side of the border,' he said, drawing an imaginary line in the air. 'And I'm the other. And please may I cross?'

'*Red rover, red rover, I'll let you come over.*'

The lad stood back and beckoned Fergus up the road.

Fergus passed. His teeth bit into his lip as he felt the boy's eyes on his back. He turned.

'What's your name?' he asked.

The soldier shrugged.

'You're not supposed to tell me?'

'I'm Owain, if you must know.'

'Owen?'

'O-wain. Spelled the Welsh way.'

'You're Welsh?'

'From the Valleys.'

'The Valleys?'

'Where the coal mines are.'

Fergus nodded as if he knew where that was, although he didn't. 'I'm Fergus.'

'Fergus? Isn't that Scottish?'

'It's Scottish *and* Irish. I'm named after an Irish high king.'

'Oh. Be seeing you, Your Majesty.'

Fergus grinned and saluted. He ran on up the road. Even though he knew it wasn't so, in his imagination the soldier was taking aim at the spot between his shoulder blades. He glanced back. The lad was lounged against the shed, his pale face lit in the sun, the gun nowhere to be seen.

They'd cut you in ribbons for that below, he thought. Up here on the mountain, the Troubles didn't seem to count. You could talk to whomever you pleased. He smiled. His legs were going strong again and the minor road fed him up to its final turning point. Then it was straight on along a ridgeway. Leitrim in its green trim came into view, and then the track arced back, so that Fermanagh, grey and flat, reappeared. Something about the lay of the land led him to the furthest brow, the place where on a map there'd be a triangulation point to mark the highest

41

bit of land. From here it was a short diversion over bracken and bog-land to where the abandoned JCB sat silent and crooked on the slope. Taut yellow tape marked the cut. He ran up close. Over the body, a great tarpaulin had been erected. Dew glinted on the bog grasses like cut diamonds.

He looked at his watch: 7:48.

Including his stretching exercises and chatting to the sentry, he'd been running for just over an hour. But how much ground he'd covered, he did not know. He smiled. The drive had taken half an hour: you had to go all around the houses to get here. The milometer said fourteen miles. Maybe today he'd run as much as seven already, and given it had been all uphill, he'd done well.

The tarpaulin around the bog child was pinned down. The place had an expectant feel to it. The archaeologists were on their way and the girl inside was waiting. He put his hand to the khaki-green side, itching to see what lay within. But the tarpaulin was weighted down and seamless. It was wrong to disturb her.

He turned back and picked his way down the mountain, avoiding the sentry box. He sprang over the turf like a rabbit on anabolic steroids. From the west, swaths of tarnished cloud moved in. By the time he was back in the Forestry Commission, a steady drizzle had rolled in, cooling him. He lapped at the raindrops with his tongue and whooped.

Running was *it*.

Seven

Back home, he flopped on the sofa, his legs dangling over the arm, with beads of rain and sweat running down his face and limbs. The mantelpiece clock chimed nine o'clock. Mam appeared.

'There you are. Look at the cut of you. You've destroyed yourself for your studying.'

'I've done my weekly revision, Mam. It's Saturday.'

She yanked his red sweatshirt. 'Take it off, Fergus. It's minging.'

Theresa and Cath drifted in, still in their pyjamas.

'*The dead arose and appeared to many,*' Fergus joked.

''S pissing down,' yawned Theresa.

'Theresa McCann!' said Mam.

'That's what Da says when it rains.'

Fergus laughed. 'We should all move south to the Mediterranean, Mam. The sun. The sea.'

'Too right,' Cath said. 'It's boring here.'

'We'd go swimming every day,' Fergus suggested.

'Swimming?' said Theresa. 'Can we, Mam?'

'You were at the pool only the other day.'

'*Please*, Mam.'

'I've no time to take you.'

'Fergus could!'

'He's his study to do. And he's going driving with Uncle Tally later. He can't do it all.'

'Aw, Mam!' Fergus groaned. The thought of the laws of stress and strain made him weak at the knees. 'Like I said, it's Saturday.'

Theresa and Cath were swarming around him.

'Please, Mam,' said Theresa. 'Ferg can study this afternoon. *After* his driving lesson.'

Mam sighed. 'You girls. You never stop.'

'I'll sharpen his pencils,' Cath offered. '*Please.*'

'OK.' Mam held her hands up in surrender. 'Off you go. But I want you home by dinner. And Fergus?'

'What?'

'Don't let them stay in the water too long. I don't want Cath's bad ear back.'

By the time the bus dropped them in Roscillin, the rain had lightened but was still spitting. There was hardly anybody about. An ancient wreck of a man, fag hanging from mouth, shuffled past, as skewed as a knotted-up lamppost. A younger woman stood in the middle of the pedestrian crossing, her inside-out umbrella hanging limp at her side, looking up as if she was Saint Sebastian and the raindrops were the arrows. The police station bristled with barbed wire, awaiting the end of all things.

Jesus, Fergus thought. The place was a blight.

At the pool, though, there was a cheerful crowd. Maybe it was the novelty of the flume, put up after the last bomb as if in compensation. There were lads

44

going down it backwards. A gaggle of grown girls swooped down, their bikini tops a-quiver. Fergus grinned at the sight of Mary Keane from school. He'd had no idea she was so endowed.

Fergus went to the main pool and swam a length. Theresa and Cath were hell-bent on the flume and he had peace. He followed the line of the lane, goggles on. For a few strokes it was as if the legs and arms worked perfectly together and he glided effortlessly from one end to the other. But when he turned for the next length, the magic left and he felt the strain and the water resisting. He was tired. The warmth of the water made him drowsy.

They took me up the mountain and it wasn't fair.

The little voice was in his head again, the child time forgot.

Theresa and Cath in their pink and orange swimsuits ambushed him in the shallow end. He'd to swim between their legs three times each. Then he'd to time their underwater swimming against the big clock at the end of the pool. Theresa had it down pat, but Cath kept surfacing as if she was too scrawny not to float. Then he'd to play 'Whale Spouting' and 'The Monster from the Deep Lagoon'. Then they went off for another go on the flume.

His eyes stung with chlorine. He heaved himself out, changed, and sat up in the spectator area, looking down at the pool, waiting for Cath and Theresa to finish. He saw them go down the flume, arm in arm. Their ponytails flew backwards and their pale legs streaked like flying fish.

He sat back and smiled at the mosaic fishes on the ceiling. A fat guppy winked at him lazily, improbably purple. He felt his lids closing as the echoes of the voices rose and clashed and began to fade. His arms and legs tingled with the day's exertions.

Somebody help me. Please. Somebody . . .

The little-girl dream-voice again, from another place, another time. She was running in a white shift, down the mountainside. Then she changed into a creamy, white goat-kid.

'Fergus! The very man.'

He snapped open his eyes. Michael Rafters, an old school friend of Joe's, was edging his way towards him along the row of seats.

'D'you mind if I sit here?'

Fergus nodded. 'Feel free. Haven't seen you in an age.'

'You here with your family?' Michael asked.

Fergus pointed to where Theresa and Cath were queuing for another go on the flume. 'My sisters.'

'They've grown. It's been a while since I saw you all. How're things?'

'Fine.'

'Are you still being crucified?'

Fergus smiled. It was how everyone referred to going to the Holy Cross School. 'I'm on study leave. For my A levels.'

'My, oh my. Joe and I never got that far. We were too busy making home-made bombs.'

Fergus guffawed. The two older lads, known at school as Dafters and Canny, had once blown up the

46

games hut at school with a mixture of sugar and fertilizer. 'They still call you "The Incendiary Devices".'

'We were only messing, Fergus.'

'The whole school knew it was you. But nobody split. And the teachers never found out.'

'I'd say they'd a shrewd idea.'

'Would you?'

'Old Dwyer dropped me a hint. But he turned a blind eye. A Sinn Fein man like him. He probably saw it as legitimate practice.' Michael squeezed out of his wet jacket. 'How's Joe?'

'Mam saw him the other day. He's studying as well.'

'Never.'

Fergus looked down at Joe's watch. 'He'll be thirty when he's out.'

'Thirty?'

Fergus nodded.

'I suppose parole and the H-blockers rarely go together.' Michael leaned over. 'He's showing no sign of joining the hunger strike?'

'None. He's more sense.'

'Fergus McCann. That's hardly the attitude.'

'I voted for Sands in the by-election. My first vote ever. What more do you want?'

'You know and I know. The ballot box isn't enough.'

Fergus shrugged. 'Maybe not.'

'With four strikers dead, the whole of the North is ready to erupt.'

Fergus nodded. 'I can believe it.'

Michael crossed one leg over the other and put his hand around the back of Fergus's seat. 'Me and the lads,' he said casually. 'We've been wondering. If we can count you in?'

He said it as if he was inviting Fergus on a fishing expedition.

'Count me in?'

'You know.' Michael's hand circled the air, like a royal wave.

'So you're—' *One of them. A Provo.*

Michael nodded. 'People are joining in droves on account of the hunger strikers. And the fiend-bitch over not listening. Maybe that's what it's all about really. Not clothes: recruitment. He was a canny man, was Sands.'

'If your numbers are up, you don't need me.'

'Fergus!' Michael hissed his name in mock admonishment. 'That's not a die-hard McCann I hear talking. You're not afraid, are you?'

'No. But I promised someone I wouldn't get involved.'

'Someone? Don't tell me. Your ma.'

Fergus felt his cheeks hot up. 'I've my mind on my studies right now. And my running.'

'The running. That's just it, Fergus. We have a job for you that involves a bit of running. You're the best runner this side of the county.'

Curious, Fergus looked over. 'Don't you have get-away cars nowadays?'

'We're not talking active operations. All we want is

a bit of couriering to and fro over the border. We've seen you jog over those mountains.'

'Seen me?'

'With that red gansey you wear, you're hard to miss.'

Fergus bit his lip. They'd been watching him, spying through binoculars.

'What better disguise would there be? And you can avoid the checkpoints altogether, if you know your way.'

'Couriering? Couriering what?'

'Nothing much. Bits and bobs.'

Fergus saw Theresa and Cath climbing out of the pool. He leaned over and waved and shouted at them. They waved back and jumped straight back in the water.

'No way,' he said, sitting back again. 'Sorry, Dafters. It's not my scene.'

'But you go running up there anyway. It's a small price to pay for freedom, Fergus.'

Fergus grunted. 'Dunno.'

'That's right, Fergus. Think about it. I'll be onto you again. You know who'll benefit, don't you? Those two young sisters of yours. By the time they're grown, Ireland will be free.'

Michael unpeeled himself from his seat and glided away.

Fergus watched him vanish through the exit, then plumped against the back of his seat.

'Jesus,' he said out loud.

From the pool, Theresa was making gestures to say

they'd be five minutes. He'd promised to buy them hot chocolates from the machine. He shook his fist and beckoned them both to hurry. They shrugged and he mimed slurping a delicious drink. Finally they got out.

Michael Rafters, he knew, was only the start. They'd never rest until they'd got him in up to the neck.

Something slithered in his belly, cold and subtle.

'Jesus,' he said again, kicking the seat in front of him.

Eight

Uncle Tally picked him up for his driving lesson at three. He got behind the wheel of the family's old brown Austin Maxi, checked the mirrors and pulled out. He was confident at the driving now. His gear changes were smooth, the pedals a natural extension of his legs, the steering finely nuanced.

The rain had moved east, leaving the day dry but dull. At the petrol station there was no sign of Da, although the shop had its lights inside on. The lough beyond looked lifeless.

'This bloody weather,' Uncle Tally grunted. 'It's like a girlfriend you forgot to phone.'

'Which girlfriend would that be?'

'Keep your eyes on the road. I'd rather not land in that lough.'

Fergus flicked a hand from the wheel. 'Is there one, Unk?'

'One what?'

'A girlfriend?'

'Nope.'

'Why not?'

'You're curious today.'

They drove on in silence.

'I did have a girl,' Uncle Tally said. 'When I was your age. We were going six years.'

'What was her name?'

'Noreen.'

'Why didn't you marry her?'

'She ran off to England with the boiler man.'

'Never.'

'She did. She's married now, kids 'n' all.'

Fergus thought of his da's story, about the other body they'd found in the bog: the woman who was supposed to have run off, but hadn't.

Uncle Tally shifted in his seat. 'Slow up for this turn. It's sharp.'

At the border, the Welsh soldier, Owain, was on duty. He waved them on. Fergus nearly told Uncle Tally how they'd got talking, and how the squaddie was a fallen Pentecostalist from the mining Valleys, but he'd to concentrate on the gear changing as they started their ascent. Above them, a chink of blue appeared in the sky. Mountainside broke through the cloud. He nearly stalled changing down on a steep run of road.

'Watch out or we'll be rolling backwards.'

'I like it up here, Unk.' Fergus tooted the horn at a sheep on the tarmac. It kangarooed off across the gorse. 'You can breathe easier up here. It's like the Troubles don't follow you. They stay below.'

Uncle Tally sighed. 'It's a bloody messed-up country, all right, down there.'

Fergus pulled in at the top. They wound down the windows and looked out at the view. The movement of the clouds was lovely. The world below was a round, swirling marble.

'Unk?'

'What?' Uncle Tally was lighting a cigarette, nodding his head as if listening to invisible music.

'Why aren't you or Da in the IRA? How come you stayed out?'

Uncle Tally blew out a ring of smoke. It hovered, expanded, then grew ragged and fell apart. 'We were too old.'

'You? Too old?'

'I'm eight years younger than your da, but that's still old. I'll be forty later this year.'

'Never.'

'I will. By the time the Troubles got going this time around, your da was already a family man. Otherwise he'd have joined up before you could say *Fenian fanatic.*'

'Fanatic?'

'You live in this place a few months, you become one. We're all deranged by now.'

'You're not.'

'Who says?'

'Everyone. You're just you, Unk. Nobody tells you what to do.'

'Wish that were true.'

'I still don't know why you didn't join up.'

'It just wasn't my scene, Ferg.'

Fergus looked at his uncle's face. It was exactly

what he'd said to Michael Rafters earlier, only in his own case it hadn't been enough to get him off the hook.

His uncle offered him the cigarette packet. 'Go on. Have one.'

Fergus took one. He didn't like smoking much, but had the occasional fag to be companionable. 'I'm leaving right after my A levels, Unk. I'm going to find a summer job over in England, then go to medical school. If I get the grades. I'll be away from all this.' He gestured to the valley below.

Uncle Tally offered him a light. It took a few goes with his lighter in the fresh wind. 'Good on you, Ferg. Get away. As soon as you can. I only wish to God I had, years ago.'

There didn't seem anything to say after that. They stared at the great bowl of life below and smoked. When they finished the cigarettes, Fergus drove on up as far as the cut. The JCB digger was still there, silent, and three cars were already parked in a line on the bridleway, the back one a smart green Renault 5 with a Dublin registration. Dotted around the hill was a handful of anoraked figures, measuring and examining. Across the bog the tarpaulin was hoisted on poles to form an awning. It flapped in the high breeze. By it, two figures stood out against the horizon. One was down in the cut, so that the bottom half was truncated, the other, tall and thin, stood to the side.

'More action,' Uncle Tally said. He lit another cigarette. 'You go and see what's up. I'll stay here.'

'Don't you want to find out what's going on?'

54

'That child is dead and gone, Fergus. Nothing can bring her back to life.'

Fergus shrugged and got out. He picked his way over to the tarpaulin. The figures there surprised him by turning into two young women as he drew closer. The one out of the cut dangled a measuring tape, as if bored. The one in it was speaking into a handheld recorder. Her voice was clear and precise, with a Dublin accent. She'd a restless gait.

'*The girl, if it is a girl,*' she was saying into the recorder, '*may have been four feet tall, if her legs were intact. Her left arm is exposed, in a position that is twisted up around her head. Her right arm is lying prone to her ribcage, with a distinctive bangle on her wrist . . .*'

She had a neat head of dark cropped hair and wore jeans with a faded blue sweater. As she recorded, she swung herself from right to left, her nose an inch from the cut's wall, staring at the body as at a masterpiece in an art gallery.

The younger woman with the measuring tape wore leggings and an outsize grey man's jumper that came down nearly to her knees. Her nose tilted up. She was biting her underlip.

'Hello,' said Fergus.

The younger girl started. She'd to shade her eyes as the sun appeared from behind a cloud. Fergus could see her more easily than she could see him. She'd white skin, almost as if she was unwell. Her hair wasn't cropped but grew flat and dark down to her shoulders.

They were surely sisters.

'H'lo. Who're you?' the girl asked.

'I'm Fergus. Fergus McCann.'

She frowned, as if the name might mean something.

'I'm the one who found her.'

A smile broke over her face. 'Mam,' she called over to the cut.

Mam?

'*The metal could be gold, and the style is in tune with Roman or pre-Roman, and the finger spools are in evidence, showing excellent preservation—*'

'Mam!'

'What?' The woman in the cut looked up. She'd the kind of face that thrived in the outdoors, with faint lines around her blue eyes and vigour in her cheeks. She looked more an older sister than a mam.

'This is the lad you asked about. The one that stopped the diggers. Fergus McCann.'

Fergus blinked. The older woman switched off the cassette and pocketed it. She laid her forearms down on top of the cut and sprang up like a gymnast. She smiled as she straightened up, rubbing dirt from her fingers like flour.

'Am I glad to meet you, Fergus,' she said, holding out her hand. 'I'm Felicity O'Brien. This is Cora, my daughter.'

Fergus nodded. 'Hi.' He shook her hand and then gestured with his arm at the car. 'That's my uncle parked over there.'

'And you found her?'

'We did.'

56

'How come?'

Fergus nearly said they'd been after some turf, but stopped himself just on time. 'Uncle Tally and I were up here early. Bird-watching. And I used the cut as a covert.'

'A covert?'

Fergus nodded. 'Then I saw the gleam of the bangle.'

The woman called Felicity whistled. 'I'd say all archaeology's in your debt, Fergus.'

Fergus looked down and ran the toe of his boot over some heather.

'In archaeology,' Felicity continued, 'usually a body like this is named after the place it's nearest. But we still don't know if this lassie here is *Drumleash Child* or *Inchquin Child*. Or even if it's a she. The police are still arguing over which side of the border can lay claim to her. So I thought I'd resort to another tradition. Which is to have the one who found her christen her.'

'You can't christen a pagan,' Fergus pointed out. 'Especially not a dead one.'

Cora guffawed. 'So you can't, Mam. He's right.'

Felicity waved their comments aside. 'We can't be sure how old she is,' she said. 'Not before carbon-dating. She could turn out to be medieval. Or even later. But somehow I don't think so.'

'Why's that?'

'The bangle, partly. And the presence of this.' She reached down and took a sod of earth. It was shot through with a soft, light-coloured layer of moss.

'What's that?' said Fergus, peering.

'It's sphagnum moss.'

'Moss?'

'It's found in bog-land like this. They used it in the First World War to dress wounds. There's a quality in it that stops decay.'

'Never.'

'It's true,' Felicity said. 'Bodies decompose because of microbes, and this moss stops the microbes.'

'They should put it in face creams,' Fergus said. 'You could make a mint.'

Felicity laughed. 'This child reminds me very much of other bodies they've found over the years, in Denmark especially.'

'Denmark?'

Felicity nodded. 'There was a ritual in Iron-Age times around this kind of terrain, across northern Europe. We don't know much but it seems that bodies were placed in the bog for a reason. And my colleagues in Iron-Age history mostly think it involved human sacrifice.'

Fergus stared. 'Sacrifice?' He looked to where he could see the little hand reaching out from the wall of earth. 'Jesus. The poor child.'

'On the other hand, they might have been criminals, guilty of something serious.'

'But a child? Surely you wouldn't execute a child?'

Felicity sighed. 'That's indeed a puzzler. Maybe she died of natural causes. It's quite likely. We'll have to get her out and do a post-mortem, just as if she was born in our time. The bangle suggests that she was a person from an important local family. Who knows? Maybe we'll have to rethink all the theories.' She crouched down by the side of the cut and reached a hand towards the place where the head would be, if exposed.

'I wish I could help you,' Fergus said.

'Maybe you can. Couldn't he, Cora?'

The girl stepped forward and put a hand on Fergus's arm, as if she was testing to see if he was worthy. 'Yes. He could.'

Cora's hand stayed on his arm for a fraction and then fluttered away.

'Really? Could I?' Fergus felt like a child who can't sleep on Christmas Eve, mad to get down in that cut and brush away the earth from the child's face.

'You can help us organize the shifting. We'll need a whole team of strong locals, because we'll have to shift the whole block of earth around her, and expose her carefully when she's safe indoors.'

'Where's she going?'

'We're moving her to the Roscillin abattoir, temporarily. They can't decide if she should go to Belfast or Dublin and until they've sorted that out, we need to keep her cool.'

Fergus thought of the dead carcasses of animals hanging and the small child lying on a slab in the middle of them. 'Ugh.'

'Ugh is right,' Cora agreed.

'It's not ideal,' Felicity said. 'Just our luck for her to turn up bang on the border. Has any name sprung to mind?'

'Sorry?'

'For our bog child?'

Fergus squinted up his eyes and examined the little hunched figure, curled like a brown gnome. In his mind she was climbing out of the bog and dancing like a plasticine model in an animation, shaking dirt from her eyes. '*I dug and delved the mountain, but it wasn't here, it wasn't there,*' she trilled. He realized it was the baby-doll voice of a pop star he'd had a crush on when he was eleven. 'Mel,' he said. 'That's her name. Short for Melanie. But everybody calls her Mel.'

'Mel?' said Felicity. 'That's Latin for honey. Maybe if she's as late as Roman period, she really could have been called that.'

'What if it turns out to be a boy?' Cora asked.

Fergus shrugged. 'Then I'll think of something else.'

Felicity grinned. She jumped back into the cut, got out her cassette and switched it on. '*Fergus McCann, the finder, has just informed us that she, if indeed she's a she, is to be called Mel. So, Mel – welcome to the light of day.*'

Nine

*Da called me to his side that dark winter. Fog was as thick as
fur and day hardly came close. 'Mel,' he said. 'What, Da?'
'I've a job for you.' 'What job?' 'It's to run to the Shaughns
over and say we've no grain or meat or milk to spare for the
payment and I am putting down my cloak across the
threshold.' 'Am I to say all that?' 'All that, and just like
that.'*

*So I ran around the mountain and down the Sky Road,
and soon I came to the Shaughns' settlement with the palings
around it. They let me in. Inside, the fires were smoking and
the men were huddled round them, eating and chatting. Boss
Shaughn stood up when I approached. He was taller and
broader than a doorway but I wasn't scared. I told him what
Da had said. And Boss Shaughn said it was some day when
a pipsqueak was sent to bring upstart news about cloaks and
thresholds and withholding payments. I stared, and he
wagged his head like a dog about to pounce and everyone
started laughing. 'Go back to your da and tell him I'll be over
to chat about the payment tomorrow. Cloak or no cloak.'*

*I turned on my heel, ready to run back up and around
the mountain, thinking how I hated those Shaughns. But I*

tripped and fell and they laughed even harder. Except Boss Shaughn's son, Rur. He came over and helped me to my feet. My head only came to his elbow but I looked up at him and he smiled. I remembered him from when I was a wee one, how he'd given me swings in the air. 'Hi, Mel,' he'd say. 'How's the shrimpling today?' and chafe my cheeks. This time, he stooped and whispered, 'Don't mind them.' His eyes were away to the middle distance and didn't meet mine. 'On you go, Mel, my girl,' he said, kneading my shoulder. 'Quick.'

I ran off, my cheeks burning. Mel, my girl. My girl, Mel. His words spun in my head. All the way home I could feel his hand on my shoulder, like the brand of a fire-iron, and see his beard trimmed neat and his shoulders narrow. And his eyes looking away into the middle distance, like the riddle of time was written there.

My life fell apart like two halves of an apple, with Rur's hand that day on my shoulder being the knife.

Fergus was so tired when he came home that he drifted off over his books, somewhere amidst a procedure to measure the breaking stress of copper. The images of figures and fog and the feel of another person's touch on his arm dissolved with the sound of the doorbell.

Felicity and Cora, he thought. *They've arrived.* They'd said they needed a place to stay for a couple of nights and he'd told them about the guest twin room. Thanks to him, Mam had bed and breakfast customers for the first time in three years. She'd been thrilled when he told her. Money was in short supply. Theresa and Cath had been drilled into hoovering and dusting. He'd helped Mam make up the beds and she'd shown him how to do neat hospital corners with the sheets. Then he'd scrubbed the room's sink. Mam had polished the mirror until it squeaked. And now they were here.

He slammed shut the book and darted out into the hallway to greet them.

But it wasn't them. It was their neighbour, Mrs Sheehan, from the top of the close. Her son Len was in the same prison block as Joe and was serving the same sentence. Often she and Mam went together on the visits, sharing the driving. She stood in the doorway in her green leather coat, a picture of faded glamour. But the coat flapped open and she was running a hand through her hairdo and her cheeks were white. Her mouth opened but no words came out.

'What is it?' Mam said, tugging at her hand. 'Come in and tell me. What is it, Maureen?'

'Oh, Pat. It's our boys. Yours and mine. Our boys.'

'You mean Joey?'

'Joey. And Len.' She tottered forward, her fingers seeking out the petals of the rose-flower pattern on the hall wallpaper. Fergus shot forward to stop her from falling.

'My God. What's happened to them?'

'They've been moved. To the H-block where the strikers are.'

Nobody said anything. Then Fergus became aware of Cath standing near him. She was staring at Mrs

Sheehan, pulling at the baubles on her cardigan. Then her jaw dropped and she screamed.

'Mother of God,' said Mam. 'Shush, Cath.' She crossed herself. 'This is not what it seems. Joey wouldn't join them. He's more sense.'

Cath screamed louder. Fergus, without knowing what he was doing, went and picked her up in his arms. He rushed off with her down the hall, through the kitchen, and out into the back yard. He put her down, still bawling, under the fluttering washing. Theresa was down at the shed, kicking a ball around.

'What's up with her?' she said.

'It's Joey,' said Fergus. 'They've moved him to another block in Long Kesh.'

'So?'

'So – maybe nothing.'

Theresa came up and spanked Cath on the cheek.

'What d'you do that for?' Fergus cried, snatching at Theresa's arm.

''S what they do in the movies, Ferg. To stop hysterics. Look. It works.'

Cath stopped crying. Her little hands grabbed at the corner of a sheet and scrunched it up, as if to stop the wind billowing through it. 'Will he die, Ferg?' she bleated. 'Will they all die?'

Fergus put an arm around Cath. 'Don't be stupid,' he said. 'Nobody's going to die. You only die if you starve yourself like Sands did for sixty days or more. But our Joe's more sense. Hasn't he?'

'Dunno,' Theresa said. 'He was always fussy with his food. Not like you. I heard Mam say the other

64

day you'd eat a load of old offal out of a dustbin.'

Cath started crying again. When Theresa tried to slap her a second time, Cath got Theresa's plait and yanked it hard and Theresa started crying too.

'Pipe down,' he shouted, but they squealed and shrieked as if the sky was coming down. They lunged at each other, bringing the sheet off the line, and fell to the grass, wrangling. Fergus gave up on them. He went down to the shed and kicked the football hard at the back fence. It missed, but an army of sparrows came darting and chattering out of the ivy. He retrieved the ball and kicked it again.

'He's more sense,' he said through gritted teeth. 'He has, he has.'

Ten

Next day, Sunday, was mass day. There was no further news from the prison, so the family went to church as usual.

Fergus had stopped believing in God when he was eight, after he'd seen his da come in with a Christmas stocking and realized Santa didn't exist. If Santa didn't exist, then God didn't either. As far as he was concerned, grown-ups had done one big cheat about the two of them. Years went by and he hadn't changed his mind.

But in Drumleash, you went to church whether you believed or not. Everyone, that was, except Uncle Tally, who never went near the place. Today, Fergus lingered at the back near the other men. He let the old words waltz around the bright benches and big windows of light.

'*Lamb of God who takes away the sins of the world, Grant us peace,*' the women intoned. The UFO-style church was a fling of the 1960s, before the Troubles. The place smelled of polish and tedium. He watched the hundred-odd parishioners sighing, fidgeting or praying their way through the service. The older women still wore triangled scarves on their heads. Not exactly Jackie Onassis, he thought as ancient Mrs Riley bustled down the aisle after communion with her belly slumping below the waistline of her floral dress. If she wasn't nearly eighty, you'd think she was pregnant. *Jesus. The place is more outmoded than Des O'Connor on a bad day.*

He thought of Felicity in her sharp jeans and short haircut and of Cora as he'd glimpsed her that morning coming out of the guest bedroom, in an outsized white T-shirt with a green-leaved tree pictured on the front.

After the post-communion meditation, the priest said something about remembering in prayer the starving people in the land. That's Joe and Len, Fergus thought. Who else? He bit his lip but no prayer came. Joe wouldn't join the hunger strikers. Not he. He'd be doing his studies and counting the days. He'd be pacing his cell and thinking about freedom. He'd be shaving in the mirror, thinking about light and refraction. And remembering the girl from Newry he'd been seeing when they arrested him. Cindy, her name was. And he'd be thinking of the next family visit. Surely.

On the other side of the church he saw Michael Rafters with his head bowed over clasped hands. *You're the best runner this side of the county. A small price to pay, Fergus. A small, small price.*

He thought of Felicity and Cora. They hadn't come to church but were up on the mountain again, investigating the earth surrounding the body. Mam had ordered the family to say nothing about Joe to them and he'd obeyed. But the secret was like a wedge of politeness. They'd arrived late in the evening. He'd felt foolish, nodding at them, showing them to their room, pointing out the bar of soap, wishing the sheets weren't old polyester and the curtains and carpet not faded brown. But they'd said how comfortable they'd be and he'd felt like a giraffe in a kennel and backed away.

'The mass is ended, go in peace,' Father Doyle said.

'Thanks be to God,' the whole congregation said loudly, as if in relief it was over. Fergus slipped out of the door without bothering to bless himself with water from the font. He escaped through the pristine grave-yard with its gravel plots and plastic see-through crosses full of plastic flowers. He'd a vision suddenly, of a burial party huddled in the far corner under the great Scots pine, where the McCann plot was, burying Joe in a pathetic, thin coffin. He slapped his head. That was not going to be. He meandered over to the bench at the opposite corner and sat down. The sun shone and made him weary. He let his eyelids shut and listened to the chatter of people leaving, the crows cawing and the wind in the hills. *Joey will be fine and I'll be out of here. Soon. Sooner. Soonest.*

When he opened his eyes, Michael Rafters was sitting beside him. *Jesus.* The man was a panther.

'So,' Michael said, crossing his legs and slouching back.

'So what?' said Fergus.

'Your brother's joined the strikers, I hear.'

'He's been moved to a different block. That's all we've heard.'

'And why was he moved?'

Fergus shrugged. 'Dunno.'

'I'll tell you why.'

'Why?'

'He and your man Sheehan. They joined the strike yesterday morning. Then the screws moved them out, before the strike could spread where they were. That's the truth of it.'

Fergus bit his lip. 'I don't believe it.'

'It's true. I had it from a good source.'

Fergus looked at the light playing on top of the Scots pine and said nothing.

'It's their choice,' Michael said. 'I'm sorry.'

'It's a bloody farce.'

'It's a struggle, Fergus. Not a farce. It's in deadly earnest.'

Fergus raised up his hands as if to embrace all the dead of the graveyard. He sucked his lips in between his teeth hard, to stop his eyes filling.

'Fergus, we need you. Just for a few bits of ferrying. Nothing more. We don't pressgang people here. We're not like the Brits. But we could really use your help. Just this once.'

'I've my exams starting.'

'I know. And with Joe and all, you've distractions enough. But this is just something to add to your regular morning run; totally safe, I promise.

But so important to the struggle, I can't tell you.'

'I want a united Republic, same as anyone, but—'

'There's no other way to get it. That's a fact. We've a Long War on our hands, Ferg. We've all to pull our weight.'

Fergus stood up. 'Dafters,' he said.

Michael smiled up at him, his lips framing a *What?*

'You've your way of doing things and I've mine. I don't judge. I just want peace.'

'You sound like those bloody Belfast wives. Soft and gooey in the centre.'

'Yes. That's me. Soft as they come.'

'You'll be getting the Nobel Prize next.' Michael playfully punched him in his belly. 'Fergus, Joe was always mighty proud of you. Your brains and speed. Mr Nippy, he called you. I remember.'

Fergus smiled. 'He was always getting me to run errands. Down the village to get his fags. Down to Roscillin for the *Morning Star* which he had on order. That was his communist phase.'

'Think of this as another errand. For Joe's sake.'

Fergus slowly shook his head.

'You're a fit man. We've watched you. You run like the wind. There's only ever one squaddie posted up there. At most. And easy to dodge. I promise you, you'd be helping the Cause big time. And helping the hunger strikers. It might even be the saving of them. Of Joe. Len. And the rest.'

'What d'you mean, the saving of them?'

Michael looked knowing. 'It's confidential. But it's an operation that's so fantastic, it will have all those Westminster bozos sitting up begging.'

'Jesus. What is it?'

Michael shook his head. 'You don't need to know. All you have to do is a pick-up and a drop. Just a few times. You'd see nobody, meet nobody and nobody would bother you ever again. I swear.'

Fergus watched his mam and the two girls walking from the church. Mam looked over and beckoned.

'A pick-up?'

'Yep.'

'What of?'

'That would be telling.'

'An envelope? A package? What?'

Michael Rafters looked around and dropped his voice. 'A jiffy bag, small enough to stuff down your running shorts.'

Fergus waved the information away as if he was rubbing it out. 'Sorry, Dafters. There's Mam waving at me. I've got to go.'

'Think about it, McCann. I need to know. By tomorrow.'

'Fergus!' Mam called.

Michael's eyebrow went up as if to say *That's mothers for you*. Then he skimmed away, merging with the crowd.

Fergus joined his mam at the gate.

'You've no business getting tangled up with that Michael Rafters,' she scolded. 'His first and last name is trouble.'

'We were just chatting, Mam. About Joey.'

'Oh?'

Fergus dropped his voice so that the girls wouldn't hear. 'He says he's already on the strike. That's why they moved him. He says he has it from a good source.'

Mam grabbed his sleeve. 'Shush,' she said. Her face froze with her eyes wide open. A wind got up in the trees and a flock of crows took off yattering into the sky. Her grip on his arm tightened, then her lips grew firm with resolve. 'Joey,' she whispered, 'I'm coming. Your mam's coming and I don't care if I sit outside that prison until midnight, they're letting me in to you.'

Fergus put his arm around her waist. 'I'll come too, Mam. I can drive you. Please let me.'

'Would you?'

'I would. I'll put the learner plates on.'

'And would you think of some arguments, Fergus?'

'Arguments?'

'To get Joey eating. You were always good at the arguments. He'd listen to you before he'd listen to me.'

'I'll try.'

'We'll go after dinner. Your da's working and he's a visit booked anyway for tomorrow. The girls can go over to the Caseys'.'

'Bake him something, Mam.'

Mam smiled. 'If that son of mine is starving himself, my rhubarb tart will have him eating again. It was always his favourite, wasn't it, Ferg? Wasn't it? And remember: not a word to the guests.'

Eleven

Felicity and Cora were still out when they got back. The door to the spare twin room was open. On one bed, Fergus glimpsed a pair of maroon, silky pyjamas, neatly folded. The other bed was unmade. The spread with the daisy pattern tipped over onto the floor, the sheets and blankets anyhow.

He'd have done anything to have been up and out with them both on that mountain, looking for relics of another age.

He went into the kitchen. Mam had the tart prepared and in the oven in record time. The family sat down to a hasty dinner of oven chips and frozen peas and burgers. Da sat at the top of the table, saying nothing. His wiry eyebrows were hunched and his mouth pursed. He toyed with his meat.

Cath and Theresa asked to be excused from the table, their plates half full. Mam nodded absently. 'Go down to the Caseys' and be good,' she said.

Da stood up. 'I'm back to work, Pat.'

'I'm sorry I didn't do a roast.'

'Never mind. We're none of us hungry.' He looked

at Fergus. 'You mind how you drive. Sunday drivers are the worst.'

Fergus nodded.

'If they let you in, tell Joe—'

'Tell him what?'

Da shook his head. 'I don't know.'

After he'd gone, it was time for the tart to come out of the oven. Mam cut it up, ready for examining by the prison guards, and wrapped it in foil, still warm. They set out.

The drive across the North was long and winding. The roads had a thoughtful quietness to them. Clouds scampered over the hills and valleys. Sun broke through fitfully. Mam sat beside him with the tart on her lap. It was three o'clock when they crossed into County Antrim.

They drew up to Long Kesh. The place, a converted RAF aerodrome, was like a low-lying colony for the miserable of the world. The sign at the main gate said HMP MAZE.

Herpes, Mastitis, Piles. A Maze of Misery. Fergus remembered reading how the Nazis had wanted to bomb the place out of existence in the Second World War. He wished they'd succeeded. When they got out of the car, all you could hear was wind and a distant lowing of cattle. The bleak and endless walls, topped with rolls of barbed wire, were barricades against the natural world.

At the entrance it was the usual routine: passports and driving licences to be shown, through the metal detector, hands up for the body search. The search was slow and deliberate. Every square inch of clothing was gone over, then a hand-held bomb detector was traced around them, as if checking their aura. Sniffer dogs were restrained on leashes. The uniformed guards were squeaky-clean, with chains and keys and 'This way, sirs, this way, madams'.

Across the yard, another gate. Then down long white corridors that smelled sulphurous, almost. This way to hell, thought Fergus.

Bars caged off every doorway. The place was like a laboratory for experiments on rats.

Unlock, lock. They went through three more gates and they'd to leave all their things, including the watch belonging to Joe that Fergus wore, in a plastic tub that was put in a cubby-hole. But they let Mam keep the tart. They looked over every piece, prodding each with a knitting needle. 'An exceedingly good pie, miss,' one screw joked. Then they were led to a waiting room. There was a guard at the door and two other people waiting silently on a bench.

'They let me keep the tart,' Mam whispered, sitting down. 'That's a good sign.'

Fergus nodded. 'If it makes Joey eat, they'll be thrilled,' he said, louder. His words hit the walls and died, echoless.

They waited. Mam's head sank down as if in prayer. Fergus looked around him. The windows were paned with frosted glass, making the light in the room dull and strange, as if the outdoors belonged to another world. He thought of the mountain and Cora standing with her hands shielding the sun from her eyes and Felicity springing up from the cut like Olga Korbut and the mysterious figure of the child he'd named Mel, lying prone, awaiting a kind of resurrection.

'Mrs McCann. Through here.'

A screw beckoned them. Mam grabbed Fergus by the arm. 'They're letting us in, Ferg. They're letting us in to see him.'

They were taken down another white corridor, around a right-angle turn and down a long passageway and around another right angle and through another locked door, with the keys jingle-jangling and a fluorescent light blinking, and then into a long room. A line of visiting booths was divided by a glass-panelled partition.

They were brought to a table at the far end. They sat down and looked through the glass to the seat opposite. There was nobody there.

They waited again.

A visit was going on three tables down. The girl on the visitors' side looked no older than sixteen. She chattered eagerly through the glass in an undertone, but you couldn't help catching a stray phrase. '*Jerry says she's raving . . . too bloody right I phoned . . . and the clutch gone again on it . . . another scan, Wednesday . . . What d'you mean, it's OK?*' It sounded like whoever was on the other side of the glass couldn't get a word in. She had her hand under her denim jacket on her belly. Fergus could see a baby on the way.

A bustle from the other side made him look back through his own portion of glass.

76

Mam's fingers tightened on his elbow. 'That's his voice. Joey's voice.'

In the faded blue of the prison garb, Joey's tall form appeared. As he sat down, his face came into view. His lips were chapped and his eyes bright, as if he had a fever. He beamed at the sight of them.

'Mam. Ferg. What a surprise.' He flopped down in the chair and stretched out his arms as if he had the whole world to embrace. Then he dropped his elbows down on the table and propped his chin up on his knuckles. 'Hi.'

'Hi?' Mam said. 'Is that all you can say? Hi?'

'Hello, then.'

'Joe McCann. You were doing the refraction on Friday. Next thing I hear you've joined the hunger strikers. Tell me it's not true.'

'Mam, I'm sorry. I should have warned you.'

Mam stared. 'You mean you *are* on it?'

Joe closed his eyes and nodded. 'We joined yesterday, Len and me.'

'Why? Why would you do that?'

'Why d'you think?' He opened his eyes again and smiled. 'I want to drop a trouser size. I've been putting on weight inside here.'

'Stop that, Joey. Tell me why you're doing this.'

'Like they say. Less is more.'

They stared at him. He was smiling now, almost euphoric.

'It's not something I'm *doing*. It's something I'm *not* doing.'

Fergus felt the three arguments he'd been

preparing unravelling. His belly churned from the hasty dinner they'd had. Calmly, Mam took the foil-wrapped tart from her lap and put it on the table. 'The guards say I can leave this for you. It's your favourite. Rhubarb. And I made it fresh before coming. And it's all butter, no margarine.'

Fergus saw Joe's nostrils widen for an instant and then he shook his head. 'You shouldn't have.'

'It came out good, Joe.'

'You have some, Fergus. My belly's a bit puffed up. With air, don't you know.' He laughed.

'This – is – no – joke,' Fergus said, his teeth clenched. He thumped the table on the word 'joke'.

The guard tut-tutted.

'Hush,' Mam said.

Joe put a hand out and touched the glass. 'It's all right, Mam. Ferg's right. It is no joke.'

Mam took a slice from the foil and held it up. 'It's good food,' she said. 'Flour, fruit, sugar, butter. Good food. Put here for us to eat.'

Joe made a motion like a priest might, blessing the holy bread. 'I know. But it's a strange time we live in. And we have to do strange things to get out of the strange time.'

'But not starve yourself, Joe. It's not natural.'

'That's my point. This is an unnatural time. See, Mam, it's like this. I'm not a common criminal. What I did was fight for freedom. I'd rather die free in my own head than live like the dregs of the earth. And that's how they treat us here, I swear to God.'

'Can't you just turn the other cheek?'

Joe shook his head. 'It's not as simple as that. It's about dignity, Mam. Human dignity. Da understands. We talked about it last time he came in. It's about freedom and dignity. Clothes, visits, the right not to muck in with the common prisoners. The right to keep ourselves apart, doing what we want to do. It's the right to hold our heads up and not be ashamed of what we've done. And me and the boys here – we're in this together.'

'Oh, Joe. Fergus. Say something to him.'

Fergus swallowed. No words came.

'You were always good with the arguments, Fergus.'

Fergus looked through the glass and caught Joe's smiling eyes. He took a breath and began the first argument he'd been rehearsing in his head.

'Joe – the Thatcher woman over – she's not for turning. She says it again and again.'

'I know.'

'When Sands died, all she said was he'd had a choice and the bomb victims didn't. That was the extent of her regret.'

'You sound like you agree with her.'

'I don't, but—'

'There are no buts. You're either for us or against us. And more are for us all the time. And that's what counts.' Joe leaned forward, his eyes shining. 'There's a sea-change. I can feel it. Even in here, I can sense it.'

'I feel nothing.'

'How can you say that, when Sands won the Fermanagh seat?'

79

'I voted for him. But I'd rather him alive than dead.' Fergus paused. He put his right palm on the glass and leaned forward. 'Joe, it's a brave thing you're doing.'

'Thanks.'

'But a foolish thing. Vain. I know in my bones. It will get you nowhere, only into a coffin. What use is that?'

'A coffin's a mighty statement, Ferg.'

'It's the end, Joe. It's worms and earth and generations coming after you that have never even heard of you.'

'They'll hear of Bobby. For years and years they'll remember him. Wasn't there a hundred thousand people at his funeral?'

'And fighting on the streets, Joe. Petrol bombs. More killings.'

Joe waved a hand as if this had nothing to do with it. 'I tell you who will remember him most.'

'Who?'

'Those who killed him, as surely as if they put a gun to his head. They'll remember him for ever. He'll be like a ghost, haunting them.'

Fergus sighed. The argument was going nowhere. It was as if Joe had an incubus in him doing the talking. It wasn't his old, familiar brother on the other side of the glass, but somebody new, with new associations, new purposes. Fergus shifted in his seat, searching for another argument, one that would bring Joe closer. Then he had it.

'Joe – remember John Lennon.'

'Who could forget him? The nearest thing to Christ in our time.'

Fergus sang *sotto voce*: '*In the middle of the night. In the middle of the night I call your name. Oh Yoko!* Your favourite, Joey.'

Joey smiled. '*My love will turn you on,*' he said. He flicked his eyebrows suggestively and did an hour-glass shape with his hands.

Fergus smiled. 'It's about love and life, Joey. Not coffins, or martyrdom. And what about the refraction? The physics. And your Newry girl waiting on you.'

'Cindy? She's history.'

'History?'

'She went off with another fellow. I told her to forget me and she did.'

'There are plenty more girls. Stacks of them.'

Mam leaned forward. 'The girls were always mad for you, Joe. I remember Sandra Gannon mooning round our back door. And you only thirteen.'

Joey splayed his fingers. 'Spare me.'

They sat in silence.

After a moment Fergus took a slice of Mam's tart and held it up on the palm of his hand. Mimicking Joe's earlier gesture, he blessed it. '*Take this and eat it,*' he said.

'Fergus!' Mam said.

'*This is my body,*' said Fergus, ignoring her. He shook his head and touched the crust. 'I don't think so. It's what it looks like. God-honest plain tart. And delicious with it.'

Joe beamed a smile. 'You're the same old clown, Ferg.'

Fergus took a bite. 'It's fantastic, Joe. Superb.'

He ate the slice up.

'You should try it.' He held out another slice. Joe shook his head. 'Please, Joe. Come off this weary strike.'

Joe shook his head. 'It's day two now. Every day gets easier, so they say.'

'Easier for you. Harder for us. Right, Mam?'

'That's right. Listen to him, Joe. You've us all paralysed with fright.'

'You mustn't worry about me. I'm doing what I want to do. Can't you respect that, either of you?'

'Your life's your own to ruin. But what about Fergus's? You're putting him off his exams.'

'I'd never want to hurt you.' Joe reached a hand to the glass. 'Oh, Fergus. Mam. Never.' Fergus saw a tear start from his brother's eye. He held his breath in hope.

'Isn't every moment I think of you starving yourself a torment?' Mam said.

Joe leaned back and Fergus bit his lip.

'Come back to us, Joe,' Mam blurted, her face pressed to the glass. 'Please.'

A spasm of something crossed Joe's face. His eyes and nose scrunched up. But then the moment evaporated. His forehead smoothed out like clean paper. 'I am in no pain, Mam. The hunger's nothing. It comes and goes and then it vanishes for good. And then you're bright and clear. Fasting is what holy men have done for centuries. All around the world.' Joe stretched his arms out like a bird. 'They say the second week's like floating. Flying and floating.'

'Joe,' Fergus called. But Joe had shut his eyes and was shaking his head, as if rubbing out all the arguments. The moment of possibility had passed.

Fergus put the slice back in the foil and wrapped it up. 'It's no good, Mam. He's not listening.'

Joe opened his eyes. He looked tired and sad. 'I'm listening, Fergus. It's you who's not listening to me.'

Fergus looked at his brother. He thought of the bog child, the archaeologists, the driving lessons and the exams. They no longer existed in this place. He opened his mouth to say something, then gave up.

'What were you going to say, Fergus?'

'Nothing. Only another thing John Lennon wrote.'

'What?' Joe's eyes opened again.

'*I don't wanna to be a soldier Mama, I don't wanna die.*'

Joe laughed. 'You're a card, Ferg. Just a song. Written in another place, another time.' His eyes shut again. 'Pacifism's a luxury, Ferg. It's not for the likes of us.' He was leaning back, arms dangling, humming the tune.

Fergus stood up and touched Mam's shoulder. 'Let's go,' he whispered.

'Have you no more arguments, Fergus? There must be another argument.'

'I can't think of one.'

'Oh, Fergus. And we nearly had him persuaded.'

83

The prison guard came forward as Fergus stood up.

'You're ready to go?' he asked.

Fergus nodded. 'We're ready to go.'

Mam buried her head in her hands. He'd to reach down to help her up from her chair.

'Come on, Mam.'

'Say your goodbyes now,' said the guard.

'Can we leave the tart for him?' Mam pleaded.

'If you wish. There on the side.'

They called a goodbye to Joe, who opened his eyes and waved. 'See you,' he said. 'Drop in for tea again, won't you? Be my guest. Any time.' He smiled, shrugged his shoulders and crossed his arms over his belly. His eyes stared past them without focusing.

'Bye, Joe,' Mam managed. The guard ushered them out, with Mam looking back over her shoulder.

'And him a reed at the best of times,' she moaned.

Fergus shook his head. Joe was a reed no more: like he'd said himself earlier, he'd put on weight in jail and that might stand him in good stead now. But Mam was weeping, quietly. Fergus steered her down the bleak corridors and through the gated doorways. When they got back outside, with the last door closed behind them, Fergus made a sound like a horse blowing out through its muzzle.

'Jesus. It's like *Alice in* Bloody *Wonderland* in there.'

Mam held him by the crook of the elbow as if she was sixty, not forty. 'Take me home, Fergus.'

He helped her into the passenger seat of the car. He fixed the mirror and reversed out, concentrating hard. Then he drove back the way they'd come. Miles, villages and houses rolled by and the Troubles were everywhere, in the barricaded police stations, the hunch of people's shoulders on the pavements, and even in the ragged shards of light. Mam said nothing the entire journey, not even when Fergus speeded up to seventy-five miles an hour on a long straight strip of A-road. She sat staring out of the window at the evening sky, kneading her fingertips with her thumbs, as if she was preparing another rhubarb tart.

Twelve

That night, in bed, the mountain called to him. He had a sparrowhawk's view, zooming in on the grasses and the gorse, the wind-stunted trees, the lichen-covered rocks. And there was the cut, with the tarpaulin over it, billowing in the breeze. And the child under it, waiting. And the JCB silent.

He heard a cough from the spare twin room, then a creak. Either Cora or Felicity had turned over in their sleep. He imagined their faces on the pillows, Cora's forehead in the crook of her elbow, Felicity on her back in her maroon silk, her straight firm nose pointing upwards, her eyelids still.

Then he was back in the prison, mouthing better arguments, and Joe was listening, reaching out through the glass, which dissolved at a touch. 'Joe, come off that weary strike,' he whispered. The memories of the years flew at him like cards in a deck: Joe showing him how to rake up cut grass, then shaking the implement up at the sky like a hellish imp's pronged fork and chasing Fergus around the house.

In the middle of the night
In the middle of the night I call your name
Oh Yoko!

Joe carol-singing with Dafters and himself, the three reprobates, shaking the collecting tins for the St Vincent de Paul Society like maracas and their songs coming out like white balloons in cartoons, getting dirtier with every doorbell. *We three kings of buggered-up Eire, selling condoms, tuppence a pair* ... Joe boogying with Mam in the drawing room on Christmas Day to the fast bit of *Bohemian Rhapsody*, Mam's favourite pop song.

In the middle of a shave
In the middle of a shave I call your name

Joe with the razor, giving Fergus his first-ever shave, and their laughing like crazed orang-utans. Joe on the football field, going for broke, and the whole school cheering him as the ball went home to the corner of the net like a kiss.

In the middle of a cloud
In the middle of a cloud I call your name

And the police coming for him on that winter's night, with Da hollering like a shot elephant and Mam gripping the back of the chair and Joe at the door, saying nothing, just taking off his watch and giving it to Fergus, saying, 'Mind it for me, Ferg. Keep it safe,' and then holding out his hands for the cuffs, smiling.

Oh Yoko! The memory cards flew off and away like scared birds. The name Yoko turned to Joey and then Fergus slept.

In the middle of a dream, Rur. In the middle of a dream I call your name.

Thirteen

'Today is the day,' Felicity said. 'Exhumation.'

The girls had gone to school and Da to work. Mam had the fry going. Fergus was helping. His head was pounding from the bad night, but he smiled as if nothing was wrong when the guests appeared for breakfast. Cora said she only wanted an egg, but Felicity wanted the works – beans, potato cake, egg, bacon, sausage.

'My school friends in Roscillin are coming over to help,' Fergus said. 'You should see Padraig. He's six foot five, and built like a truck, with a Mohican on him.'

'We'll need every one of you.'

'Have you ever shifted something like this before?'

'Never. But Professor Taylor's arriving down from Queen's University, and the police pathologist. Between us all we should get her up in one piece. And the army's helping.'

'The army?'

'They're coming in a truck. They built a crate for her.'

Mam came in with the plates. Her face was white, the top button of her jeans undone. 'Fetch the sauce, Fergus.'

She put the plate of food down by Felicity. Fergus got the brown sauce and ketchup from the press. Mam reappeared carrying an eggcup with a brown egg popping out. She put it on Cora's side plate and vanished, shutting the door behind her.

'Sit down, Fergus,' Felicity coaxed.

He sat down. 'I don't want to intrude.'

'You're not intruding. Tell me, have you any theories?'

'Theories?'

'About Mel. She's your girl, after all.'

'Some girl. A bit leathery round the edges.'

Cora giggled, cracking open her egg. 'My theory is that she was a royal child. And buried there as a mark of honour when she died of measles. Or something simple like that.'

'Did they have measles back then?' Fergus asked.

Felicity speared a sausage. She munched thoughtfully. 'The Greek writer Thucydides might have been describing measles when he referred to a plague hitting Athens in the fifth century BC. I suppose Mel might have caught measles from traders coming up from the south. Maybe.'

'I don't think it's as simple as measles,' Fergus said.

'Why not?'

'You said there was an Iron-Age ritual of sacrifice. And she's lying strangely, like she fell or was dumped.'

'Don't forget the bangle,' Cora said.

90

Felicity nodded. 'There is that.'

'Maybe she was sacrificed to the pagan gods because the crops were failing. And a child with jewellery on her was a valuable sacrifice.'

Felicity offered Fergus some toast and he took it.

'Like kidnappers. They go for children to get the most ransom, don't they?'

'Interesting,' Felicity said. 'But my guess is, they didn't have much notion of childhood. She was old enough to work, so she was a person. You were either a baby or a worker, with nothing in between.'

'Not much fun to be young.'

'It probably wasn't.'

Cora put her spoon down. 'We've no evidence of how she died.'

'No,' Felicity agreed. 'We must see what the post-mortem brings. Finish your egg, Cora.'

Cora picked up the spoon again. She took out a dainty bit of white. 'I think Mel was like any child. Long-haired. Laughing. Naughty. I see her running around the mountains and going for boat rides on the lough, just like kids today. What d'you think, Fergus?'

He nodded. 'I'm sure her life had its joys.' He took another segment of toast and munched. 'Sometimes it's like she's alive still. At night, I've been dreaming of her. It's as if she's trying to tell me all about herself. As a warning or something.'

'The curse of the mummy's tomb . . .' Cora rolled her eyes and flicked her fingers. 'Wooo-hooo.'

Fergus laughed.

Felicity leaned over to pour tea into her cup.

'Fergus is right. That's what history is. A warning. For all of us. Only mostly, we don't listen.' She downed her tea in one. 'Now hurry on, Cora, so we can make strides. I don't want Professor Taylor getting his oar in before us.'

Fourteen

Fergus tried to persuade Mam to come up the mountain with them, but she was in no humour for it.

'The last thing I want to see is a dead child,' she said over the washing-up. 'And just you say nothing about Joey to anyone. D'you hear, Fergus?'

Fergus promised. He joined Felicity and Cora in the Renault and they set off. The ride around the lough was jaunty. Two swans swooped down, setting off a trail of water disturbance. Cora wound down the front passenger window and air rushed in, biting, exhilarating. The feeble strip-lights and smell of Long Kesh seemed a bad dream from another world.

The army checkpoint was empty.

'I think half Drumleash is coming,' Felicity said as they joined a procession of cars turning off up the bog road.

Sure enough, cars were parked yards back along the bridleway. They'd to walk the last stretch. A crowd milled about the peat workings, with a mix of Gardai and RUC men keeping order. Sunshine blazed down on the gorse. The peace of the place was gone. There were cameras, movement, laughter, like a pantomime in a church.

Felicity went straight over to where a grey-haired man with a grizzly beard was talking to an RUC officer. Cora and Fergus lingered by the silent JCB.

'You know, I've just realized,' Cora said, shading her eyes. 'Mel was buried with her head to the east. Like the song.'

'The song?'

'You know. The old John McCormack: *Will ye bury me on the mountain, With my face to God's rising sun.*'

She had a light, trilling voice but when she got to 'sun', she stopped and flushed.

'Go on,' Fergus urged. 'I don't know it.'

'I can't remember any more.'

'It's pretty.'

'Sentimental, more like.' Cora twisted the end of her baggy jumper round her finger. 'Quite a turn-out.'

'I wonder if the fact that she's facing east meant something.'

'You'd have to ask Mam. That's Professor Taylor she's talking to. He's top of the field. After Mam, that is. D'you know what they call her in Dublin?'

'What?'

'The Iron Lady. They leave out the "Age".'

Fergus chortled. 'She's a much nicer iron lady than Thatcher over.'

'Dunno. Mam's tougher than she seems.'

'Is she?'

'Yep. She grounded me for six months last year.'

'What for?'

94

Cora bit a lip. 'You won't laugh?'

'No.'

'I posed in a Warner bra. For a lingerie ad.'

Fergus stared. 'You never!'

'I did.'

'For a magazine?'

'A poster. My friend Laura put me onto the photography people. Only they never used it.'

He couldn't help staring at her front. There wasn't much to it going by the way the sweater skimmed straight downwards. He flushed up, then laughed.

Cora elbowed him in the ribs. 'You said you wouldn't laugh.'

Fergus gulped. 'Did they pay you?'

'Thirty punts.'

'Jay-*sus*. Would they take me on, d'you know?'

Cora clouted him, laughing too. She elbowed him and he elbowed her back and they laughed like goons. Then he froze. He saw Michael Rafters waving over to him from across the gorse. *We need to know, Fergus. By tomorrow.*

'Shush,' Cora said, stopping laughing too. 'There's Mam coming over, with the professor.'

Felicity drew up, beaming. 'Professor Taylor, Fergus. He wants to meet the discoverer.'

Fergus felt like Christopher Columbus the way the professor kept shaking his hand in congratulation, while Michael Rafters's eyes needled into him, like a blade in his back. 'Cora and I were wondering,' he blurted. 'Her head is towards the east. Does that mean anything?'

Professor Taylor considered. 'The Danish finds were every which way,' he said. 'But here in Ireland, we've little to go on.'

'We'd better get organized,' Felicity said. 'Talking of Denmark, we don't want another disaster on our hands like what happened there.'

'Why? What happened?' Fergus asked.

'When they lifted out the Tollund man, thirty-odd years ago, they planked him up into a box where he lay. And the ground being too soft for a crane, they'd to hoist it by manpower alone. One of the helpers had a heart attack and died. *The bog claimed a life for a life*, so they said. The villagers were petrified.'

Fergus shivered. 'The curse of the mummy's tomb. Like Cora said.'

'We've a simpler system here today. The army are supplying some tin sheeting for us to use. We're going to slip that under her and lift her out that way. Since her legs have already gone, there is less to remove – although we'll be sifting all around the area in case there's anything buried with her.'

'More jewellery?'

'Maybe a comb or some beads. Who knows? Anything at all would be a godsend. It would help us to date her. Give us a context.'

As Felicity spoke, a soft-topped Bedford truck drew right up on the track: the army. Four soldiers jumped down. One of them was Owain, the fallen Pentecostalist. He lounged in his fatigues, a bit apart from the others. The officer in charge came up towards them.

'Professor Taylor?' he enquired politely. He'd the same clipped English you heard in war movies, an accent of quiet, self-appointed leadership: *The empire's safe in our hands.*

Fergus drifted over to a quiet rock before Owain could have a chance to talk to him. He hoped Michael Rafters wouldn't follow. As he leaned up against a rock, he couldn't help catching Owain nodding at him, half smiling. Fergus bit his lip, unsure if he should respond. Then he nodded back, the merest tilt of his head, hoping nobody noticed. Seconds later, it was just as he thought. Michael Rafters was on to him.

'Have you decided, Fergus?'

Fergus looked at the bog grass beneath his boot. 'Yes.'

'So you'll do it?'

'I didn't say that. I said I've decided.'

'What have you decided?'

Fergus dropped his voice. 'Michael, when you join the Provos, is it *official*?'

'How d'you mean?'

'In the old days, when you joined, you read an oath. There was a chain of command. You were a soldier. Is it like that now?'

'More or less.'

'So Joe is under orders?'

Michael considered, leaning back against the rock next to Fergus. 'To a degree.'

'What does that mean, *to a degree*?'

'He's in prison, isn't he? Can our orders reach him there?'

97

'He's allowed visits. Mam and I saw him yesterday.'

'I'm sorry, Fergus. That must have been tough.'

There was a movement of the people towards the tarpaulin. Cameras began flashing.

'Michael, I don't want to join you. I'm leaving for Aberdeen when the summer's over. Whatever my results. If I can't go to college, I'll dig the roads. But I will do this thing for you, if—'

'That's great. It's just a bit of couriering, between now and the end of June.'

'*If.*'

'OK, OK. If what?'

'If whoever the man is who gives the orders tells Joe to stop.'

'Stop what?'

'His hunger strike, of course.'

'His hunger strike?'

'Yes.'

Michael whistled softly. 'He was never *ordered* onto it in the first place. It was his own choice, Fergus.'

'He's a soldier, right?'

'Absolutely. That's the whole point of the strike. We are an army fighting another army. He's a prisoner of war.'

'And a soldier obeys orders, right?'

Michael shrugged. 'I know what you're driving at, but—'

The word seemed to float off into the sky. After a moment he put his hand on Fergus's arm.

'I will talk to the man you mean. I will put the word through. But I can't promise the result you want.'

'But you promise to try?'

'I promise.'

'Fergus! We're waiting for you at the cut.' Cora ran over and yanked him off the rock. Fergus looked back over his shoulder. Michael nodded. 'Good man, Fergus. Go for it.' He slouched back and yawned, taking out a fag. 'We'll talk more tomorrow.'

Fergus ground his upper front teeth hard into his lower lip and turned away. 'Now I've done it.'

'Done what?' said Cora.

'Nothing.'

'Mam wants you at Mel's head. Over here.'

Five minutes later, a group of eight strong men, including Fergus, had formed a semicircle around the tarpaulin. They watched as Felicity and Professor Taylor directed two soldiers slicing the tin sheet through the cut, well beneath what you could see of the buried child.

It was as if the child was on the cusp of a second coming.

The bearers gathered round and started to lift. It was awkward, like getting the first slice out of a cake.

'Careful. Her hand jogged,' someone said.

'There's a strand of hair. Reddish brown.'

'The colour's probably down to the tanning of the bog.'

'Dunno. Looks auburn to me. And thickish.'

'OK. In position. After three, gently, lift.'

'Padraig. Get in there on the middle section. Fergus and you, there, lad. To the top.'

'One, two, three . . .'

Fergus found himself next to Owain. The two breathed in and hoisted. He was aware of the fine sandy hairs on Owain's arm brushing against his.

'Hey there,' said Owain.

'Hey,' Fergus grunted.

'Bit gruesome, huh?'

'Uh-huh.'

'Like *Dawn of the Dead*.'

'Hey?'

'The movie with all the zombies in the shopping mall.'

Fergus's cheeks glowed hot. 'Oh. Yeah. That.'

The group began to carry the tin sheet with its ancient remains and mounds of peat across the uneven ground.

'Watch out,' the professor called. 'A great clump's fallen away from the top.'

A sod fell by Fergus's foot. He had to half hop, half skim over it, trying not to shake his corner of the bier.

'Mark that spot, where the earth fell.'

'Oh my God.' It was Felicity's voice. 'Her face. Part of her face.'

'Keep going, team. There's a shower coming in.'

More helpers arrived to take the strain. There were ten or twelve of them now, shouldering the strange load. Gingerly they picked their way over the bog. Fergus could see only the patch of ground ahead of him and the feet of the bearers, army boots on some, trainers on others. He and Owain had taken the head-end of Mel, but somehow they'd ended up at the back of the team.

When they got to the waiting truck, it was as if

Professor Taylor's and Felicity's command yielded to that of the army officer. Rope was fed under the tin. On his count, they lowered her. Then the soldiers took over, manoeuvring her into the waiting crate on the open-topped truck.

'She's landed.'

It started to spot with rain.

Fergus was flushed with exertion. There was sweat between his shoulder blades.

Felicity came up beside him, her hand on his shoulder. 'Fergus, look at her. The peat fell away from part of her head when we shifted her. I think she really is a girl.'

He saw first the smoothness of a cheek. The skin around the jaw was wrinkled, as if pressed by the centuries. But the nose was strong and Roman, and the lips shut, pursed, as if ready to kiss. The one visible eye was shut, and over her head was part of a bonnet made of something like wool. She was like a girl of the last century in a nursery story, tucked up for the night. How dainty she was; he'd never seen a more peaceful expression.

'It's as if she just lay down and fell asleep,' he whispered.

Felicity nodded. 'That's what the Victorians used to put on people's graves. *She fell asleep.* I always thought it a silly euphemism for death. But here, it seems quite apt.'

'She's unbelievable. She's sweetness itself.'

Cora was crying by his side. 'Oh, Mam. Fergus. Look. Beneath her chin.'

Fergus peered. What he'd taken for a bonnet string was thicker, more like a slender coil of rope, neatly made and extending down by her folded arm.

'God have mercy,' Felicity whispered.

Fergus stretched out a hand, as if to touch her. 'Mel?' he said. The crowd was silent. Rain fell in earnest. 'Oh, Mel.'

The rope was a noose.

Somewhere a car engine started. An order was given. A soldier unfurled the truck's khaki canvassing, hiding her from view.

Part II
SECOND SIGHT

Fifteen

When I told Boss Shaughn's message to Da, Mam drew her shawl around herself and the new baby, saying nothing.

'The payment's unfair and should be resisted,' Da argued. 'The winter's the cruellest I've ever known. Our stores will never last out until spring if we make the payment.'

The baby cried. Mam hushed it, her own eyes filling. 'We should send Brennor away,' she said. 'Let him take a boat over the lough, away from this. Southwards. There at least he'd have a chance.'

Da shook his head. 'This is Brennor's home. He's too young to go.'

He saw me listening and shooed me out the door. I found Brennor outside, eavesdropping.

'Mam wants me gone,' he whispered, his face a zigzag of hurt.

'No,' I whispered back. 'She wants you alive.'

'When Boss Shaughn comes tomorrow,' Brennor said, turning the shaft of his boy-sized spear in his hand, 'he'd better watch out.'

'Brennor,' I said, 'you're too young to remember what happened three years ago. When Boss Shaughn came, he and

Da shouted and shook their weapons. Then they went up the bog road to fight it out. Then they made a pact and came down again. Boss Shaughn's payment was deferred to the summer.'

Brennor shook his head. 'Da knows and I know.'

'What?'

'The payment isn't fair in the first place.'

I frowned. 'What is fair? Is it fair that we hunt wild things and eat them up when they've done nothing to hurt us?'

Brennor laughed and tickled me under the arms and on the belly, which is what very annoying younger brothers do the minute they've outstripped you in size and strength. I pinched him hard above the kneecap and he jumped in the air like a laughing stoat.

'I'm off to hunt down a deer. I saw some earlier through the mist, over by Inchquinoag forest.'

'Happy hunting,' I said. He ran off, spear in hand.

I turned to where on a fine day you could see a view of the lough. 'Fat chance you'll catch anything in this murk,' I muttered. I bit my lip. In the swaths of mist, I saw Rur's face, staring into the middle distance. And whatever way I looked into the coming weeks, I saw death. But whose, I did not know.

Fergus shook himself awake. *Christ.* He'd dozed off during the exam with only half of his multiple choice questions done. He looked at Joe's watch then breathed out in relief. He'd only lost ten minutes. But that left twenty questions with only thirty-four minutes to tackle them in.

His tongue felt furry, his brain slow. Ahead of him ten lads worked, heads down in a slant of afternoon sun. The air rippled with concentration, shuffles, sharpenings, creaks. Mr Dwyer, invigilating at the top desk on the dais, was intent on the *New Scientist*. What Fergus would have given to swap places.

He'd a hundred and two seconds per question.

Get your act together, stupid.

His pen had rolled onto his lap. He picked it up.

In multiple choice, you'd five possible answers. Two were usually way-out wrong, one could be excluded after a moment's calculation, but the last two were close contenders. One trick would be to identify the two and make a guess between them. That way, he could hope for a percentage of 50 on the second part. If he'd scored 70 per cent in the first half, he'd have 60 per cent overall.

Good, but not good enough for his place in college.

His stomach tightened. He stared at the calculation he'd been stuck on and guessed Answer B.

Nineteen left.

Joe. Eleven days of starving.

He knew about the focal length of a lens. He quickly checked the box which said: *Gradient = 0.119.*

Yesterday he'd read in the newspaper what one of the other strikers had said. *You drink four pints of water a day. Every time you drink, you retch. Your stomach cramps up like you've poisoned it with bad mushrooms. The water's cold. You're freezing. No amount of blankets can keep you warm.*

Another lucky question, about measuring the refractive index of a glass block, but he'd to guess the next two.

Fifteen left. He checked the time. Ninety seconds left a question.

He dug his knuckles into his eyelids. *Joe, I am banishing you from my thoughts.*

He speed-read the remaining questions and found five he could do. He did them and then began using his principle of guesswork for the last ten.

'*Time.*' Mr Dwyer said it quietly but every soul heard. Every pen went down. Fergus checked E in the last box without looking at the question at all. He dropped his biro.

He sat in his chair, waiting for the command to leave. He was in the last column, at the back. The first column of candidates filed out. He heard their voices in the corridor, urgent but subdued, growing louder as the footfalls faded.

Mr Dwyer nodded at the column next to Fergus's. They got up, leaving their work behind them. Fergus saw his friend Padraig ambling past the desks, sneaking a glance at the abandoned exam scripts.

'The last column may rise,' Mr Dwyer said. He made it sound like a last stand in battle. They all stood up and filed out. Fergus felt dizzy with the need to be out of there. He saw somebody had ticked A for the last question where he'd ticked the E. A or E. Pass or fail. Leave Ireland or stay. Perhaps that one tick in that one box would fix his groove into the future. As he passed the dais, he saw Mr Dwyer smiling down at him, a brow raised. Fergus shrugged a *So-so*.

Outside, Padraig was waiting. 'How d'you find it, Fergus?'

'Dunno.'

'I thought it was OK.'

'Did you?'

'Yeah. I like multiple choice. You only have to tick a fecking box. It might be the wrong box. But the ticking bit's easy.'

Fergus chuckled. 'Too right. We'll both get a hundred per cent for the ticking of the boxes.' They approached the male toilets and Fergus paused. 'And d'you know another good thing?'

'What?'

'The exam is ended. Go and piss.'

Padraig slapped his knee. 'Thanks be to God,' he quipped. They yelped and fell about the corridor like mad buffoons, then reeled into the toilets. Fergus laughed so hard he'd to grip his side. His eyes watered. He half collapsed against the wall, groaning.

'Go and piss,' Padraig shrieked over the urinal. 'Thanks be.'

A moment later, Fergus felt the laugh go out of him. He realized he'd got the one on Young's Modulus the wrong way round. It was stress over strain, not strain over stress. He wiped away a film of sweat from his forehead and laid his arm flat to the wall. His head collapsed against it. 'Bugger,' he said.

''S anything wrong?' Padraig asked.

'No,' he said, swallowing. 'Nothing.'

'Fergus?'

'Catch you later, Padraig.'

He walked out of the toilets and down the corridor, seeing the boxes and the ticks, the grooves into the future and Joe on the narrow prison bed with the blankets over him, retching up nothing. Somewhere off in the distance, under the old Scots pine of the churchyard, a dark funeral party was huddled and, strength over strain, a coffin was being lowered.

Sixteen

Michael Rafters was waiting for him by arrangement at the chip shop, a newspaper bundle of chips in hand. 'Hey there, Fergus.'

'Hi.'

'Did it go OK?'

'The exam?'

'No. The—' Michael tilted his head. 'You know what.'

'Oh, that. Yeah. Fine.' Fergus had been up the mountain that morning at 6. As instructed, he'd picked up a packet from an old lorry tyre lying thirty yards off the bridle track in the Forestry Commission and exchanged it for a packet in a loose rock in a dry-stone wall a mile around the other side of the mountain. Then he ferried the second packet back over to the tyre in the Forestry Commission. Both ways, he'd avoided the sentry post on the dead-end road. *Pick up. Drop off. See nobody. Talk to nobody. Don't even think about what's in the packets. Don't even ask what they're for. Not a word to anyone.* The packets consisted of a small brown jiffy bag, soft, not too heavy. They were done up securely with gaffer tape. There was no address on them or writing of any kind.

'Have a chip.'

'Thanks. I'm starved.'

They munched, turning off Roscillin's main street and into the park. There was a bandstand in need of paint, some wilted pansies in the beds and a children's play area, empty. Michael headed over there, climbing over the low railing. They finished the chips sitting down on the children's swings.

'I've put the word through,' Michael said. 'About Joe.'

'About time. Joe's in a desperate state. I don't see how he'll ever last sixty-six days like Bobby did.'

Michael sighed. 'The problem is, Fergus, the lads in Long Kesh are following their own rules. Your man McFarlane's in charge there. He and Bobby had a plan drawn up, a rota for starving. He meant there to be a death at regular intervals.'

'Jesus.' He'd heard as much from the media coverage of the strikes, but hearing it from someone in the know chilled him.

'There's no shortage of volunteers like Joe and Len. They're mad to starve in there.' Michael shrugged. 'I'm having to go right up to the top on this one: the IRA Army Council. And that takes time.'

'Time?' Fergus swung on the swing, watching his black shoes, the school trousers over them, thinking of how, if you were Einstein, you could maybe find a way to bend time.

Time was the enemy. At home, Mam was white and

drawn, her own appetite gone. Fergus was eating as if for two, incessantly hungry. Theresa and Cath were fractious, fighting every other minute. Da was grim and calm. He kept saying, like a broken record, how Joey was a grown man and this strike was his right and he for one was proud of him. He may as well have punched Mam in the belly. She didn't argue with him, but her silence spoke anguish. The girls were sent down to play at the Caseys' after school and weekends. Mam and Mrs Sheehan were off to the prison most days or to meetings with mothers of the other strikers. Fergus was told he could not come. Mam said he'd to do his exams and put Joey out of his mind. The house was a stricken place. The only bright speck on the horizon was the prospect of Felicity and Cora. They'd returned to Dublin after the bog child was safely delivered to Roscillin's abattoir, but were due back tomorrow, when the archaeological investigations were to begin. They'd not been told about the strike.

'Fergus,' Michael urged. 'There is hope.'

'What hope?'

'Some members of the Council think the strike should end.'

'That's not enough, Michael. I can't go on with these packets. Like I said, it's not my scene.'

Michael reached over and gave Fergus's swing a playful yank. 'Sure you can. For old times' sake. You remember "We Three Kings", right?'

'*Selling condoms, tuppence a pair.* Yeah.'

'It's a small thing, the packets.'

Fergus put his foot to the ground to stop the swing dead. 'So what's in them?'

Michael shook his head. 'Don't ask. Don't even wonder.'

'Do *you* know what's in them?'

Michael glanced about, dropping his voice. 'I know what the mission is. But not every last detail.'

'The mission?'

'The target.'

'It's not a civilian target – is it?'

Michael said nothing.

'Is it?'

'Shush. No. It's a *legitimate* target.'

'I don't want to be part of killing anybody innocent, Michael.'

'There is no such thing as innocence any more, Fergus.'

'There is. Children are innocent. Our Theresa and Cath. They're innocent.'

'They're part of a war, Fergus. This is a nation at war. But the target's not a child. Or a woman. Or anybody that doesn't deserve to die. I promise you.'

'It's a military target?'

Michael nodded. 'Now forget everything I've said.'

A woman approached the play area with a buggy and a young toddler.

'I'll say nothing,' said Fergus.

'But you'll keep on with the packets?' Michael whispered. 'There's another planned for tomorrow.'

Fergus groaned.

'It's only a few more, Fergus. Then that's the end of it.'

'And what about Joe?'

'He'll be hearing from the top, don't you worry. When the word comes, he'll have no choice but to come off the strike.'

Michael got up from the swing as the woman and child entered the play area through a little gate. He hopped over the low railing and Fergus trailed after him. They stopped at the bandstand. Michael rested a hand on the flaking red paint of the round dais. 'It's only a matter of time, Fergus.'

'Time,' said Fergus. He looked down at Joe's watch. It said 13:10.

Michael smiled. 'Joe's watch?'

Fergus nodded.

'Will you be seeing him?'

Fergus shrugged. 'Dunno. I hope so.'

'How's he doing?'

'How would you be doing in his place?'

Uneasiness flickered over Michael's face. He shook his head. 'Same time, same place, Fergus? Can we rely on you?'

'OK. For now.'

'Good man.' Michael saluted and walked briskly off, tossing the chip wrappers into the rubbish bin as he left the park.

Seventeen

When Fergus got home, the house was empty. There was nobody to ask him how his exam had gone. He got a packet of Jaffa cakes out of the biscuit tin and munched through the lot, standing at the window, staring out at the washing as it dried in the wind. Mam had hung up the sheets for the twin room in readiness for Felicity and Cora's return the next day. Then she must have gone out prison-visiting. Pegged up next to the sheets was the coverlet Cath had inherited from Joe, the one he'd loved as a kid with the 101 Dalmatian dogs plastered all over it. Fergus smiled then felt a sob threaten to convulse him.

He shut himself into the front room. *Three Bs and you've a place for medicine, Fergus McCann. A whole new life.* He put on *London Calling* by The Clash at top volume. He sat head in hands at the drop-leaf table where his textbooks were piled. Then he opened his Nelkon and Parker.

But after a few minutes he gave up. Instead, he took a fresh piece of paper and started to write.

He tore the paper up, threw it in the wastepaper

bin and restarted on a fresh page. The bin was filled with crumpled balls of paper and London had been calling three times over by the time he was done.

He looked at what he'd written.

Dear Margaret Thatcher,

My brother would not want me to do this so I cannot tell you my name. My brother is a hunger striker and I do not want him to die. You say that crime is crime is crime and there is no such thing as political crime. But there are times when we've no choice but to fight. My brother believes this is one of them. I don't know if he's right. I just don't know. But one thing is sure. This is a time of hate and it's getting worse.

There are no winners in this strike, just losers. My brother will lose his life. I will lose my brother. On the streets, more lives are being lost every day. You will lose votes and supporters, maybe even your place in history. And hope – we'll lose that too. All of us. Is there no way out?

The strikers won't budge. I have visited my brother and seen his face. He is happy to die. You are the only person who can save him, Mrs Thatcher. It may go against what you see as your principle. But you will save his life and many others, and isn't this a better principle than not giving the strikers the special category status they want?

Every death makes peace more distant. Every funeral makes more hate. Save us from this violence, this despair. My mam prays to God every Sunday in church, 'Only say the word and I shall be healed'. Please. Over there in Westminster. Say the one word. 'Yes.' You will never regret it. Never.

From a sincere citizen.

Fergus stared at the words. Death. Peace. Hate. Principle. Crime. It was as if an older, more seasoned Fergus from twenty years into the future had bent time and returned to the brain of his younger self to write this letter. Surely it was persuasive. Surely anyone would think twice on reading this. Surely—

Put it in an envelope. Address it to the House of Commons. Before you change your mind.

Then he thought of the long corridors of power, of the secretaries screening everything, of mailbags groaning with letters from sincere citizens, the manifold pleas of the kingdom; and the grating, intransigent voice of the woman herself.

She'd never see it. Let alone be moved by it.

Send it anyway.

He frowned at the words 'a sincere citizen'. He crossed them out, thinking of the running he was doing for Michael Rafters. What was sincere about that? And what country was he a citizen of? Britain? Ireland? Who was he? What had he become?

He dropped the pen and tore up the letter. Then he took the bin with all the drafts out into the garden and burned them to ashes. When the flames died, he upended the ashes over the flowerbeds, cursing under his breath.

'What on earth are you doing, Fergus?'

It was Mam, back from wherever she'd been, standing at the back door, the lapels of her shell-pink jacket flapping, her eyes troubled.

'Nothing, Mam.'

'That's ashes you've flying about everywhere. What have you been burning?'

'Just notes, Mam. Old revision notes.'

'But you might need them, Fergus. You should've kept them.'

'Not those, Mam. They were rubbish.'

She nodded as if she believed him. 'OK, Fergus. Come on in. I'll make some tea. We'll have something sweet on the side.'

'Oh, Mam. I'm sorry. The biscuit tin's empty.'

'And I only bought a fresh supply yesterday.' She shrugged. 'Just the tea, then.'

She made a pot for them both and they drank it in silence at the table. The telephone rang. Fergus was about to answer it, but Mam shook her head.

'It's that man from the *Roscillin Star*, I bet you. I told him already we'd no comment.'

No comment. Mam and Da didn't agree on much nowadays, but they'd agreed on those two words. Neighbours, newsmen, friends: *If they don't ask, say nothing. If they do, say 'No comment.'* A freak gust of wind shook the washing on the line outside. Dalmatian dots danced in the air.

'I forgot to ask. How was the exam, Fergus?' Mam stretched out her hand and placed it on his, leaning towards him. He could see miniatures of himself

119

reflected in her eyes. The smile she attempted cracked her haggard face in two.

'It was a breeze, Mam. A breeze.'

Eighteen

He was up at six o'clock the next morning for another run, courtesy of Michael Rafters. He put on the trainers and stretched. His limbs were like lead.

He let himself out the front door and stood for a moment, breathing. The sun was up and shining. Mam's roses were at their height. The mountains looked as if they'd been freshly created overnight. It was the kind of day to put springs in your legs. But as he jogged down the street, the thought of the packets weighed him down.

Joey, he thought. *I'm doing this for you. So help me God.*

His breathing was uneven and the pavements jarred his knee joints. It was a relief when the tarmac ran out and packed earth and weeds took over.

The first mile was always the worst, but this was hell. His throat raged with thirst. Maybe it was the smoked kippers Mam had made for tea last night. The sun burned his forehead. His stomach felt rough.

The hunger striker nearest to death was nearly forty days into his strike. Going by the average of those

121

who had already died, he was almost two-thirds of the way to his death. Joe at twelve days surely had a long way to go. Anything could happen. Any*thing*-huh-huh. Hap*pen*-huh-huh—

He nearly tripped on a rock on the path. He staggered, then saved himself.

Get a grip, McCann.

He drew up to the gate into the Forestry Commission. Normally he vaulted it. Today he clambered over, puffed. Once in among the trees, he stopped. He panted, feeling the sweat trickling down between his shoulder blades. The peace of the place unfurled around him. The dark-green shades were friendly ghosts. The smell of resin calmed him.

He strolled to the tyre and took out the waiting packet, stuffing it down his front.

I am doing this for you, Joe. I am running for your life.

He started up again, getting a better rhythm. He thought of Felicity and Cora – the Dublin ladies, as he called them – coming today: Cora with her boyish clothes over and sleek girlishness under, Cora with a lacy Warner bra on. He smiled. Mel was waiting, with all her secrets. *We'll be going over every inch of Mel's skin*, Felicity had promised. *We'll be photographing, measuring, assessing. It's not for the faint-hearted. But maybe we'll find out how she died. Maybe she'll tell us her story. Maybe. You're welcome to join us, Fergus. We'd be honoured.*

He broke from the cover of the forest. He came up to the place where he always turned, running on the spot, to look back. Today there was no haze. Beyond the tops of the sunlit firs the valley sprawled: the jumble of buildings that was Drumleash, his home, and the lough, clear and flat, the patches of fields and dark ribbons of roads.

Whatever way I looked into the coming weeks, I saw death.

He shook his head. Wherever had those doom-laden words come from? He started running again. He came to the point where he normally cut off from the road to avoid the sentry hut. It meant missing the little stream and he was parched.

What the hell. He ran straight up the road. The stream was just a trickle but he managed to get some scoops of water down him and felt better. The border checkpoint, the tiny hut in the middle of nowhere, would surely be empty. The British soldiers had better things to do in these tense days of the strikes. Sure enough, as he drew close, he saw it was locked up, abandoned as if for good. He grinned. He'd saved himself half an hour at least of rough terrain.

He ran on, over the line of the ridge where Leitrim appeared. He made for the wall, dislodged the loose stone with the dab of white paint on it and exchanged packets.

Why don't they just drive it over? He sighed. The answer was obvious. All the signed-up Provos in the area were probably suspects by now. Their movements were watched. He put the second packet into the waistband of his underpants and let his puma sweat-shirt hang loosely over it.

What was in them? *Don't ask. Don't even wonder.*

He started jogging again, looking about. No living

thing was in sight save some sheep, baaing as if they thought he'd come to feed them.

'*Baaa,*' he called back to them.

He remembered the question he'd got wrong in the multiple choice. Stress over strain, not the other way around. He felt his calf muscles taut and firm as he jogged back the way he'd come. But maybe he'd got it right after all. He frowned, trying to remember. His brain was addled with all the questions in all the papers. And he'd only one more exam to go, but it was the one he was dreading most, Applied Physics. On this side of the border, the exams were over and the schools were closed for the summer already. Cora had her university all sewn up, no doubt.

Mam and Dad, he thought. *Why didn't you move down south when the Troubles started? Why?*

He came back up over the top and the answer came with the view. *Because of this. All this. It's home.* He reached out a hand as if he could touch the round, brown shrubs that crawled up the far hillsides like giant hedgehogs. He imagined it was Cora's hair he was touching, smoothing it off her face, ready for a kiss. Her eyes were slanting upwards at him, and she was singing 'Will Ye Bury Me on the Mountain'. *Not pretty. Sentimental more like, Fergus.* They were nose-to-nose, then lip-to-lip.

Over beyond the Forestry Commission he glimpsed a stark flash: a lens, glinting. Bird-watchers. Or man-watchers, more likely: the Provos, training their binoculars on him.

He was nearly back at the sentry hut. It seemed

124

deserted still. He slowed, considering. Then he looked at Joe's watch. He'd made bad time today. It was 7:15. He pressed on.

He drew level with the hut just as the squaddie called Owain drew up the hillside behind the wheel of an army Land Rover. Fergus's right ankle gave with the shock. He stumbled for real this time. He landed flat on his belly in the middle of the road.

Maybe he blacked out briefly or maybe time bent in on itself. The next thing he knew, Owain was standing right over him and he'd an uncanny feeling of *déjà vu.*

Frantic, he checked the packet was still secure in his waistband. Then he rolled over and half sat up.

'Hey, there,' said Owain, offering a hand. His rifle was over his shoulder, its long line truncating the sun. There was a sizzling in Fergus's ears and a sick feeling in his stomach as if he was going to faint. He swallowed. He took Owain's hand and heaved himself up, and then quickly doubled over. Yellow streaks danced in his eyes. Slowly he straightened up. He stretched out his sweatshirt and fanned his belly with the hem.

'Thanks,' he said. Blood trickled down a knee. His right ankle throbbed.

'D'you want to sit down a minute?' Owain offered.

'I'm late as it is.' He tried to walk but a stabbing pain shot up his calf. 'Youch.'

'Come over to this rock and sit for a bit.'

He'd no option but to hobble over with Owain

supporting his elbow. He sat down on a boulder and stretched out his leg.

'I'll get the first aid,' Owain said. While he was back at the Land Rover, Fergus checked the packet again, shoving it down further. He sat forward so that his sweatshirt hung loose down his front. There was sweat pouring off his forehead. He was shivering.

Owain was back with an antiseptic wipe at the ready.

'I'll do it myself,' Fergus insisted. He took the wipe and cleaned up his leg. The cut was superficial.

He scrunched up the used wipe, wondering what to do with it. He looked out across the valley as if there might be an answer there. There was no glint of a lens, but somehow he still felt on public display.

'How's the ankle?'

''S nothing. A small sprain.'

'I could run you down the mountain, maybe, only—'

'You'd be abandoning your post?' Fergus suggested.

Owain smiled. 'Something like that.' He looked out across the emptiness. 'Not that anybody'd notice.'

'Don't you soldiers get shot at dawn for things like that?'

'Not these days.'

They sat in silence, watching the advance of the morning.

'I heard the archaeologists saying it was you who found her,' Owain said.

'Sorry?'

126

'The child. In the bog.'

'Oh, that.' Fergus shrugged. 'Word gets around.'

Owain smiled. 'Normally, we hear nothing of what you locals get up to. It was just when we were carrying her on that piece of tin, I heard the talk.' He sighed. 'One day we're helping out with a bit of archaeology, shoulder to shoulder with you lot. Next day we're out escorting the coffins of the hunger strikers and we may as well have been beamed in from another planet. Everyone treats us like freaks. And before you know it, the petrol bombs and stones are flying.'

'And the plastic bullets,' said Fergus.

'And the plastic bullets.' Owain raised his hands palm upwards. 'And as far as my unit's concerned, you're the taigs. A crew of mad, bad Irish bog-men, straight out of the Stone Age.'

Fergus snorted. 'That's us all right.'

'But that dead child, she really *is* Stone Age, isn't she?'

'Iron Age.'

'What's the difference?'

'Stone Age is older than Iron Age. Iron Age is only two thousand years ago.'

'Plenty old enough for me.'

'I couldn't get over her bonnet,' Fergus said. 'Did you see that?'

'That hat thing? Yeah. And her legs, chopped off.'

'That was the JCB.'

'Christ.'

'She was already dead. Very dead.' Fergus stretched out his own leg.

Owain wandered over to the edge of the track, looking down on Drumleash. 'You come from down there?'

Fergus nodded. 'My father's family's lived there for generations.'

'It rains a lot.'

'It's the saddest place in the northern hemisphere.'

'Not as sad as the Valleys.'

'The Valleys?'

'In Wales. Where I'm from.'

'Oh, yeah. Well, they can't be as wet as here. They're further south, aren't they?'

Owain took his rifle from his shoulder and looked through its iron sights, turning on his heel, as if following the arc of an invisible bird. 'Less rain,' he said. 'But more soot.'

Fergus checked the packet again while Owain was turned away.

'Slag heaps and streets of miserable houses, ready to slide down the hill. *Krepow.*' Owain mimed firing the gun.

'Some rifle.'

'It's the latest SLR.'

'SLR?'

'Self-loading rifle. *Krepow.* That's the Valleys I've just shot down. The Rhondda. The Sirhowy. The whole bloody lot.'

'You don't sound homesick.'

'No.'

'You were glad to leave?'

'Telling me.'

'Is the army any better?'

Owain's shoulders slumped. He turned to face Fergus. 'It's the short straw, being sent to Ulster.'

'And the Irish are meant to be so welcoming.'

Owain laughed. 'At least I'm not underground all day.'

'Underground?'

'In a coal mine. That would finish me. I'm claustrophobic.' He slung his rifle back on his shoulder. 'The army or the mines. That was the choice.'

Fergus considered, trying to rotate his sore ankle. 'At church, we had a priest visit a few weeks ago. And he was just back from the hill tribes of Laos.'

'Laos?'

'You know. The country near Cambodia. In Asia. Anyway, your man had visited this remote village and the people there cooked a mammoth feast in his honour.'

'They weren't cannibals, were they?'

'No. But when it came time to serve up, he was offered a choice of two dishes to eat.'

'What?'

'Dog or rat.'

'Yuck. What did he go for?'

'Rat, on account of his boyhood memories of his wee springer spaniel. What would you have gone for?'

'You had to choose one?'

'Yep. Or starve.'

'Dog.'

'Dog?'

'They're cleaner. They don't go down the sewers.'

'They lick their asses, though.'

''S true. Still. A dog.' Owain wrinkled his nose. 'Did the priest say what the rat tasted like?'

'He said it was delicious. Like chicken. That was the whole point of his bloody sermon. What's made with love tastes of love.'

'Yuck times three.' Owain turned back to see the view. 'Priests, reverends, they're all the same. What would you have gone for?'

Fergus considered. 'Rat.'

Owain slapped his thigh. 'You Irish. Pied pipers, the lot of you.'

There was a faint drone of a car, climbing the mountain from far below.

Fergus stood up. 'I really must go.' He limped, winced, limped again.

Owain watched him. 'You need a stick.'

'I'll find something in the Forestry below.'

'You sure you're OK?'

'Course. It's nothing.' *Twinge.* He grabbed his middle to protect the package. With all the talk, he'd nearly forgotten about it. He'd a vision of it falling down through his Y-fronts.

'Sure you're OK?'

'Sure as sure.'

'Bye then, Mr Ratty.'

'Bye yourself, Mr Bow-Wow.'

Owain rattled his gun in mock anger. 'You watch

what you say, you miserable taig. Or I'll be setting my sights on you.'

Fergus put a hand up in mock surrender.

'So long, Fergus.'

Fergus glanced back, surprised the squaddie had remembered his name. 'See you, Owain.'

He hobbled fast down the road and was relieved when he turned a corner.

'Shit,' he whispered to himself.

His heart was hammering it. 'That was chancy,' he gasped. He stumbled down the road, a stitch in his side. The oncoming car was an armoured Land Rover. It passed him without stopping. 'Christ Jesus.'

The place was crawling with British soldiers.

He got into the cover of the forest and collapsed on a log. He retched, but nothing came up. Then his heartbeat slowed. The silence of the trees calmed him. Feeling better, he got up and found a stick. He hobbled over to the rubber tyre and flung the packet in.

There you have it, Michael Rafters. Hate you. Hate this place. Hate everything.

He limped with the stick back down the hill, swung himself over the gate on his belly and staggered back to Drumleash. The morning cool was gone. The sun was glaring down.

He stood on the outskirts of the village. It was the worst run he'd ever had. He looked back up the stark, blameless mountain. *I'm not doing it again,* he thought. *No more packages. I don't care if the Provos take a gun and shoot me through the head.*

Nineteen

He limped his way down the main street pavement, passing Finicule's Bar just as Uncle Tally drew up in the van.

'Hey, Unk.'

Uncle Tally switched the engine off. There was a frown of concentration on his face.

'Unk?'

'Fergus! What's new?' Uncle Tally got out and slammed the door of the van.

'Nothing, Unk. I've been running and twisted my ankle.'

'Not badly?'

'No. Just a sprain. Unk?'

'What?'

'Are you busy?'

'Me? Busy? What would I be busy at?'

'Can we talk?'

'Talk away.'

'Not here.' Fergus jerked his head. 'Indoors?'

Uncle Tally looked taken aback. 'My room's a tip.'

'I don't care.'

'Give me a minute to clear the fag-ends off the bed, will you?'

Fergus laughed. 'OK.'

He rested his stick against the pub wall while Uncle Tally opened the side door to the bar. There was a narrow flight of stairs straight up to his bed-sit. He ran up ahead of Fergus, and a minute later re-emerged, switching on the stairwell light.

'It's a bit more decent now.'

It was ages since Fergus had been at Uncle Tally's place. He limped up the stairs and into the room. Within, the curtains were still drawn. Uncle Tally went to open them. The place smelled musty, but there was a pleasant smell muddled up with it. Fergus sniffed. It reminded him of Christmas.

'Smells nice in here,' he said, puzzled.

'Must be the aftershave,' Uncle Tally joked. Fergus saw a bottle of Old Spice by the sink and chortled. With the curtains now parted, light toppled into the room. There were cardboard boxes stacked against the wall, an overflowing ashtray and no lampshade on the overhead light. The purple blanket on the bed was all in a heap.

'*More* decent, you say, Unk?'

'You should have seen it before,' Uncle Tally said. 'Have a seat on the bed.' As he lifted a cardboard box out of Fergus's way, the top flapped open, revealing the contents.

'Cigarettes!' Fergus said. 'Stacks of them.'

Uncle Tally looked sheepish. 'Your man Harry and myself. We've been flogging fags over the border. With the Irish punt the way it is, there's a pretty difference in the price. Everyone's at it.'

Fergus grinned. 'You're over your duty-free limit, Unk.'

'Well. The dole wouldn't make a rat fat.'

'What if the army stopped you?'

Uncle Tally shrugged. 'They've bigger fish to fry.'

Yeah. Me. Fergus plonked down on the bed.

'What did you want to talk about?'

Fergus thought of the squaddie, Owain, the brown packets, and Michael Rafters. He longed to tell Uncle Tally the whole lot. But he'd been sworn to secrecy. He bit his lip. 'It's Joe, Unk.'

'Oh. Joe.' Uncle Tally moved another box from the armchair by the window and sat down.

'You and he were great friends. Weren't you? It was he who called you Unk when he was a wee one. And then it stuck.'

Uncle Tally shrugged. 'So it did. Unk the Monk. I don't think.'

Fergus grinned. 'I remember you taking us fishing. And the time we all developed the black-and-white photos of the fair in Roscillin.'

'We used the old coal shed below for a dark room. They were a bit streaky, as I recall.'

Fergus laughed. 'Every Saturday we'd play football in the park. You never let us win.'

'That would've been patronizing you.'

'And in the summer we'd drive over to Bundoran strand,' Fergus said. 'Remember the time you saved Joey's life?'

'I only scooped him back when he'd gone out a bit too far.'

'I remember. The current was strong.'

Uncle Tally waved a hand as if to dismiss it.

'Saturdays were the best bit of our week, Unk.'

'I was only taking you out from under your mam's feet. On the weekends when your da had to work.'

'Joe and myself were always fighting. But somehow, when we were with you, we never did.'

'No. You were good lads. Mostly.'

Fergus stared at the boxes. His ankle throbbed still. He leaned over and took off his trainer, then his sock.

'That looks sore,' said Uncle Tally. He went to the sink, got a flannel under the cold tap and squeezed it out. 'Take this, Ferg.'

Fergus draped the flannel over his ankle. 'So, Unk.'

'What?'

'Why d'you never go to see Joe?'

Uncle Tally sat back down on the armchair, silent.

'What do *you* think of the hunger strike, Unk?'

'God, Fergus. What am I supposed to say? You know me. I try not to get involved.'

'Da's all for it. He's like a recruitment advert for the Provos the way he goes on.'

'Your da was always a die-hard.'

'But my mam, Unk.'

Uncle Tally tutted. 'She's looking shook all right.'

'Mam says I'm not to visit Joe. But Unk, you could visit him. He might listen to you.'

135

'Listen to *me*?'

'If you told him to eat again. He might listen.'

'I doubt it.'

'He'd a mighty opinion of you. Always.'

'I'd like to help, Fergus. But would they even let me in? I'm not immediate family.'

'They might. It's worth a try.'

'I'd go like a shot if I could help. But there's nothing I could say would sway Joe.'

'But even if you just went in and said nothing. It might make him think.'

Uncle Tally stood up and opened the sash window. He stared down at the street. The primary school bell was being rung amidst the sound of young children at play. 'There's something I must tell you, Fergus.'

'What?'

'Joe and I had a falling out.'

'A falling out? You never.'

Uncle Tally nodded. 'It's why I haven't been over to see him.'

'But he's on hunger strike now, Unk. He's weak. Dying, maybe.'

Uncle Tally's head dropped into his hands. 'Don't I know it.'

'Surely whatever falling out you had wasn't that bad?'

There was no reply.

'Was it about the Provos, Unk? Did you disagree about him joining up?'

Uncle Tally shook his head. 'That was none of my business. You know I never get involved.'

136

'So what was it about?'

Uncle Tally looked up. 'D'you really want to know?'

'Yes.'

'It was about a girl.'

'A girl? Not that lassie from Newry? Cindy?'

Uncle Tally said nothing. Fergus recalled Joe saying she was history now.

'Did you steal her off him, Unk? Did you?'

Uncle Tally reached over to the open cardboard box and took out a pack of cigarettes. He removed the wrapping and popped a fag in his mouth, then offered one to Fergus.

'No thanks.'

Uncle Tally lit his own and breathed out the smoke. 'It's water under the bridge, Fergus. Go on, have one. Have a whole packet.'

Fergus sighed. He took a packet but didn't open it. 'So you won't go in and see him?'

'No. I'd only make things worse.'

'He didn't seem that fussed about Cindy when I saw him last.'

'Maybe not. But he's not fussed about me, either, let me tell you.'

Fergus took the flannel from his ankle. 'I'd best be going. The ankle feels better.'

'I'm sorry, Fergus.'

Fergus folded the flannel and put it over the side of the sink. He hobbled to the door. 'Are you still seeing her?'

'Who?'

137

'Cindy, of course.'

Uncle Tally tapped a long finger of ash into the sink. 'Sort of.'

'So it's not serious? Not like it was with – Noreen, was it?'

'No. It's not like it was with Noreen.' Uncle Tally smiled.

Fergus opened the door. 'I'll let myself out.'

'Mind how you go. And Fergus?'

'What?'

'You just get through those exams. Don't worry about anything else. Just the exams. D'you hear?'

Fergus bit his lip. *Easier said than done.* 'I hear you, Unk. You sound just like Mam.'

'When are they over?'

'Tomorrow.'

'Come in for a pint then, tomorrow night. On me.'

'Can I?'

'Yes.'

'And will we do some more driving lessons?'

'As many as you like. You should apply for the test.'

Fergus nodded. 'I will. I've the application form ready.'

'And Fergus – if you do get in to visit Joe again, don't say a word about our chat, will you?'

'No.'

'Just give him my – my greetings.'

'Your greetings. OK.' With a hand on each banister, Fergus swung himself down the narrow stairs. 'S'long, Unk,' he called at the door below.

As he came out onto Drumleash's main street, the

school bell clanged a final time. The uproarious sound of the pupils, Theresa and Cath among them somewhere, retreated into the building. He remembered what Sands had said before he died: *Our revenge will be in the laughter of our children.* Fergus picked up his stick, wishing he was back at their age, in that simple, ordered time, filing between the small, intimate classes. *Greetings?* The word was quaintly formal, redolent of birthday cards from great-aunts or postcards from watering places. He was exhausted, he realized. He tried his weight on the injured foot and winced. He shuffled along through the village, sweating under the morning's heat, and turned with relief into the close and home.

Twenty

At home, Mam was cross about the ankle. 'The running's becoming an obsession, Fergus.'

'It keeps me fit.'

'Cripples you, more like.'

'It's the only thing keeps me sane.' He thought of the packets. 'Or halfway sane.'

Mam raised her eyes to heaven and ran him a bath. Afterwards she bandaged the ankle up tight for him. Then he helped her get the twin room ready for the Dublin ladies. He turned the mattresses over and did the hospital corners with the sheets. Together they had scrambled eggs on toast for dinner. Then Mam said she was off to a meeting with the priest who served as chaplain at Long Kesh. He was a man in the know, she said, a man who wanted to help.

It was Fergus's turn to raise his eyes to heaven. 'It's beyond the power of prayer,' he said.

Mam's face looked worse than the Pietà. He wished he could bite back his words. 'Nothing's beyond prayer, Fergus,' she said, her eyes filling. 'Nothing.'

'No, Mam. Of course. There's always hope.'

'And Fergus?'

'What?'

'Not a word to the guests.'

'No, Mam.'

After she'd driven off, Fergus sneaked into the front garden with the scissors and snipped an orange rose that was coming into bloom. He rooted out a Belleek vase nobody ever used from the dresser in the front room. It had a cream-coloured glaze with hokey green shamrocks sprinkled on the front. He filled it with water and put the rose in. Then he added a spoon of caster sugar, because he'd heard somewhere that cut flowers thrived this way. He put the orange, cream and green creation on the bedside table between the twin beds.

The Renault drew up just as he finished. He stood at the front door and watched Felicity's trim figure hop out. She moved around to the boot, getting out the luggage, while Cora emerged on the passenger side. She was dressed in a mustard coat that looked like a blanket. The sun beat down on it like a jealous rival. Her hair was cut short like a boy's, making her face seem larger, more definite.

'Hello there, Fergus,' Felicity said.

'H'lo,' Fergus replied.

Cora said nothing. She just shrugged and looked up at the sky as if to say the whole world was on the road to ruin. She caught Fergus's eye and winked.

'We've the room ready for you,' he said. There was a wobble to his voice. He pretended to cough, holding the door open.

'We'll just dump our things inside and go,' said Felicity. 'Mel is waiting for us. Do you want to come too, Fergus?'

'Can I?'

'Of course.'

'Let me take those.' He darted forward before they could protest and took the two holdalls. They were heavier than they looked and his ankle rankled as he hobbled with them back into the house. Felicity and Cora followed him down the hallway.

'It's very patriotic in here,' Felicity said in the twin room. She nodded towards the vase. He realized it was the colours of the Irish flag.

'Oh, that. It was a notion of my mam's.'

'It's nice,' said Cora. She picked up the vase and smelled the rose. 'From the garden?'

Fergus nodded. She replaced the vase and wriggled out of her mustard coat, flinging it down on the coverlet. Under it, she was wearing a black sweater and khaki trousers. The style was military but made her look very girlish. She flopped on the bed, yawning.

'Cora!' Felicity scolded. 'I told you to eat that sandwich. Now look. You're fit to wilt.'

'No, I'm not. I'm fine.' She bounced back up like Zebedee from *The Magic Roundabout.*

Felicity sighed. 'Let's crack on. They're expecting us in Roscillin.'

They got back in the car. Felicity insisted Fergus sit in front as navigator. Cora sat behind him, her heels drawn up onto the edge of the back seat, her hands clasped around her knees. As they drove to the head of the lough and up onto the main road, Felicity admired the sunshine, the swans with their new cygnets, and the unusual sight of two people on a tandem, pedalling downhill at such a pace it was hard to overtake them.

'You'd never think there was anything wrong here in the North,' Felicity said. 'Would you?'

Fergus looked out at the green tunnel of trees ahead and the idyllic roadside flowers. 'No.'

'With the hunger strike and all, the news would have you believe the whole place was at its own throat.'

Fergus swallowed. *Maybe it is.*

'They teach history like that,' Felicity said. 'Battle after battle – as if there was no ordinary living in between.'

Then she asked him about his exams, his family and whether he had summer plans. He answered with half his brain. The other half was aware only of Cora, behind him, saying nothing, her knees pressed up into the back of his seat. She was quiet, but alive to the power of ten. She reminded him of the laws of electromagnetism:

$$F = qv \times B$$

where F, force, was Cora, and q the charged particles in his body and v the rate at which they were being sucked backwards towards her. B was the inside of the Renault, a moving magnetic field, with the sun dappling, the air rushing and Felicity chatting and the white lines of the road flicking past, like heartbeats.

143

'Turn right here,' he said, just in time.

They pulled up at the low-slung white shed with the corrugated iron roof that was Roscillin's abattoir, the place where the resurrected bog child lay waiting.

Twenty-one

Mel's truncated body had been laid out on a wheeled trestle before they arrived. Experts had cleaned her down. They stared in silence in their surgeon's gowns, donning latex gloves. She looked different indoors, hunched, almost ungainly. She was less an organic part of the earth, more a ghoulish murder victim. Her brown skin was wrinkled, as if she'd died of old age. The shift was a rag, torn at the back so that her spine and buttocks were revealed. Her face slumped onto the plastic sheeting that covered the trestle, less peaceful than it had seemed up on the mountain. The bangle on her wrist had been removed. Her short arms were plump. One hand lay relaxed, open; the other was clenched into a fist. The rope around her neck was revealed as deftly made, precision-coiled by a craftsman.

'We've established two things for sure,' Felicity said.

'What?' asked Fergus.

'The bangle she was wearing is consistent with an Iron-Age date. Late BC or early AD, the expert says.'

'So she *did* live around the time of Christ?'

'So it would seem. We've sent off samples of the body tissue for radiocarbon-dating for a more accurate date. We should get results in six weeks.'

'What's the other thing?'

Felicity pointed to the girl's lower abdomen. It was a shrivelled mass of cloth and flesh, but there was no sign of a male organ. 'Definitely a girl.'

'Poor Mel,' said Fergus. 'She looks so sad.'

'We'd all look sad if we'd been buried that long,' Cora said.

'Other bog people have been found hanged like this.' Felicity traced the loop around Mel's neck. 'If you believe the historians, a cult prevailed across much of Northern Europe from the Bronze Age through to the Iron Age, surrounding a goddess called Nerthus.'

'Nerthus?' asked Fergus. 'Who was she?'

'Mother Earth, if you like. Tacitus describes rituals surrounding her in his *Germania*. She's always depicted wearing a neck-ring or torque. Archaeologists think the instances of hanged bog people connect with this. The noose could be a symbol – the threshold between life and death.'

Cora put a hand to her own throat. 'Ugh.'

'Another interesting pattern with bog people,' Felicity continued, 'is the contents of their stomachs. They all seem to have died in the winter.'

'The winter? How can you tell?'

'There's no summer fruit in there, only grain. It's as if they were given a frugal meal, a kind of porridge, of last year's grain before being sacrificed. Perhaps to protect next year's crop.'

'Didn't they eat meat?'

'They must have. But we've never found any in the stomachs of those who were hanged like this. But who knows what Mel's stomach will tell us? Maybe she'll be different.'

'You're going to look in *there*?'

'In the cause of science, Fergus. And history.'

Fergus's own stomach somersaulted but he nodded. 'D'you think she *was* sacrificed then?'

'Possibly.'

'I think the sacrifice theory's a load of rubbish,' Cora said.

'Really? Why?' asked Felicity.

'It's just us looking back and thinking they were savages.'

Felicity walked around the trestle, smiling. 'You know, Cora, you may be right. Tacitus talks about the tribes of Britain and Germany as if they were primitives. He calls them barbarians. It's what the Romans always called the supposedly remote peoples they conquered. But we know from archaeology that Iron-Age people had villages, social systems, even coinage. They had well-made clothes, furniture, farms. On the other hand—'

She paused at Mel's back, riveted.

'On the other hand, what?'

Felicity pointed to a spot just below the back of Mel's shoulder. 'Do you see what I see?' she gasped.

Fergus and Cora peered. In a fold of tanned skin

147

was a neat split, about an inch long. Fergus reached out his hand, following the line with his forefinger.

'A cut,' he whispered.

Cora winced. 'Hanged, then stabbed in the back.'

'Or maybe stabbed then hanged,' said Felicity. 'Poor child.'

'Whichever way you look at it,' Fergus blurted, 'it must have been a brutal time.'

Felicity took a cotton bud and gently cleaned the area further, so that the stab wound was more apparent. 'Another thing Tacitus tells us,' she said as she worked, 'is that the Germans of the time punished crimes in two separate ways: deserters and traitors were hanged as a warning. Other criminals – those guilty of truly shameful crimes – were "drowned in miry swamps".'

'How could Mel have done anything shameful?' Fergus protested. 'She was a child. It *must* have been a sacrifice. Perhaps they just drew lots. And she pulled the short straw.'

He noticed Cora shivering, turning her eyes away from the wound.

Felicity sighed, straightening up. 'Perhaps we'll never know what happened to Mel. The evidence points every which way.' She shifted her examination to Mel's arms and hands. Her gloved fingers gently touched the clasped hand. She leaned forward again, peering. 'Pass me those tweezers, Cora.'

'What?'

'They're on the side.'

Cora looked dazed.

'I'll get them.' Fergus found the little metal implement in a dish and handed it to Felicity.

Cora had turned away, gripping the radiator by the wall.

'I'm trying to get something out of Mel's hand, Fergus, without damaging her.'

Fergus felt his heart pumping as Felicity worked. Tiny shreds of hair were appearing, bog-tanned in colour.

Cora turned round again, just as Mel's thumb flopped back on itself, almost breaking away from the hand. She gasped. A whole knot of hair appeared, tied up with a tiny thong.

'I've never seen anything like it,' Felicity said. She whistled through her teeth, holding it up to the light. 'It's like an Iron-Age love knot. Sweet Jesus.'

There was silence.

Fergus became aware of Cora gripping his arm. 'I can't take any more of this, Mam. I feel sick.'

Felicity put down the knot of hair, then the tweezers. She came over and gave Cora a hug. 'Would you rather wait outside?'

'Yes please.'

'Fergus,' Felicity said. 'Why don't you and Cora have a walk around the town? I'll meet you back at the car in about an hour.'

Fergus nodded. 'OK. We'll go to the café in the park.'

Cora made straight for the door, almost colliding with Professor Taylor and another gowned man as they came through. The professor beamed at Fergus and rubbed his gloved hands, as if anticipating a splendid dinner. 'Hello, Felicity.'

'Hello, Angus.'

'I've a date made for the radiography in Omagh for Friday, Felicity. And here's Dr Lavery, to get a sample of the stomach's contents.'

'Great. But come over here, Angus. Just you take a look at this.'

Fergus made his escape too.

Twenty-two

Cora and Fergus walked into the centre of Roscillin in silence. His ankle gave odd twinges but he could walk without limping, almost.

'The one thing I don't want to talk about,' said Cora as they strolled past the shoppers, 'is *her*.'

'Mel?'

Cora nodded. 'Mam's obsessed. It's all she thinks about.'

'I can understand it. Mel's a way of getting under your skin. She's an odd-looking girl. All hunched and leathery.'

'You'd look odd if you'd been pulled out of a bog after two thousand years.'

Fergus shook his head. He didn't know what he meant but it wasn't that.

'Let's talk about anything else,' Cora pleaded. 'Not her. Not now.'

'OK.' They passed the chip shop where he'd been with Michael Rafters yesterday. He picked up his pace. 'The park's this way.'

'Is she still talking to you in your dreams?'

151

'Sometimes.' Fergus laughed. 'I s'pose it's just my subconscious.'

'You talk about her as if she's still alive, the pair of you.'

They paused at the second-hand TV shop. Twelve identical screens of the weather map flickered in the window. Symbols of clouds, partial sun and rain were spangled across England, Scotland, Wales and Northern Ireland, but stopped short at the border, as if the Republic had no weather at all. Then they went on down the steps, through the alleyway and past a wall on which somebody had painted in white BRITS OUT. This had been crossed out in red paint and under it, in small letters, was written the familiar joke: *What's Sands's phone number in the afterlife? 8nothing8nothing8nothing.*

Fergus pointed the graffiti out to Cora. She frowned, pinched her own wrist, then groaned, leaning against the wall. 'Jesus. This place,' she said. 'Dunno if I could live here.'

Fergus looked at the smeared walls and flaking paint of the town, the northern heaviness of it, the grimness even when the sun shone. 'Can't say I blame you. It's a vale of tears, all right.'

They walked on.

'You're limping, Fergus.'

''S nothing. I twisted my ankle when I was out running this morning.'

'Running?'

'Yeah. I go running up the mountain most mornings. You should try it.'

'I couldn't run to save my life.'

At the park café, Fergus bought tea and two currant buns for himself and a Diet Coke for Cora. When they'd settled down at a quiet table outside, he watched Cora drink through a straw. The tiny hairs on her lower arm were dark. Her wrist was slender with the bone prominent. On her hands, the slender blue rivers of her veins showed through her white skin.

'D'you want a bun?'

'No thanks, Fergus. I'm sorry I was rude.'

'Rude?'

'About your home town.'

'I don't think of Roscillin as my home town.'

'No? What is, then?'

Fergus considered. 'Drumleash. The mountains. The lough. Ireland, really. All Ireland.' He swallowed half a bun at once and grinned. 'I'd love to see Dublin.'

'You've never been?'

'No.'

'It's a dump. Beggars everywhere and junkies jumping in the bloody Liffey.'

'No!'

''S true. I prefer Belfast. At least there's a posh shopping centre. A bit more action.'

'You *could* say that.'

'Mam and I were there last year for a conference. We were up in this B & B on a hill. And I loved how you could look down on the docks below. Packing, unpacking, crates, cranes. Activity all night long. And there was stained glass everywhere, even in this pub we went into. And the people were dead friendly.'

'You should've gone down the Falls Road. Dead friendly is right.'

'Next time I will.'

He caught her eye and laughed. 'You wouldn't like it down there any more than the abattoir.'

'You weren't that keen on the abattoir either.'

'Who says?'

'I do. I saw you go green when they took us through the main part.'

He remembered the long hall with cattle carcasses hanging in rows. 'I wouldn't like to work there,' he admitted.

'It would make you think twice about eating meat.'

'Not me, it wouldn't. There again, Mam says I'd eat the contents of the hoover.'

Cora giggled, brushing the bun crumbs off the table. 'It's not the butchery so much. It's more the way dead things look. Humbled. Apologetic.'

'Apologetic?'

'As if they're sorry they ever lived.' Cora's hand stopped the brushing. It hovered over the tabletop, right by his own hand. It would be the simplest thing in the world, Fergus thought, to take her hand in his. His fingertips tingled. *Should I or shouldn't I?*

Cora's hand clenched into a fist. 'And the thought that one day you'll end up like that,' she whispered.

Fergus stared into his tea. He thought of a photo of a dead hunger striker he'd seen recently in a Republican paper. The man was lying in his open coffin, eyes shut, hands folded in prayer. He looked like a man in his eighties, not his twenties. His ravaged, waxen face spoke of a hideous journey to the grave. *Joey. Oh, Joey.*

'I'm sorry. It's too morbid,' Cora said. 'Let's talk about something else.' She drained off the Coke and then crushed the can between her fingers with surprising strength and rested it back on the table.

Fergus shook his head as if to expel Joe and the strike from his mind. He picked up the dented can. 'Whoa, Cora. Miss Iron Fingers.'

'Yeah. Bet I could beat you in an arm wrestle.'

'Bet you couldn't.'

'Wanna try?'

'OK.'

He put down the can and they clasped right hands. His thumb-pad rubbed up against her finger-joints.

'My elbow's half off the table,' Cora protested.

'OK now?'

'Yep. Let's go.'

Fergus got her hand down in one second flat.

'I wasn't ready!'

'OK. Another go.'

'After three. One, two, three—'

Fergus laughed. She'd a fair bit of strength but it didn't take much for him to keep his own arm upright. *That would have been patronizing you,* Uncle Tally's voice echoed. Gently, he forced Cora's hand down.

'There.'

Cora shook out her hand.

'I didn't hurt you?'

'No.' She smiled. 'You're stronger than you look.'

'Thanks.'

'Must be the running.'

They sat in silence. On an empty table nearby, two goldfinches fought over crumbs, their frantic wings hovering in one place, like tongues of Pentecostal flame. Fergus nibbled at the second currant bun, then discarded it, leaving it to the birds. 'D'you believe in an afterlife?' he asked.

'Me? No.'

'You're not religious?'

'No. Nor is Mam.'

'I noticed you didn't go to church that Sunday you were here last.'

'Mam and I aren't Catholics.'

'You mean you're *Protestants*?'

'We're not anything. Mam was brought up a Unitarian.'

'A Unitarian? What's that?'

'It's a kind of Protestantism, I s'pose. It says Jesus was just normal, like you or me. Not God.'

'I never heard of a Unitarian Irish person before.'

Cora shrugged. 'We're not really Irish. Mam was brought up in Warwick in England. She moved to Dublin to study when she was eighteen.' She shrugged. 'My dad's the Irish one.'

'Your dad?'

'He and Mam split up. He lives in Michigan nowadays. With a new woman. And kids. Good luck to him. I haven't seen him in years.'

'I'm sorry. D'you miss him?'

'No.'

There didn't seem anything to say to that. He picked up the Coke can again. 'I'm not religious either, Cora.'

'No? So there's no afterlife in your book either?'

'Unless you count cells breaking down and re-forming. Or Mel, being unearthed. With her noose and her knot of hair.' He frowned, thinking of what Mel had been hiding in her fist. 'Strange.'

Cora put a finger to her lips. 'Shush. Remember?'

Mel was not to be spoken of. They'd agreed. They sat in silence. The goldfinches had gone. Fergus turned the wrecked Coke can around his hands. Cora leaned over and took it from him.

'Say, Fergus?'

'What?'

'What d'you think an archaeologist would make of this in two thousand years' time?'

Fergus chuckled. 'He'd probably say it was a late-second-millennium torture device. Used by the barbarians of that time.'

She put her little finger in through the opening at the top. 'You put the victim's digit in like so and *smash*.'

'You're certifiable.'

She waggled the crunched-up tin at him. He tried to catch it and she jerked it away. Then his hand landed on it and carefully he prised the tin off her. She caught his eye and made as if to tuck a strand of hair behind her ear, as if she'd forgotten her new cropped hairstyle. She shivered. 'Fergus?'

157

'What?'

'I'm cold. Let's go back to the car.'

The sun was blazing. Even the grass was wilting. He was in a T-shirt, she was in her sweater, absorbing heat like a black hole. There was a taut look to her face. She was pale.

'Course, Cora. If you like.'

When they got to the car, she realized they'd no keys to get in.

'I'll run in and get them from Felicity,' he offered.

Cora shook her head. 'I'm all right now. It's a sun trap here.'

She leaned against the smooth green metal and glass of the Renault 5's hatchback and tapped the place next to her. 'Try it.'

His heart was hammering as he went and leaned back against the metal next to her.

'Nice day,' he said.

Cora slapped him, laughing. 'You don't say so.'

'Youch. The metal's scalding.'

'Stop messing.'

He shuffled, then she did. Then they were arm to arm. Her elbow jutted into his side and somehow the wool of her sweater became bunched up in his own hand. He wasn't sure if she pushed him or he pulled her but he'd his arms full of her and they were hip-joint to hip-joint. He'd an image of them like two Halloween skeletons on the make. He wanted to laugh and whoop and discovered her mouth brushing against his.

'Jesus,' he said.

158

His body shook as if he'd cracked an all-time gag. She was laughing too and then they were kissing for real. He'd a hand on her back and another ruffling her short hair. Roscillin and its troubles, the peeling paint and graffiti and the dead of the abattoir flew off like sparks. It was just Cora and himself joined at the hip like Siamese twins and tongues of flame coming down on them and the metal hotness of the hatch-back. The sun blared down, egging them on, and why wasn't the whole world doing this all the time, why?

Twenty-three

Boss Shaughn and the gang came through the fog the next morning. They stood in the curve of the track with their dogs and weapons. Da laid his kidskin cloak across the threshold. Mam was within with the younger ones. Brennor and I hid together by the goats' pen, looking on.

Words were exchanged, challenges, then spears were shaken, just as I'd foretold to Brennor the previous day.

'You'll be sorry if you don't pay up,' Boss Shaughn said. 'Won't he, Rur?'

The figure to Boss Shaughn's right made a gesture with his arm. 'The whole mountain's sorry these days.'

Boss Shaughn cackled. 'D'you hear that, lads? That was my son. He's a sense of humour, has my son.'

The silhouettes in the curve of the track laughed to order. Boss Shaughn raised a hand. They fell quiet.

'Shall we go up the track, Shaughn?' I heard my da say. 'And fight it out?'

'Told you,' I hissed to Brennor. 'They'll go up the bog road and come down friends with the payment deferred.'

'Up the track?' Boss Shaughn laughed, doubling up. His

cronies slapped their thighs. All save Rur. He stood with his spear, motionless.

'Fight it out,' Boss Shaughn wheezed. 'D'you hear that, lads?'

'We did, Boss.'

'He's a scream.'

'A scream with cheek, Boss.'

The band of men approached. Dogs were let loose. They yapped around the yard, chasing the hens. The men came towards where Brennor and I were hiding. I grabbed Brennor's hand, but he shook me off and I fell over in the straw. I pinched his calf and dragged him by the hem of his coat and he fell over too. The men were upon us. They opened the pen and drove out the goats, shouting and swaggering.

One of them saw Brennor in the straw. 'A brat,' he said. 'Nearly took it for a kid.'

Brennor bit his heel.

'Wee shite!' The man kicked Brennor hard in the ribs and hounded out the last goat. Its little talisman tinkled as it sprang up the track.

As Boss Shaughn's men herded the goats away, Da shouted, 'You'd have us starve, Shaughn, would you?'

Shaughn's men's laughter was the only answer, apart from the tinkles of the talismans. But Rur lingered. He stood motionless in the curve of track, his spear loose in his hand.

'I'm sorry, friend,' he called over when the last tinkle faded. 'It's the fog. It's driven every last one of them demented.' His voice was like that of a ghost coming through the murk.

I heard Brennor spitting. 'Sorry, my ass,' he hissed. 'You Shaughns. You'll pay for this.'

The figure of Rur retreated into the fog. The moanings and gurnings of Mam and the wee ones started up in the hut. 'It'll be the dead you rule, Shaughn,' Mam wailed. 'Only the dead.'

Deeeaaaadddd . . . Fergus started over his books. The cries in his dream drifted off. He shook himself awake. He'd been reliving the afternoon. He'd been doubling and trebling every second of the kissing like compound interest. The letters of the equations he was working on kept turning into waists and necks and tongues and short-cropped hair. He'd finally slumped over the drop-leaf table, exhausted. Falling asleep had been like diving into a warm swimming pool.

Felicity and Cora were out to supper with Professor Taylor. Cora had said Felicity wasn't to know about the kissing or she'd ground her again. Meanwhile, Mam was baking in the kitchen. Theresa and Cath were watching TV in the lounge. And he'd another exam tomorrow, the last but the worst. Applied Physics, the one he'd been dreading.

His ankle was throbbing again.

The door opened. Cath put her head in. Her hair was plaited over her head like a girl out of *The Sound of Music*. She'd a banana in hand, unpeeled.

'Mam says, d'you want this banana and d'you want a cocoa?'

Fergus looked at Joe's watch. Nine o'clock and he was wrecked. 'Yes.'

'Yes, what?'

'Yes, I'll have the cocoa. And yes, I'll have the banana.'

Cath handed over the banana reluctantly. Fergus turned it over in his hand, examining it.

'Say, Cath. Here's Padraig's latest joke. Why can't boys eat bananas?'

Cath looked hard at the banana. 'Dunno, Fergus. Why can't boys eat bananas?'

'Because they can't find the zip.'

Cath shrieked and slapped his arm. 'Stupid.'

'Don't slap me. Slap Padraig.' He peeled the banana, gave her half and shooed her away. He turned back to the equations, munching.

Mam came in ten minutes later. She brought the cocoa over to him and two fresh-baked scones. She stood for a moment, looking over his shoulder.

'How's the ankle?'

' 'S fine.'

'I'd never make any sense of all those figures.'

'You would, Mam. They're not as difficult as they look.'

He felt her fingers brushing over his crown. 'They are as difficult as they look.'

'OK. They are.' Fergus threw down his pen. 'Mam?'

'What?'

'Can I see Joe? It's driving me nuts, thinking of him but not seeing him.'

'Have you any more arguments thought up to persuade him?'

'No. But maybe I'd think of one on the spot.'

'Your exams—'

'They're over tomorrow. Remember?'

'So they are.' Mam frowned, confused.

'I'm not a child any more. I'm eighteen. And Joe's my brother. I've a right to see him.'

Mam nodded, her eyes filling. 'Maureen's changed her tune, Fergus. Did you know?'

'What d'you mean?'

'She's gone all patriotic. She's giving interviews to the radio saying how her son Len is the brave warrior and martyr and she supports him to his death. Should that be what I say, Fergus?'

Fergus shrugged. 'Joe would like it if you did.'

'He would.' Mam walked to the window and looked out on the close. The streetlamps were just coming on, a light violet, turning white.

'But it would be a lie,' Fergus said. 'Wouldn't it?'

Mam didn't answer. Even though there was still blue left in the evening sky, she drew the curtains. 'Before Joe went on strike, we had a family visit organized for tomorrow afternoon,' she said. 'I haven't cancelled it.'

'So I could come then?'

Mam nodded. 'But not Theresa or Cath. They're too young to see Joe in the state he's in. Just you, myself and Da. OK?'

'OK.'

They were silent. 'How bad is he, Mam?' Fergus whispered.

'He's lost a good few pounds. The doctors check him over every day.' She scrunched up a corner of curtain in her hand. 'He's quieter now. Tired. But just as determined.'

'Is there no talk of the strike finishing?'

'None.'

'I heard different.'

'Who from?'

'Michael Rafters.'

'What does *he* know about anything?' She gestured at the cup of cocoa. 'It's getting cold.'

Fergus took a sip. 'What did the chaplain fellow have to say to you today?'

Mam smiled wanly. 'He said that what Joe's doing isn't a sin. It's not suicide.' Her lips tightened. 'You know, Ferg – the lads inside – they're more a family to Joe now than we ever were. And what I want to know is, what did I do wrong? What?' She kneaded the rough curtain fabric between her red workaday fingers.

'Nothing, Mam,' Fergus said, touching her elbow. 'You did nothing wrong.'

She let the curtain go and shook her head. 'Good luck with the study, Fergus,' she whispered. Biting her lip, she left the room.

Twenty-four

That night, he dreamed not of Mel, but of Cora.

Cora floated into his room and slipped into his bed. He'd his hands under the soft cotton of her out-sized T-shirt and they lay still like two quiet question marks. Somewhere over them, a goldfinch hovered like a tongue of fire, frenzied. Then Cora was gone and he was calling her name, running down the corridors of the H-block, past the blue-painted gates, searching, desperate. He'd a can of Coke in one hand and a lock of hair in the other, but she was nowhere. A pale face appeared instead in the darkness. It was Michael Rafters, in prison garb. 'Dafters!' he yelled. 'What are you doing here? Did they catch you too?' Michael shook his head and his skin started drooping from his cheekbones as if he was melting. He turned into beige dough, with eyes of currants. 'Fergus,' he said, 'don't forget the packets.' He laughed as if he'd cracked a gag. As Fergus watched, Michael's body tilted upside down and floated from the ceiling. Fergus's body followed suit. They roared, laughing, the two of them, like characters out of *Mary Poppins*.

Then Fergus realized. They were hanging from hooks, with the blood flowing into their faces, suffocating them. They were laughing carcasses, the pair of them. He bolted awake.

Jesus. A slither of lamplight fell across his coverlet through a crack in the curtains. He panted. Outside, he heard a distant clatter, as of a dustbin lid falling on the pavement, then nothing. He breathed out long and slow. He picked up Joe's watch from beside the bed and made out the time in the half-light: 4:17.

He lay back down, calling Cora's name under his breath. He willed the door to open, but there was no sound through the paper-thin wall. He shut his eyes, flat on his back, his arms crossed behind his head. Everywhere inside him the heavy silence grew, as of the sleeping dead.

Twenty-five

The next morning, Felicity and Cora emerged from the twin room just as he was leaving for his exam.

'Hi, there,' he said, pausing at the bungalow's front door.

'We're off up to Omagh,' Felicity said. 'For Mel's X-rays. We'll call you if anything interesting emerges.'

'Good luck with the exam, Fergus,' Cora called.

'Thanks. I'll need it.' He smiled, looking back at her, as Felicity went through to the kitchen and started a bright, polite conversation with Mam. Cora lingered on her own in the dimness of the hall. He stepped towards her but she put out her arm, palm upward. Her finger went to her lips. She nodded her head in the direction of the two mams' voices.

'Fergus,' she whispered.

Her face gleamed white under her short dark hair. In the half-light, her eyes were incandescent.

'Cora . . .' He reached his hand out to hers, and for a magical second she let her fingertips trace his. Then she shooed him away.

'On you go,' she hissed. 'Scram.'

He grinned and stepped out of the house.

Outside, the day was grey and uncertain but he jaunted into town on the bus as if the whole world was an electromagnetic field set up by the fingertip-touching. But the pulse faded when he got to school and filed into the exam. The equations he'd been working on the night before crumbled to pieces in his head. He turned over the paper. *Three Bs and you've a place for medicine in Aberdeen, Fergus McCann. A whole new life.* Maybe he'd got a B in chemistry and biology. No way would he get one in physics. He dropped his head in his hands, afraid to look at the questions.

You're stronger than you look, Fergus.

It was Cora's voice, with the goldfinches hovering and the charged particles sizzling. He smiled, picking up his pen, and read question one.

Two hours later, he had to admit the exam wasn't as bad as it could have been. Mr Dwyer, invigilating again, said, 'Time.' With weary relief he put down his pen. His eyes were sore from staring at the ruled feint. His right hand felt like dropping off. But all he could think was, *It's over. Three Bs or no, it's done.*

Once released, he and Padraig capered down the corridor, punching the air, bounding out through the school vestibule and across the concrete yard. '*School's out for summer. School's out for ever,*' shrieked Padraig as they sailed through the school gate. He shook out his head and played air guitar, sounding the spit of Alice Cooper.

'*School's – been – blown – to – pieces,*' crooned Fergus.

They waited for the bus together, Padraig

head-banging and strumming through the hits of their youth. Fergus shadow-boxed the bus stop, his knuckles stopping just short of the metal, then he did knee-bends and ran on the spot until the bus came. They got on, flashed their passes and went to the back.

'Jesus. I could drink a crate of beer,' Padraig moaned.

'Come over to Drumleash later,' Fergus suggested. 'We can go to Finicule's Bar. My Uncle Tally said he'd stand me a pint or two.'

Padraig laughed. 'How would I get home? Walk over the surface of the lough, like Jesus?'

'You could crash at our place.'

'Wouldn't your mam mind?'

'Why should she mind?' Fergus said.

'You know. What with Joe 'n' all. Hasn't she a lot on her mind?'

It was the first time Padraig had referred to the trouble in their family. Fergus bit his lip. 'She wouldn't mind. She's always liked *you*, Padraig.'

Not like some of Joe's friends, Fergus recalled. Not like Michael Rafters.

The bus picked up a final passenger and, talk of the devil, it was Rafters himself, getting on like a regular punter. He'd his hands in his bomber jacket and a new haircut. It was sleek and layered, like a pop star in a new romantic band. He saw Fergus at the back and approached, sitting in the seat in front. 'Hi, Fergus.'

'Hi.' Fergus shrugged. 'Where's the car?'

Michael was famous for his metallic-blue Triumph TR7.

'In the garage. Being serviced.'

'D'you remember Dafters, Padraig?'

'Sure.' Padraig grinned. 'One of the two Incendiary Devices. Who could forget?'

'Whisht.' Michael smiled. A woman sat down opposite. 'People might get the wrong idea.'

The bus started up again. They travelled the eight miles towards Drumleash in silence.

'My stop,' Padraig said.

'Are you on for later?' Fergus asked.

'Definitely. I'll call before I leave.'

'Great. S'long.'

'S'long, Fergus.'

Fergus stared out of the window, watching Padraig retreat up a side road, strumming his air guitar. The bus rumbled on.

'D'you mind if I sit here?' It was Michael.

'Feel free.'

'How's it going?'

'How's what going?'

'You know. Our . . . little arrangement.'

Fergus lowered his voice. 'Terrible.'

'What d'you mean?'

'I've twisted my ankle. I can't do any more runs.'

'I saw you just now at the bus stop. You looked as if you were doing kung fu.'

Fergus recalled the capering. Dafters must have bionic eyes, he thought. The man missed nothing. 'OK. So my ankle's mended. Almost. But yesterday, I'm telling you. I nearly got caught.'

'Shush.' Michael lowered his voice. 'How?'

171

Fergus relayed the story of how he'd fallen over at the sight of the squaddie, and the squaddie chatting away to him all the time he had the packet hidden down his underpants.

Michael chuckled. 'Close shave,' he said.

Fergus grunted. 'I'm not doing any more pick-ups. Or drops. Nothing.'

Michael tut-tutted. 'You're not frightened by that little accident, are you?'

'No. I just don't want to be involved any more. That's all. I'm out. That's final.'

Michael sighed. ''S pity. And the hunger strikers nearly ready to call it a day.'

Fergus frowned. 'That's not what my mam says.'

'It's not certain. But things are' – Michael wiggled his hand – 'shaping up. At the top, there's talk of a deal.'

'I'm seeing Joe myself. Later.'

'You're seeing Joe?'

Fergus nodded.

'Jesus. Give him my best.' Michael Rafters drummed his fingers on the bar of the seat in front. 'He won't have heard about the deal. Not yet.'

Fergus sighed. 'D'you know, Dafters – deal or no deal, it's not the point any more.'

'So what *is* the point?'

'I'm saying this in confidence, right?'

'Fire away.'

'It's the squaddie.'

'The squaddie?'

'He's not just a squaddie. He's Owain. He's Welsh.

172

He's just like you. Or me. And I don't want to be involved in the killing. That's all.'

Michael stared. 'You've taken a shine to him, have you?'

Fergus shook his head. 'No. But he's just a bloke. Normal. He'd no choice but to join up. It was that or go down a mine.'

'A mine would've been better for him. Trust me.'

'Trust *you*?'

'OK, don't trust me. But he's no business being here in the Six Counties. Just you remember that.'

The bus pulled into Drumleash. Fergus was about to get up, but Michael didn't move.

'Can I get past?'

'In a second.' Michael had his eyes half shut. 'Fergus.'

'What?'

'Keep on with those packets.'

'No.'

'I would, if I were you.' His words were almost sinuous.

'Why?'

'Because otherwise that squaddie of yours will end up a has-been.'

'A has-been?'

'You know. Tatty-bread.'

Fergus stared.

'Rhyming slang, McCann. Remember?'

Tatty-bread, dead.

Fergus thought of Owain with his pale, freckled

173

face, his fallen Pentecostalism, his rifle tracing the arc of a bird.

'Jesus.'

'So you'll keep on, Fergus? Just another wee while?' Michael got up from his seat, smiling and nodding, as if he'd just invited Fergus round for tea.

Fergus bit his lip. He nodded.

'And Fergus?'

'*What?*'

'Remember to send Joe my best.'

Michael skimmed his way up the bus, waving his hand over his shoulder as if they were all-time friends.

Fergus sat frozen to his seat.

'Last stop, Drumleash,' the driver called.

Last stop is right, Fergus thought. He kicked the seat in front of him and winced. His ankle pain returned, sharp. Cursing under his breath, he got up and limped out. The sun came out as he walked up the street towards home. He thought of the dismal smell of the prison blocks awaiting him and remembered the dream he'd had the night before.

I'd rather be dead meat, he thought. *Hanging from a hook. Or cells breaking down in the ground. Anything but this. Anything.*

Twenty-six

The prison visiting room was bright. Light filtered through the frosted glass, making the glass dividers glow. Across from him, Joe sat huddled up to himself. Spasms of shakes came over him. It was warm in the room but around Joe was a chilly penumbra.

Mam and Da passed the time of day with him, while Fergus was struck dumb. Joe was gaunt-looking, older. His cheekbones jutted through his skin, his eyes were downcast. There was a weary resignation to him, like a lamb being led to slaughter. He remembered a picture he'd once seen in a book, of Christ crowned with thorns. The face of the Saviour had been elongated, the eyes calm, the complexion only one step removed from the pallor of death. Joe looked the same. The struggle of fear and temptation was over. He was going with the flow, on cruise-control to his coffin.

'Couldn't you take the water hot?' Da was saying. 'It wouldn't be breaking the fast, would it?'

Joe shook his head, not answering. He looked up and caught Fergus's eye. A flicker of a smile crossed his face.

'Mam, Da,' he murmured. 'D'you mind if I have this visit with Fergus? On his own?'

Da got up. 'You see us all the time, Joe. That's fine. We understand. Don't we, Pat?'

Mam bit her lip and nodded. She got up, touching the glass panel. 'We'll wait outside, Joe.'

A guard approached, and after some hushed conversation they were led away. Joe settled back into his huddle. Fergus stared at the ceiling wondering what to say. No words came. No arguments. Nothing.

'You still don't agree, do you?' Joe said. His voice was hoarse.

Fergus shrugged. 'Like Da says, it's your choice, doing this. I respect that.'

'So you understand, Fergus?'

'I suppose I do.'

Joe nodded.

Fergus leaned forward. 'Joe?'

'What?'

'Is it true that a deal's being made?'

'A deal?'

'To end the strike?'

'No. There's no deal.'

'You sure?'

'Sure.' Joe coughed and shivered. 'They say your man Adams is delighted. Nobody could have foreseen the rallying around. Nobody.' He coughed again, grabbing his belly.

'You all right?'

Joe shook his hand as if to say not to worry. The coughing subsided. 'The strike, Fergus. It's worked.'

176

'If it's worked, can't you come off it? What more can you achieve?'

'Special category status. Remember? The whole point.'

'You'll never get that, Joe.'

'Wait and see.' Joe moved in his chair as if all the bones of his body were sore with pressing on the hard seat. 'I might not live to see it. Others will.'

'Oh Joe.' A terrible thing was happening to Fergus. His shoulders convulsed and a great sob came from him. He was crying like a woman. Like Mam. Here, in this place, in front of his brother. He buried his head in his hands. 'Joey.'

There was silence. When he looked up, he saw a tear gathering in Joe's eye.

'Fergus.'

'What?'

'You know. Love. That stuff.'

Fergus scrunched his fists to make the crying stop. 'Yeah, I know.' He forced the crying feeling back down his throat. He sucked his lips between his teeth and bit the flesh, hard. He felt like a toddler crushing the jack-in-the-box back in.

A bleak silence fell on them both.

'Tell me, Fergus?' Joe rasped.

Fergus swallowed. 'What?'

'How's your man with the van?'

'Who?'

'Uncle Tally.'

Fergus smiled. 'Uncle Tally? He's grand. I saw him yesterday. He said to send you his . . . "greetings".'

' "Greetings"?'

'That was the word.'

'I miss him,' said Joe. 'But this prison – it's not his scene.'

Fergus shrugged. 'Whose scene is it?' He looked around at the hard, cold floor, the Spartan plainness of the place. 'D'you want me to tell him you'd like to see him?'

Joe seemed to consider this. Fergus thought he heard a sigh. 'No.'

'No?' It was on the tip of his tongue to ask about the Cindy affair, but Uncle Tally had said not to.

'Just tell him something,' Joe said. 'From me.'

'What?'

'Tell him, "It was all for the best." '

' "All for the best"?'

'Yes. Tell him that. Those words.'

'I will.'

Joe shifted in his seat. 'Any more news from Drumleash?'

'Not much. I saw Dafters earlier. On the bus.'

'Dafters on a *bus*? What's happened to his TR7?'

'Nothing. It's in the garage.'

'That Dafters. His eyes always on the main chance.'

If that's how you remember him, thought Fergus, good on you. 'He said to send you his best.'

'His best? You know what Dafters's best is?'

'No.' *A brown jiffy bag. Crammed with explosives.* 'What?'

Joe hummed a tune.

178

Fergus made out the air of *We Three Kings*. 'Jesus. Not that again.'

Joe stopped humming and laughed softly. 'Those were the days, Ferg. You, me and Michael. Wassailing Drumleash. D'you remember what we did with the money?'

'No. What?'

'We bought three giant-sized bottles of cider. And you were sick.'

'I wasn't.'

'You were. You threw up all over Dafters's shoe.'

'You're having me on.'

'I'm not. You were too drunk to remember.'

Fergus shook his head. 'I'm off out boozing tonight, Joe. I'm going out with Padraig, down to Finicule's. We're celebrating the end of the exams.'

'The exams?'

Fergus nodded. 'They're over.'

'Of course.' Joe flicked his wrist as if to say exams were part of another world. 'I should have asked. How were they?'

'So-so.'

'That's what you always say. Then you come top.'

'Not this time. They *were* so-so. Honest.'

'You'll be fine, Ferg. You could do those exams standing on your head. You crack on with the study, Dr Fergus. The first McCann ever to go to university. Mam and Da – they're that proud.'

Another spasm came over Joe. His eyes dilated and he retched. Then he doubled over, grabbing his guts. Fergus got a whiff of something stale, like a breadbin that badly needed washing out, mixed with something chemical, like pear-drops.

'You'd better go,' Joe gasped.

Fergus realized he'd exhausted him. Slowly he got up. 'Are you all right?'

'Never better.' Joe looked like torture itself. 'Only, Fergus?'

'What?'

'Don't come back. I'd rather not see you again.'

Each word was a stabbing.

'D'you understand?' Beads of sweat formed on Joe's forehead.

Fergus nodded. 'S'pose.'

'Nothing personal.'

'OK, Joe. I won't come in again. Not until all this is . . . over.'

Joe rocked on his seat. 'Not until then, Ferg.' His face grimaced with another spasm. 'Christ. Goodbye, Ferg. Fight the fight.'

'Bye, Joe.' But he couldn't move. Joe looked up in anguish. The whole eighteen years of their lives together were in his face. 'Go on, Ferg. This will pass.'

'Joey.' Fergus pressed his palm to the glass panel. With an effort, Joe pressed his palm up to the other side, so that their hands matched. Fergus noticed his own hand was now the larger. Joe's hand shook a little, then fell back to his lap.

'Bye.'

'Bye.'

Fergus stumbled from the booth, towards the other end of the room. The floor lurched like a boat in a bad sea. The guard reached out to steady him at the door. 'Bye, Joe,' he called again as he left the room. He followed the signs to the exit, retracing the steps Mam, Da and he had taken earlier. As he walked the weary corridors, the thought that he'd never see his brother alive again pressed on him with numb certainty. The words of the Lennon song careered around in his head:

> *In the middle of a cloud*
> *In the middle of a cloud I call your name.*

He dragged his knuckles along the peeling paint. There was all his life till this moment and that was the past. There was all his life after this moment and that was the future. He could hear the mouth organ, jauntily playing the tune, the piano bouncing along. *Oh Yoko! Oh Yoko!* The present was the fulcrum, holding all of time. Old war planes took off from the old aerodrome, men banged the bars of their cages with bedpans, weeds of the future grew through the crumbling concrete. The piano died away. Only the mouth organ was left. It too faded into silence as he emerged from the H-block into the blinding whiteness of the sun.

Twenty-seven

It was gone tea time when they got home. Felicity and Cora hadn't returned from Omagh. Mam sent Fergus over to collect the girls from playing at the Caseys'. Theresa helped Mam put out some bread and cheese. They snacked on that with quartered tomatoes.

'Mam?' Cath said.

'What?'

'How thin has Joe got?'

Mam looked over at her. 'No thinner than you'll be if you don't eat your supper.'

There was silence.

'Mam?' said Theresa.

'*What?*'

'Did you tell Joe about my part in the panto?'

Mam smiled. 'I forgot. I'll tell him next time, Theresa. Promise.'

Fergus looked up from a doorstep sandwich he'd been eating. 'What panto?'

'The end-of-term panto, Fergus. We're doing *Snow White and the Seven Dwarfs*. And I've the best part.'

'Not Snow White?' He gaped at Theresa's flaming red hair and freckles with mock horror.

'No. I'm the evil stepmother.' Theresa leered. '*Mirror, mirror . . .*' She gave a hideous cackle and scratched the air under Fergus's nostrils with her fingernails.

'Whisht,' Mam said.

Fergus shielded his face. 'I get the picture. What are you, Cath?'

'I'm a dwarf,' she said, skewering a tomato quarter.

'Not Grumpy?'

'No.' Cath pouted at the tomato. 'I'm Sleepy.'

'Go to bed, then.'

Theresa chortled and scratched the air with her fingernails some more. Cath stuck out her tongue.

'Don't wind them up, Fergus,' Mam scolded.

Fergus munched through his sandwich and made another. 'Mam?'

'*Now* what?'

'I said to Padraig he could come over tonight. We're off to Finicule's to celebrate.'

'Celebrate? What in God's name is there to celebrate?'

Fergus shrugged. 'The end of the exams. Uncle Tally said he'd buy me a pint.'

Da looked over at Mam, who was frowning. 'Pat,' he said. He put out a hand. It hovered, but didn't land on her wrist. 'Let him go. Let him leave off some steam. He deserves it.'

Mam's eyes went up to heaven. 'OK, Fergus. Only

don't be talking about – you know. Not to anyone.'

'No, Mam. I won't. Can Padraig sleep here? I'll put the sleeping bag out for him in my room.'

Mam smiled. 'No. I'll make up the bed in Joe's room.'

Everyone fell silent. Joe had moved out when he was eighteen, after getting a job in a brewery in Newry. Then, a few weeks before his arrest, he'd moved back in. He'd said at the time it was just until after Christmas. Perhaps he'd already known the RUC were onto him. Nobody had slept in there since the night of his arrest.

'I'll give you a hand,' Fergus offered.

Mam nodded. 'OK. You can get the sheets down from the press.' She and the girls started to clear away. Da handed Fergus a fiver, putting his finger to his lips, then shuffled out into the garden, jangling the loose change in his pocket.

Fergus found the bed linen and went into Joe's old room. The bed was stripped bare. The place was full of his things. Soccer albums, clothes, Airfix models, the mandolin he'd never mastered, the schoolbooks he'd hardly opened. His green-and-white striped Celtic football scarf was draped over the back of the desk chair. Fergus sniffed. There was a faint odour of old trainers, a whiff of Joe's familiar sportiness.

He went and stood at the window, pulling back the net curtain. If you looked out sharp to the west, you could make out a fold of hillside, a patch of meadow with sheep grazing. On the sill he found some old conkers Joe must have kept since last autumn. He'd always been fond of conkers, Fergus recalled. He'd had some crackpot theory about how the life trapped in their shells gave you magical energy if you carried them round in your trouser pockets. Aphrodisiacs, he'd called them. They were dusty and wrinkled, nut-brown.

He scooped them up one by one and polished them with his sweatshirt. He thought about pocketing them, but somehow it didn't feel right. He put them back on the sill in a neat ring.

'There, Joe,' he whispered. 'There.'

He opened the window to air the room and set about making the bed.

Twenty-eight

There was a good crowd in Finicule's. Padraig and Fergus sat propped up at the bar, two beers in. Uncle Tally was behind, mopping the glasses, pulling the pints, juggling the custom like a pro.

Padraig drained his off. 'I've a wicked thirst on me.'

'Me too. I'm parched.'

'If it was pints of water, we wouldn't be that fussed.'

'We wouldn't.'

'The lure of the beer. What the hell is it?'

Fergus held up his glass. 'It's the amber light, Padraig. It sends you off in a trance.' He drained his off. 'I'll get another.' He flashed Da's fiver over the counter. Uncle Tally grinned and pulled another two. He refused the cash. 'Save it for the next round,' he said.

Glasses recharged, they re-examined the amber. 'Bottoms up?' suggested Padraig in a posh English voice.

'May we all be alive this time next year,' Fergus responded. He thought of Joe and winced. Padraig

186

clinked his glass and together they took a good slug.

Fergus slooped some spilled beer off the counter with his beer mat. 'D'you know our Theresa and Cath?'

'Yep?'

'They're in the school panto. *Snow White and the Seven Dwarfs*. I ask you. You'd think they'd put on something pacier.'

'Like what?'

'Dunno. *Grease?*'

'That's way too advanced for Drumleash.'

'OK. *The Sound of Music*. Wouldn't the nuns like that?'

Padraig giggled. 'That reminds me.'

'What?'

'I know this joke about the seven dwarfs.'

'I've a pain in my belly starting.'

'Honest. 'S funny.'

'Go on.'

'Snow White sends the seven dwarfs off to convent school, right? So they can learn to read and write. And while they're there, they all go off on a school trip to the Arctic Circle.'

'The Arctic Circle?'

'Yeah. To find the North Pole. See the Eskimos. Whatever.' Padraig swallowed some beer. 'Anyway, Grumpy goes up to Sister Mary. She's the class teacher, right? And really pretty, if you can imagine her out of her habit.' He sketched an hour-glass shape with his hands. 'The works. "Sister Mary?" goes Grumpy. "What, child?" "Did Dopey spend last night with you?"'

Fergus chuckled.

187

'And she says, "No, Grumpy. Don't you know, I've taken a vow of chastity."'

'Hi-ho, hi-ho. Then what?'

'Grumpy goes back to the other dwarfs. "Hey, Dopey," he goes. "I've bad news for you." "What?" goes Dopey. "That wasn't Sister Mary you screwed last night. It was a penguin."'

Padraig slapped the bar and waddled on his stool and hooted. Fergus laughed, even though he'd heard a million variations of the penguin-nun joke. Padraig was practically off the barstool, when Uncle Tally came over with two whiskey shorts.

'What are these?' said Fergus.

'They're chasers. They're not from me. They're from Mr Casey over there. For the exams. He says good on you, the pair of you.'

'We haven't passed them yet. We've only finished them.'

'He said to give them to you anyway.'

Fergus swivelled round on the barstool and raised the whiskey glass to Jim Casey, who shook his head and smiled as if to say, *It's the least I can do for the brother of a hunger striker.*

Soon after, Padraig went off to the porcelain receptacle, as he put it.

'Uncle Tally?'

'What?'

Fergus beckoned him over and leaned over the counter. 'I saw Joe,' he whispered. 'Today.'

Uncle Tally looked around to check nobody was listening. 'How was he?'

'Awful.'

'God. I'm sorry.'

'He asked after you. So I gave him your "greetings".'

'Thanks, Fergus.' Fergus was about to give him Joe's message, about it being "all for the best", whatever that meant, when a customer approached the bar, a man Fergus didn't recognize. Uncle Tally picked up a cloth to wipe a glass.

'Can I have two pints of Guinness, Thaddeus?' the man said.

Fergus smiled. Nobody around Drumleash ever called Uncle Tally by his real name. The man must have dropped in from another planet.

Padraig came back. Together they downed the chasers, then returned to the beer.

'D'you wanna hear one about the three pigs?' Padraig said.

'Christ. Spare me. OK.'

Padraig was halfway through the joke when Michael Rafters came in. Fergus nearly choked on his beer. He swivelled round so as to have his back to the door and grabbed Padraig by the wrist.

'Let's move to that snug,' he said.

'OK. If you insist.' They shuffled over. Fergus settled into the shadowy corner, praying Rafters wouldn't come near him.

'Where was I?' asked Padraig.

'Something about the wolf. Huffing and puffing.'

'Oh, yeah.' The walking encyclopaedia of jokes finished that gag and three more besides, when

189

Uncle Tally came over with another round of beers.

'Who are *these* from?' Fergus asked.

'Michael Rafters. He says they're for Mr Marathon Man and his friend.'

Uncle Tally put them down. Padraig burped. 'There's a powerful mood of generosity in Finicule's tonight,' he said. He leaned out of the snug and caught Michael's eye. 'Here's to the Incendiary Devices!' he roared. The whole pub laughed.

Fergus sat back in the shadow of the snug, all mirth evaporated. He was exhausted suddenly. His stomach churned and his limbs had shooting pains. He remembered the spasms of Joe, the stale-breadbin smell of starvation.

'And the angry neighbour goes, "You should be damn well hung, you bastard."'

'What?'

'The punch-line, get it?'

'Oh yeah. Damn well hung. Ha-ha. 'Scuse, Padraig.' Fergus got to his feet, pushing his beer to one side. He lurched to the door at the back of the bar and made it to the gents just in time. Everything he'd eaten earlier and drunk in the pub got thrown up in three violent retches.

Afterwards, he splashed water on his face. His brain tilted. The urinals rocked.

'Jesus,' he moaned, gripping the porcelain edge. He retched again, his throat and mouth stinging with the acrid taste of nothing.

He splashed himself again and rinsed his mouth out. The seismic shifting of the tiles and urinals slowly settled. He breathed in and out and dried his face, feeling better. Then he slipped out of the toilets, down the passage and out the back of the pub. The night was fine and cool. There was a freshening breeze off the mountain. His heart was pumping. His collar felt tight. He undid the top button of his shirt. Stars pulsated overhead.

'Good job,' he heard a voice say.

He looked around. There were two men talking out by the parked cars. He didn't recognize them, but their voices carried over in the stillness.

'Give it here.' He saw one man pass something that glinted in the dark to the other. 'Let's get out of here.' They got in a car and drove off.

When Fergus got back to the bar, another chaser had appeared alongside Michael Rafters' pint.

'Where did that come from?' he said to Padraig.

'Colm Fahey this time. You're one popular man.'

Fergus plumped down. 'I've had enough beer. I'll stick with the chaser.'

'Sure?' Padraig picked up Rafters' pint with an expression of boozy satisfaction.

'If I have another bubble, I'll burst,' Fergus said. 'Swear to God.'

'That reminds me. Have you heard the one about the Catholic man from Sligo?'

Fergus groaned. 'God. No.'

'Your man was blowing bubbles through the wee ring you get with those bubble-solution yokes. You know the kind?' Padraig mimed the action by making an O with his finger and thumb and blowing through it.

'I know. What then?'

'He keeps trying to get the perfect bubble and cursing when each bubble bursts. So this Derry guy who's watching him, a Proddie, goes, "Why d'you keep cursing and taking the Lord's name in vain?"'

Fergus laughed. Padraig had the Reverend Ian Paisley's voice off to a T.

'And d'you know what the Sligo fellow says?'

'No. What?'

'You'd curse too if your condoms kept bursting.'

He screamed with laughter at his own joke. Fergus grabbed his side, groaning. He slapped the tabletop. 'Where the hell did you get that one from?'

'I made it up.'

'Jesus, Padraig. You'll be wasted on electrical engineering.' They clinked glasses and Fergus took a swig of the whiskey. As it went down his gullet, its warmth swelled inside him, like bread rising. He looked around the bar. The place was full to bursting now. The smoke in the air, the carved wood of the snug, the jaunty windows and round bowls of light were a consolation in a vale of tears. He took another sip of whiskey and smiled.

'Tell us another, Padraig. Keep them coming.' Somewhere out there, he thought, Cora was on her way back from Omagh, with her short-cropped hair and surely another round of the kissing to come. Here at his side was Padraig with his crazed jokes, with all Drumleash standing him drinks and the exams done. He didn't care if he was half cut – 'stocious', as Uncle Tally would say. When Colm Fahey got out his accordion, Fergus bellowed out *The Siege of Venice!* Everyone thumped approval. Colm nodded. Soon the whole bar was mad, delirious with the clapping, the toe-tapping, the laughter. The night spun like a top. Colm's fingers flashed over the buttons and the keys. And the smell of starvation was nowhere, gone, obliterated somewhere in the beat and the golden glow of the whiskey.

Twenty-nine

Things got better before they got worse.

The morning after he stole our goats, Boss Shaughn was found dead in the lough, drowned. On his head was a fierce gash.

He hit it on a rock falling from his boat, drunk out of his skull, people said. This cold, foggy winter would drive anyone to drink.

Others whispered, Someone thumped him and dumped him.

Even I wondered, Did my own Da do it?

Da said nothing.

Boss Shaughn's body was carried to the greensward at the head of the lough and buried there in accordance with our custom. Then Rur took over the leadership of the land. He gave us our goats back. He made atonements to the people Boss had robbed. Rur said the payments could resume in the summer, with backlogs written off.

But still spring didn't come. The cold murk lingered even when the bluebells should have been and gone. Crops failed. People got hungrier. Old folk died. Mam's baby died. And the whispering got louder.

A crime has been committed with no recrimination. The gods are punishing us.

At another funeral, I saw Boss Shaughn's widow eyeing me across the sward. She spoke words to her daughter with a spiteful slant to her eyebrows.

I'd never believed in the gods taking an interest in our small lives, but even I started to pray to them for the sun to return.

A day came when narrow fingers of light grappled through the cloud. I went up the mountain and looked down on the settlements: bonfires, men tending the animals, barren, brown fields. I'd a glimpse of Rur's tall, fit frame, doing the jobs with the other men. He caught sight of me up there and, to my delight, downed tools and climbed up to me.

'So, Mel. What's new?'

Just then a full beam of sunlight prised its way out, like the first daffodil. I pulled off my bonnet and shook my hair loose. I undid my belt and then the knot of my shawl and stretched out my arms.

'Mel?' he laughed. 'What are you doing?'

'I'm catching the sun,' I said, 'to keep it here with us.'

Rur chuckled. He sat down and patted the limp grass beside him. I sat down.

'Do you know what they say about you, Mel?'

'No.'

'They say you're a spirit from the Sidhe. And I'd say they've a point.'

I punched him. 'I don't believe in no Sidhe, Rur. That's baby stuff. I believe in now. That's all there is. Here and now. Today.'

Then my hand travelled over and found his. He ruffled

195

my hair like I was a pet. We sat together in the weak sun, watching the banks of cloud shift, showing up silver glints of the lough.

'I loved a girl once,' Rur said.

'Did you?'

'Yes. She was beautiful. Too beautiful. My father sent her away to the Brannans down south. He sold her. On account of her fine eyes.' He looked intently at me. 'Beauty comes at a price, Mel.'

I stroked down my hair and rolled my eyes. 'Don't I know it.'

Rur chuckled and chafed my hand.

We sat in silence. But silent words are the loudest.

'Rur,' I said, putting on my bonnet. Down on the lough shore, I saw Rur with a stone, held aloft, with his father in a drunken sleep in his boat.

'What?'

'I see it now.' I pointed down to the water.

'What do you see?'

I smiled. 'What might have been.' I turned to him. 'What has been, maybe?' I picked up the two strings of my bonnet and showed how the two lines could cross.

'What about what will be?' Rur said.

I shrugged. 'That I don't know.'

Rur tied my bonnet strings up in a knot. 'Go on home, Mel. Look after yourself. And your family. And your goats.'

So I went back over the mountain and the sun shut its door on the world. I smiled. I held the life of the person I loved most like a frail moth in the palm of my hand. But it was safe there. Safe always.

* * *

Fergus woke from sleep, his fingers chasing a sensation of butterfly wings passing over his face.

He started, scratched his nose. It was a current of air coming from somewhere.

His head thumped. He remembered the beers and the chasers, the swaying urinals, the madcap jokes.

He sat up, groping for the coverlet. It had slid off him onto the floor during the night. Then he gasped. The draught was coming from the door. It was open, with a ghost standing at it.

'Jesus.'

'Fergus?'

The 's' slithered over to him, making him breathless. 'Cora?'

'Shh.'

Now he could see the white of her oversized T-shirt, the slope of her shoulders, a pale glimmer of nose.

'You've the exams finished?' she whispered. She stepped towards him.

He nodded. '*Cora?*'

'Shh. Mam's just the other side of the wall, remember.'

His heart was hammering it as she got into the bed, pulling the coverlet up and over them both.

'Smells like a brewery in here,' she giggled.

He groaned. 'We were out celebrating. A real session.'

'We tried to phone you this afternoon from Omagh. But there was no one in.'

'We were out visiting—'

'Visiting?'

'Nobody. Nothing.' He felt her hand searching for his. She was trembling. 'Are you cold?'

Their fingers interlocked. 'Frozen.'

He drew her into a firm clasp.

'Cora?'

'What?'

'I've no – you know what. Protection.' He'd been falling around laughing about condoms all last night, but now Cora was next to him he couldn't say the word.

'I've it all organized, Fergus.'

'But Cora?'

'What?'

'I've not ever. You know. Never—'

''S fine. We can just lie here, if you like. Together.'

His head thumped. Joe with his conkers would be on the third go-round by now. He ran his hands over her ribs and waist and hips. There wasn't a spare inch of flesh anywhere. Then she turned and they lay like they had done in his dream, two quiet question marks. His hands and fingers traced her skin. She breathed deeply. When he reached her jaw line, he felt a trace of wet.

'You've been crying,' he said. Her shoulders shook. She buried her head in his armpit. 'Cora? What's wrong?'

'Oh, Fergus. It's Mel,' she said.

'Mel?' Strange fragments of a dream came back to him. 'I was dreaming of her just now.'

'Were you? What was she doing?'

'I can't remember. I was seeing the land, through her eyes. Settlements, cattle, fields. It was cold. And the lough was down there somewhere. You could glimpse it when the clouds shifted.' He sighed. 'No different from today.'

He smoothed her fringe over her forehead and got his lips up to hers. They started again on the kissing. He was inside-out with it, frantic. He'd to stop to draw breath.

'D'you know what it's been like since yesterday?' he said.

'No.'

'It's been Kissus interruptus.'

Cora giggled.

'Now it's Kissus continuus.'

'You're daft, Fergus.'

They had another long kiss. It was like running for his life.

'So,' Cora said.

'So what?' he gasped. The T-shirt was up around her armpits. The coverlet was tangled between them. It was hard to know whose limb was whose. He was about to explode.

'D'you want to know what we found out? In Omagh?'

'Yes. After another kiss.'

She pushed him off and pinched his arm.

'Ouch.'

'*Shush.*'

He untangled the coverlet and spread it neatly

over them, his heart thudding so hard he could've sworn it would wake the whole house. There was a sudden creak through the paper-thin wall. *Felicity. Waking?* He froze, listening intently. The night went silent again.

'Phew,' he breathed out. 'Did you hear that?'

'Yes.' Cora crept out of the bed. ''S too risky, Fergus,' she whispered. She glided towards the door. Her T-shirt fell back into place.

'Cora. Wait.'

She paused, touching the door handle.

'What did you find out in Omagh?'

She shook her head, with a finger to her lips.

'Please. Tell me.'

She crept back and sat on the edge of the bed. She sighed. Then she leaned over and whispered two words in his ear:

'Wisdom teeth.'

He frowned, thinking it through.

'You mean . . . ?'

'Yes.'

'Jesus.'

'Shh.'

'I should have known it.' Fergus's heart raced. He slapped his forehead. All the mentions of Snow White and he hadn't made the connection. Studying medicine and it hadn't occurred to him. He remembered the strange hunch of Mel's little body as he'd seen it in the abattoir, the plump, short arms and stout fingers. It was obvious all of a sudden. 'She's not a child at all. Is she?' He sat up.

'No.' Cora took his hand and cradled it to her cheek. 'She was a dwarf, Fergus. That's why they killed her.'

With terrible clarity he saw the party of execution, leading Mel up the hillside, shouting and castigating her with a noose around her neck. Diamonds of frost sparkled on the stiff grass. The sun rose crimson over the horizon. Her small feet slipped and they yanked her on, threatening her with the naked blade of a knife.

'The child time forgot,' he whispered.

'What?'

'Nothing.'

'Mam's thrilled. And Professor Taylor. You'd think they'd discovered America.'

'Jesus. Poor Mel.' He put his hand to his neck as if he could feel the noose, tightening.

They sat together, saying nothing. Outside, a grey dawn got underway. He thought of the long corridors of the H-block, the brown packets, the exam questions that had thrown him. He thought of Mel looking out over the glories of the morning mountain for the last time.

'Cora?'

'What?'

'Stay. Please.'

She paused, listening intently, then nodded. As she got back under the coverlet, a chaffinch gave out its first hesitant trill of the day. Cora's ribs pressed hard up against his. Then there was no sound or sight, just feeling, a pure toppling, free-falling *swooooooosh*, as of a sparrowhawk swooping down from the sky. He'd to clamp his teeth over his inner lips with the sweet agony of keeping silent. *Suffering Saviour. Dying's like this*, he thought. *Painful. Beautiful. You stretch out your hands. You meet it like a lover, on cruise-control to your coffin.* And he heard all the priests of all his mass days intone the familiar words. *In the midst of life, Fergus. In the midst of life we are in death.*

Part III
FIGHT OR FLIGHT

Part III

FIGHT OR FLIGHT

Thirty

The funeral party fanned out from the open grave.
Photographers, journalists, soldiers were thrown
together with the mourners. Half of County
Fermanagh was there. You could hardly move a leg.

Father Doyle's voice led in prayer. The polished,
ornate coffin gleamed in the sunshine on its trestles.
Whoever had paid for the top-of-the-range model, it
wasn't the Sheehans. Fergus stood twenty yards away,
his hands clenched, his eyes trained on the great Scots
pine at the far end of the graveyard. '*Pray for us sinners,
now and at the hour of our death,*' the crowd intoned.
At the graveside Mrs Sheehan stretched a hand out
over the waiting cavity. The Sheehan men, directed by
undertakers, slid the coffin from the trestles over the
grave. The lowering ropes were put in place. There
was a hush. Nobody moved. A late July breeze got up
in the surrounding trees, amid the questioning calls of
crows.

Lennie Sheehan had died forty-five days into his
strike. He'd caught an infection and died sooner than
expected. The morning the news of his death broke,

205

women across the North had taken to the streets with dustbin lids, crashing them down onto the tarmac, cymbals of protest. That was the new ritual. Would the dustbin lids of Drumleash ring out soon for Joe? Fergus wondered.

Joe clung on to life still, drifting in and out of consciousness, emaciated. The McCann house was already in mourning. Whenever the phone rang, everyone feared the worst. Previous plans to go south for a family holiday had been discarded. Mam and Da were hardly talking.

Just before Lennie's coffin was lowered, three men in balaclavas topped by berets, in makeshift army uniforms, appeared from the far side of the church. They took position by the central mourners and fired a round of three shots into the air. Fergus had been expecting it. All the dead hunger strikers had been saluted in this fashion. Some had even been carried to their resting place by balaclava'd pall-bearers. The police and army did not intervene.

The Provos' volleys of gunfire set the crows cawing off the trees. Shots ricocheted across the valley, reverberating between the church and the mountain. Mrs Sheehan keened, then stumbled, almost as if she'd been hit. The British soldiers posted out on the surrounding road stiffened, their weapons at the ready. Fergus recognized Owain, stationed at the church gate. His face was pale, uncertain. His hands gripped his SLR. Fergus tensed. The whole cemetery teetered on the brink of something. Panic leaped through the crowd, like flame to a paper.

There were swayings, rustlings, mutterings. One false move, there'd be a bloodbath.

Then the moment passed. The Provos paused, looked at each other through their eye-slits. One gave a low command and they retreated the way they'd come. There was a familiar Drumleash slope to their shoulders. The gait of the last figure was eerily like Joe's, as if Joe's spirit had somehow escaped his prison hospital bed to do this last thing for his comrade in starvation.

Joe, Fergus thought. *You'll be next. Maybe tomorrow, maybe in two weeks. We'll be here again, in this place. But this time we'll be grouped around the McCanns' family plot, under the great Scots pine.*

Len's coffin was lowered. Fergus heard his mam, standing behind him, start up the '*Hail, Holy Queen*', her favourite prayer, under her breath. '*To thee do we send up our sighs,*' she muttered, '*mourning and weeping in this vale of tears.*' The words had made him giggle as a child. He'd gurn and smite his breast, enjoying their lugubriousness. Today they suffocated him. Prayers, mourners, rifles: he'd had enough. He stumbled away through the crowd.

Vale of tears is right. When this is over, the afternoon of Joe's funeral, I am taking the ferryboat and getting out of here. For ever. He pictured the bouncing waves, the receding town of Larne, the trailing gulls. Then the first sighting of Scotland, the stepping ashore to a whole new life and country. *Three Bs or not, I'm off.* He pushed his way through the graveyard, past the seat where Michael Rafters had first recruited him with the packets, down the crowded gravelled pathway. By the time he reached the gate, the service was over. Everybody was leaving.

Owain stared at him as he walked by. Fergus raised his eyes to heaven, as if to say the world was a show. Owain half nodded, half grimaced and turned away. His superior barked the order to retreat.

Dog or rat, Fergus thought. *Do what you're told, or run free? Rather a rat, any time.*

As he turned onto Drumleash's main street, he noticed Michael Rafters lounging by a wall. He'd a small backpack at his feet, no doubt containing his balaclava and other Provo attire. For the past three weeks Rafters had been away. There'd been a welcome hiatus with the packet deliveries. He was back like a bad penny, his face brown as a nut. He emanated relaxation, as if he'd been on a world cruise. He'd probably been off to a Provo training camp in some foreign clime.

'Hi, Fergus.'

Fergus quickened his pace.

'Fergus?'

'What?'

'Tomorrow?'

'Tomorrow what?'

'You know.'

'Not *again*?'

'Yes again. Or else.' Michael beamed as he mimed a throat being cut. He nodded over to where the soldiers were climbing aboard their Bedford truck. 'You know what.'

I know. Fergus nodded and walked past, fast. He

turned into the close and let himself into the house. It was silent in the hallway. Dust motes floated in a stream of light. He shut his eyes, listening to the quiet. It was as if his ears were preternaturally sharp. There was a faint scrabbling, as of underground rats in the bungalow's foundations. He felt his way down the hall, fingering the rose petals of the textured wallpaper, then crept into his room, shutting himself in.

He opened his eyes with relief. From a paperback on the bedside table he retrieved the two postcards he'd hidden between the pages. They'd arrived that morning, his secret. It was a miracle he'd got to the post before anyone else. He stroked the two glossy photographs. He put one of them up to his nose and sniffed it as if to catch the heady fragrance of another place. Both cards were from Rome, dated two weeks ago. One pictured the Colosseum and read:

Dear Fergus and family,
    Wish you were here to see the layers of history. Ancient times, Renaissance and Mussolini cheek-by-jowl. On to Pompeii tomorrow. Could we book in for Tuesday August 2nd? We have an important meeting arranged with Professor Taylor regarding Mel. See you then.
    All best, Felicity and Cora.

The other was of a nude nymph, sitting cheekily on the lap of a hairy, pagan Pan. It read:

    Soon, sooner, soonest . . .
    Maximus kissus resumus.

Thirty-one

When the alarm beeped the next morning, Fergus jolted awake and remembered. He groaned, stuffing a pillow over his head. Another packet delivery day. He dragged himself up and got into his running things.

Outside, the weather continued fine with a soft white sky. The village nestled in the valley's side, dormant. The first bee of the day explored some hedgerow clover.

If it weren't for these bloody packets . . . Fergus ran from the close and down through Drumleash without limbering up. *If it weren't for Joe* . . . He vaulted the Forestry Commission gate, picked up the packet, ran without bothering to hide it in his shorts. He stopped for a splash in the stream that was now a trickle. *If it weren't for the Troubles* . . . He stuck to the tarmac road and went straight past the sentry hut. He hardly cared if he was caught. He swapped packets at the dry-stone wall and ran back the way he'd come. *If it weren't for Ireland breaking off from Britain, aeons ago, or Britain breaking off from Europe* . . .

He froze. A strange sound emanated from the

sentry hut: a high note, caught, strangulated. For a moment he thought it was a strange breed of cattle. He looked around. The note fell downwards into a perfect scale. It didn't belong here on the mountain. It wasn't the wind, or an animal, but an instrument. He stopped and listened. Silence. Then the breeze brought over to him another snatch, a broken chord, mounting with rising sadness. He remembered TV footage he'd seen of President Kennedy's funeral eighteen years before, the year of his birth: the small child saluting, the lament of the bugle, a nation in mourning.

He shoved the packet down his front. Not a moment too soon. A figure emerged, walking into the open, playing a silver instrument, now with circus-like cheeriness. *Pad-da-tum-tum-pom, pad-da-tummy-tummy-pom.*

The player was Owain. He was dressed in regulation trousers, but his khaki shirt flapped open. At the sight of Fergus, the instrument jerked away from his lips. 'Oh. Phew,' he said. He smiled, gesturing with his trumpet, or whatever it was. 'Just you.'

'Just me.'

'How's it going, Fergus?'

'Never better.'

'You must be fit for the Olympics by now.'

Fergus shrugged. 'Not quite.' He gestured to the instrument. 'What's that?'

'This? A trombone.'

'Never knew you could play.'

Owain looked at the trombone like an old friend

211

of whom he was weary. 'There wasn't much else to do in the Valleys but join a silver band.'

'D'you still play in one?'

Owain shrugged. 'Off and on. More just on my own, to practice. Sometimes I fill in for the locals here. The UDR fellows are always short of a trombone. I've a concert booked with them next Wednesday.'

'The UDR? You'd be shot for playing with them round here,' Fergus warned.

'You'd be shot for breathing these days.'

Fergus thought of the packet hidden in his shorts, the lowering of Len's coffin, the keenings of Mrs Sheehan. He nodded. 'True enough.'

'It's a bloody mess, this whole place.'

'Bedlam.'

'At the funeral, yesterday. We were *that* close.' Owain held out a finger and thumb, as if only the thinnest sheet of paper would fit between. 'I saw you there. Were you a friend of the dead man?'

'Len Sheehan? I knew him. In a place like Drumleash, you know everyone. He was three years older than me, more a friend of my brother's.'

'Your brother? Was he there too?'

'No. He's . . . away. In Rome. For the holidays.'

'Lucky him.'

'Yeah. Lucky him.'

Owain shook his trombone to get the spit out and blew on the mouthpiece. 'Those hunger strikers. I don't get why they do it. It's not like we're torturing them. Or sending them off to the salt mines. Do you get why they do it?'

212

Fergus stared at Owain, then looked out across the valley. 'No.' Fermanagh rolled serenely away, its green lands tumbling into the pale horizon. 'I've no idea. Unless it's this.' He gestured across to the view.

'What?'

'Land. Freedom. Whatever.'

Owain smiled. 'If it was the Welsh Valleys, y'know what?'

'No.'

'Guess.'

'You'd fight to the death too?'

'Hell, no. I'd say, welcome to it, slag heaps 'n' all.'

Fergus smiled. 'Owain?'

'What?'

'Play us another tune.'

'No.'

'Go on. Please.'

Owain shrugged. 'OK. But promise you won't tell?'

'Who would I tell?'

'Dunno. But I'm supposed to be on duty. Not practising the bleeding trombone.'

Fergus grinned. 'I won't tell.'

Owain put his lips to the mouthpiece and started on a slow, rollicking waltz. The tune was familiar. It gathered pace. It brought to mind ball gowns, chandeliers, frock coats, champagne. Fergus shut his eyes, smiling. He and Cora were dancing, her in a silken amber dress with layers that floated like feathers as she turned. Her shoulders gleamed like living marble, her eyes were dark, sleepy. They were whirling

213

around the crumbled ruins of the floodlit Colosseum, the mosaic-tiled floor empty just for them. Onlookers circled around them, clapping with white-gloved hands . . . Then the tune changed to a lyrical, hymn-like air. Fergus recognized it from an old TV advert for sliced brown bread. He opened his eyes and lounged up against the rock he'd sat on the last time he'd met Owain. Soon he couldn't help but hum along. The trombone notes crescendo'd upwards to a bittersweet conclusion, as if a question posed by the tune was being answered, but not as expected. The final chord died away amid the nearby baas of sheep. The wind settled.

Jesus. The man's a genius.

The trombone fell from Owain's lips. 'Sorry.'

'Sorry? What for?'

'I changed the ending. I went into the minor key. Dunno why. It felt right somehow.'

'Sounded fine to me.'

'D'you know what they call it when you finish sad like that?'

'No. What?'

'A feminine ending.'

'Feminine? Why feminine?'

'Guess it's like the pop song says.'

'What pop song?'

'*Only Women Bleed.*'

Fergus grinned. 'Alice Cooper. I thought that was all about you-know-what. Periods. That stuff.'

'Nah. It's about women getting a raw deal. Being beaten up.'

'Never.'

''S true.' Owain grinned. 'Only all the women I've ever known give the men the hard time. Not the other way round. You should have seen my mam. She went for Dad once, with the flat side of the iron. That's Welsh women for you.'

'Sounds like Irish women. The beginning and end of all sorrow.' It was what his da said when he wanted to bait Mam. 'Irish women and this bloody place, all rolled together. It's enough to make you weep.'

Owain put the trombone to his lips and did a short rendering of *Only Women Bleed*. When he stopped, a nearby sheep baaed shrilly. It sprang up the mountain, veering off to the right and left as if in panic.

'What's got into that fella?'

'Dunno. Must have been scorned in love.'

They laughed, then stopped at the sound of an army Land Rover coming up the hill.

'Better put this away,' Owain said.

'Yeah. You better had.' Fergus started to run on the spot, tensing up. He checked the packet, flapped his sweatshirt. 'Gotta run myself.'

'I'll say. Never seen anyone train so hard.'

'Owain?'

'What?'

He thought of the lie he'd told about Joe being in Rome, Len's coffin being lowered, the hopelessness of it all. He'd a desperate need to talk to somebody. Anybody. The approaching Land Rover changed gear as it climbed. 'Nothing. Bye.'

Owain waved with his trombone. 'Bye.'

Fergus sprinted down the road, trying to make cover before meeting the oncoming vehicle, but the vehicle was soon upon him. He stepped onto the verge, almost stumbling in the gorse. Against the sun, he could see silhouettes of broad shoulders, bristling rifles, army berets. The horn beeped. The Land Rover sped up past him. He ran down the hill and didn't stop until he reached the place where the view of the entire lough opened up. He paused, panting. Nobody could see him now. He felt like taking the packet from his waistband and hurling it as far as he could down into the wilderness. Maybe it would land in the forest and blow up and start a fire. Or maybe it would arc outwards, land in the lough and sink, to be eaten by unsuspecting fishes. Or maybe it would reach Drumleash and land *bang!* on Rafters' head and kill him outright.

Land. Freedom. Whatever. He ran down into the Forestry Commission and flung the packet in the abandoned tyre.

Thirty-two

Mam had the garden shears out when he got home. She clipped at the lawn's edge, *thrapp-thrapp*, with a face to send Jack the Ripper running.

'There you are. The wreck of the *Hesperus*.'

'Mam?'

'What?' *Thrapp-thrapp*.

'I had a card. From Felicity and Cora.'

'So?'

'From Rome.'

'Lucky them.' Mam scraped a strand of hair behind an ear. 'I always wanted to go to Rome. Father Doyle used to run the pilgrimages. But money. Time.' Mam shrugged as if to say, *Never enough.* 'This place,' she sighed.

'Maybe you can still go, Mam. After. After—'

'After what? After Joey's died? Is that what you were going to say?' She stood up and attacked a rose bush, snipping off buds along with the dead heads. 'When Joey's dead,' Mam said, 'there will be no afters. No trips. No messing. No nothing.'

Thrapp-thrapp. The shears, wide-open, flopped

from her grasp, threatening to stab her leg. Fergus grabbed them and steadied her as she swayed. 'Oh, Mam. Please.'

She pushed him away, eyes closed. 'I wish to God I'd never met your da. That I'd never crossed that border. That I'd never come anywhere near these Troubles.' Then she opened her eyes and nodded at the shears. 'Shut them,' she said. 'They're a menace. On a fine day like this. A bloody menace.'

Fergus blinked, confused. He eased the handles of the shears together. The rusty blades scrunched up with difficulty. 'There.'

'That's better.' Mam spread out her hands over the mangled rose bush, as if granting it absolution. She breathed out. 'What was it you were saying?'

'Sorry, Mam?'

'About the Dublin ladies?'

'They want to stay again. Next Tuesday.' *When Joe may still be alive. Or not.*

Mam shook her head. 'No, Fergus. We need the money badly, I know. But I can't deal with them. Not now.'

'I'll look after them, Mam. I'll get the breakfasts. Please. If nothing else it will be a—'

'What?' She was glaring again.

He mouthed the word instead of saying it. *Distraction.*

Mam must have lip-read it. 'I'm distracted enough, Fergus.' Then suddenly she relented, smiling. 'You've taken a shine to that young girl.'

'Cora? How d'you know?'

'I know. I'm your mam. I've known you all your life. That last morning, when I came in with the breakfasts. You were gazing at her over the rashers.'

'I wasn't.'

'You were. Pie-eyed. The same look you used to have when I'd cut up the Christmas cake. You were mad for the marzipan, remember?'

'Yes, Mam. I remember. I liked the marzipan, but Joe preferred the royal icing. So the two of us would do a swap.'

Mam stared, tears gathering.

'Sorry, Mam. Didn't mean to—'

'Don't be sorry, Fergus. It's a nice memory.' Joe might as well have already been dead, the way she said it.

'Mam?'

'What?'

'Can I phone and tell them to come then?'

'Who?'

'Felicity and Cora.'

Mam sighed. 'Do what you want, Fergus. I'm beyond caring. If anything happens while they're here, we can send them over to stay at the Metlins'.'

'OK, Mam. That's what we'll do.'

'What's the time, Fergus?'

Fergus looked at Joe's watch. 'Nine forty-five.'

'Sweet Mary. I must fly. I've an important meeting.' She rushed indoors, almost skidding on the doormat. Fergus followed, watching as she grabbed her handbag, keys, a tube of Polo mints. 'Fergus. Take the girls out. Swimming. Anything. To give the Caseys a break.'

'OK.'

She was out the door in a whisker, with the car roaring to a start. She turned hard right out of the drive, nearly scraping the passenger side on the gatepost. She zoomed off, an accident waiting to happen. He could see the newspapers, in a whirling sequence of cinematic headlines, like a game of consequences. SON ON HUNGER STRIKE. WORRIED MOTHER IN CAR CRASH. GRIEF-STRUCK DA KILLS HIMSELF.

He knuckled his eyeballs to get rid of the images.

'Theresa, Cath,' he yelled. 'D'you fancy a swim?'

From their bedroom at the far end of the hall he heard a rumble, like horses' hooves pounding over the plain. He braced himself. The door flew open.

'Fergus,' Cath wailed. 'My costume stinks. Mam never washed it.'

'Fergus,' Theresa shouted. 'I've a new stroke invented.'

'Have you? What's that?'

'It's called Killer Shark. You use your elbow as a fin.' She bared her teeth and swam up the hallway. 'It's good, Fergus? Isn't it?'

ORPHANED GIRLS ESCAPE FOSTER HOME AND TAKE TO CRIME. 'Terrifying, T. Makes *Jaws* look a tadpole.' *Oh, Joe. The consequences. On you, on us, on all of us. Did you think of them? Did you?*

Thirty-three

That night, he rang the Dublin ladies. The previous time they'd left, he'd carefully inscribed their phone number under the 'O's for O'Brien in the address book, but he'd never dared dial it before. Cora answered.

'H'lo?' she said, sounding as if she was munching something.

'It's Fergus.'

The munching stopped. 'Fergus.' The 'r' in her voice was like a rug unrolling inside him. Words deserted him.

'Are you still there, Fergus?'

'Yes. Cora?' His blood was pumping in his temples. 'How was Rome?'

'R-R-Roma.'

The way she said the 'r' again made his ears burn. 'OK. So how was Rom*a*?' He couldn't roll his 'r's, so he stressed the 'a' instead.

'Romantic.'

'Never.'

'It was. There were motor scooters everywhere.'

'Did you ride one?'

'Mam would have had a fit. But guess what?'

'What?'

'You couldn't hail a taxi.'

'Why not?'

'Dunno. Some rule to do with the mafia or something. You had to call up from a phone box.'

'What about the Vatican? The Sistine Chapel?'

'Awful.'

'Awful?'

'I got a crick in my neck from staring up. The ceilings dripped with blood and gore and gold.'

'Yuck.'

'Telling me. I liked Pompeii best. The whole place is frozen at the precise hour, day, year that Vesuvius erupted. AD seventy-nine. All the bodies are turned to statues.'

'Christ.'

'Telling me. And Fergus?'

The 'r' did him in again. 'What?' he gasped.

'When we got back, the radiocarbon-dating result for Mel had arrived.'

His heart skipped a beat. 'Don't tell me. Was she—?'

'Mam was so nervous reading the report, her hands trembled. She was sure Mel would turn out to be Victorian or something awful like that. But it was AD eighty. She nearly had kittens with relief.'

'AD eighty? Oh.' For some reason, Fergus had cleaved to the idea that she'd walked the earth at the same time as Jesus. 'How accurate is it?'

'Dunno. Pretty accurate. Ask Mam.'

'I will. Cora?'

'What?'

'About Tuesday?'

'Yeah?'

'You can still come. Only my mam's a bit busy visiting some relatives. So I'll be doing the breakfasts.'

'You can *cook*?'

'Sort of. Can't you?'

'Not to save my life.'

Fergus had the receiver crammed up to his ear. He lowered his voice. 'Cora?'

'Yeah?'

He'd the wire corkscrewed around his fingers and wrist. He whispered, 'Kissus resumus.'

'Kissus maximus resumus.' Cora giggled.

He grinned and looked at the mouthpiece as if Cora's face was imprinted there. He pressed it back to his ear. 'Be seeing you.'

'Yeah. Tuesday, Fergus.'

That 'r' again. 'Bye,' he whispered.

'Bye.'

Her end clicked dead. He was about to put down the phone, when he saw Theresa eavesdropping on him by the door to the lounge. She fluttered her lashes and patted her heart. 'Kissis whatsits,' she crooned.

'Shush, T.'

'Mam, Da,' she caterwauled. 'Fergus is in love. I heard him.'

'Shut up!' Fergus dropped the phone and chased

223

her. He picked her up bodily, clapping his hand over her mouth. With muffled squeals, she shook her legs out. He marched her down to the girls' bedroom and flung her down on the lower bunk.

'Booty?' she said.

'Yeah. Booty. And if you eavesdrop again, I'll boot the booty. Right?'

'Right, Fergus. Only if you do, I'll put a curse on you.' She did her Evil Stepmother hideous cackle, scratching the air.

He pinched her kneecap. 'Curse away. I'm cursed already. One more curse won't hurt.'

He left her to her cackling and went back to the hall. *Soon, sooner, soonest.* Two and a half more days till Tuesday morning. Sixty hours. Every hour would bring Cora closer.

And take Joe further away.

The phone receiver was still dangling over the table's edge. He replaced it, biting his lip. The lounge door was ajar. He could hear the sound of football on TV. He sighed and went through.

Da was watching *Match of the Day*. Cath was stretched out on the carpet, cutting out pictures of food from old magazines and arranging them on a piece of yellow card. Mam normally read magazines, filed her nails or sewed when *Match of the Day* was on. Today, she sat in her chair, staring at the screen. The sewing box was open at her side. In her hand she held a large leather-covered button. Da's cardigan, from which it came, was bundled on her lap. Her eyes were vacant.

'Mam?'

'What?'

'I rang the Dublin ladies. They're coming.'

'Shush,' said Da. 'And close that door. There's a draught.'

Fergus shut the door. 'What are you doing, Cath?'

'I'm making a get-well card for Joey.'

'I said, shush, the pair of you,' Da snapped. The sound of the football crowd, relayed from the Glasgow stadium, crescendo'd, then died away. Da groaned. 'Celtic nearly scored. If you two hadn't been gassing, maybe they would've.'

'But Da—'

Da flapped his hand. Cath gave Fergus a *Dunno-what's-up-with-him* look. She went back to cutting out a steaming bowl of soup. Mam sighed and unfurled the cardigan on her lap. She got a needle out of the sewing box and set about threading it.

Fergus was about to leave them to it when the football play was interrupted by a newsflash. '*We are interrupting tonight's programme to bring news of a car bomb that has exploded in Londonderry,*' an announcer said. The scene panned to a female reporter, stationed by a police cordon on a nameless street. Her long blonde hair flew about her in the night breeze. She'd a microphone at the ready. Ambulance and police cars flashed. People milled around, some looking at the camera, some turning their faces away, others hurrying off. The sound hooked up to the waiting reporter. '*Three people are thought to have been killed and several hospitalized in a bomb that went off about one hour ago,*' she

225

said. '*The device is thought to have been planted in a car parked outside the local Ulster Defence Regiment quarters, and reports are coming in that two women passers-by, who were out celebrating a friend's wedding engagement, are among the dead. Nobody has yet claimed responsibility for the attack . . . A witness says the street was busy, as it usually is on a Saturday evening, then a sound like "giant metal sheets" crashing together was followed by screams and flying debris. It seems as if the bomb was intended to do maximum harm.*'

'Why would they interrupt the football with a report like that?' raved Da. 'Another bomb? What's new about that?'

'Nothing,' Mam said, stabbing the button with her needle. 'Nothing's new about it. Not nowadays.'

Fergus fumbled with the door handle and backed out of the room. Quietly, he closed the door after him. He stood with his forehead dropped against its smooth, blank wood, with a sensation of drowning overwhelming him. Gasping for air, he went outside into the back garden.

He fingered his throat, staring at the pegged shirts hanging on the line. *Jesus. Two women dead.* He saw them, high as kites, arm in arm, laughing as they swayed down the street, the worse for wear after a night on the vodkas, boozed out of their brains. Then that awful sound, the clash of metal sheets, the flying parts. Was anything left of them? Did they even know what hit them? *Nobody has yet claimed responsibility for the attack . . .* He imagined a quiet backstreet room, maybe right here, in Drumleash. A man worked in the bright light of an angle-poise lamp, his face in shade, his nimble hands opening the brown packet, fixing explosives to fuses, setting the timer. *Deus at work. The Incendiary Device himself.* Michael Rafters.

And himself, Fergus McCann, the courier.

I killed them, he thought. *As surely as if I'd planted the bomb myself.*

Thirty-four

The frail moth grew strong, but the people grew weak. Rain fell, rust-coloured, the same day that three children died. They were buried on the sward in a freezing fog. 'Enough is enough,' I heard the mourners mutter. I walked from the sorrowing place behind my father. I passed the great dripping pine that grew by the palings and spun round, as if it was a game of peep-behind-the-curtain. But this was no game. The settlement stared at me with a hundred blazing eyes, coalesced with hate.

I felt small then. It was as if I was less than knee-height, truly a creature from the Sidhe. My bones ached with the endlessness of urging them to grow. I saw myself as they saw me. I almost believed in the image of Mel the witch, as reflected in their hostile eyes.

Rur stood at the gatepost as we filed by, his eyes fixed to the impenetrable mists of the middle distance, his intentions inscrutable.

Fergus lay prone on the lawn, dressed only in his pyjamas, drifting. The sun slanted down, almost strong enough to burn. Visions of Mel died away.

Instead, in and out of his head, the voice of Michael Rafters ebbed and flowed. *A legitimate target, Fergus. The Incendiary Devices? We were only messing, Fergus. The ballot box isn't enough. Can we count you in, Fergus?*

'Fergus!' Theresa yelled from the back door. 'Mam says shake a leg. Mass time.'

He shut his eyes fast. *Lord I am not worthy to receive you.* 'Tell Mam I'm not going.'

'But—'

'No buts. I'm staying put.'

She must have darted off. A minute later, he heard Mam's voice. 'Fergus?'

'I'm staying here, Mam.'

'Are you sick?'

Why not say yes? There'd be no more argument or fuss. 'No.'

'Hurry on, then.'

'No. I'm not going. I don't believe a word of it.' *But only say the word and I shall be healed. Fat chance.*

'Fergus?'

The plea of generations of Irish Catholic mothers was in her voice. Fergus sat up and glared. 'I'm not coming.' She looked aghast, as if the Devil himself had taken possession of him. He fluttered a hand. 'I'm sorry, Mam. I'm just worn out with all the praying.'

'C'mon, Pat,' he heard Da say. 'Leave him be.'

Fergus flopped back on the lawn. Gradually the sounds of the family departing faded away: the calls, the doors slamming, the gravel crunching, voices retreating down the close. He opened his eyes. The clouds inched their non-judgemental path across the sky. He drifted with them. Mel's voice returned.

First I was a child. Then I became a woman, trapped in the body of a child. But now I was a malign being, an incubus, sent to bring havoc and grief to the world of giants around me.

A magpie chortled nearby, bringing him back to the present.

'What should I do?' he whispered. The sun skimmed behind a shallow cloud. 'Do nothing?' This was doing nothing and it was hell. Maybe the Devil really had moved into his soul. 'Do something? But what?'

Inside, the phone began to ring. He tried to ignore it. But it didn't stop. Then he thought it might be Cora. Perhaps there was a change in their arrangements. Or maybe it was news of Joe.

He rushed indoors, grabbing the receiver before it rang off. 'Hello?'

'H'lo, Fergus. It's me. Michael.'

'Christ. You.'

'Thanks very much.'

'What the hell d'you want now?'

'You weren't at church, Fergus. You're slipping.'

'Ha-ha.'

'I was hoping to see you there. I don't like talking on the phone. You know why.'

'I can guess.'

'One more run, Fergus. Tomorrow.'

'You always say that. Then it goes on and on. And what about last night?'

There was a silence. Then, 'What about last night?'

'How can you say that? The bomb. In Derry.'

'Shh. You never know who's listening.'

'I don't care who's listening. They can listen away.'

There was silence. 'That . . . little incident, Fergus?'

'Yes?'

'It wasn't us, Fergus.'

'No? Who then?'

'Does it matter?'

'To me it matters.'

'Whoever it was, it wasn't us. Ours is a strictly military target. Remember?'

'I remember. But what difference does it make?'

'All the difference. And it's the last time I'm asking you, Fergus.'

'The last time?'

'Swear to God. This is the last phase of this . . . mission.'

Fergus snorted. He nearly said, *You can stuff your mission up your backside.* But something shifted in his head. 'The last time? You're sure?'

'Sure as sure.'

Fergus thought. 'OK. I'll do it.'

'Good man, Fergus. The lads won't forget this. Never.'

'I don't care if they remember or forget. This is my last act. You'd better remember.'

'I'll remember, Fergus. The last act. Same time, same place?'

'Fine.' Fergus replaced the receiver. He went back into the garden and flopped back on the grass. He

231

numbered the people in his life that he loved. Mam. Joe. Da. Uncle Tally. Cath. Theresa. Padraig. Cora. Felicity.

Do nothing. Do something. A cortège of dark clouds moved in from over the mountain. He waited. The first drop fell on his cheek. He squeezed his eyelids shut. *The last act.*

I passed Rur on the sward and I turned to face the hostile crowd. I clasped my wrists together and held them out before me, offering them up to be bound with rope. 'Take me,' I said. 'Do what you will with me.' What else was there for me in that world of starvation, with my stunted body an object of such loathing?

Soon rain pelted down, swift and furious. Fergus didn't move. His pyjamas were sodden. He imagined a lightning bolt crackling down to earth, finishing him. *Take me.* 'OK, Mel, my girl,' he whispered. 'If you can do it, so can I.'

Thirty-five

Uncle Tally came in through the back door after dinner.

'Look what the cat brought in,' said Mam over the washing-up.

'No need to bite his head off,' Da snapped, shaking out the *Roscillin Star*. It was plastered with pictures of Lenny Sheehan's funeral.

There was silence.

'I'm here to take Fergus out driving, Pat. His test's coming up.'

'Your test?' Mam said, glaring at Fergus.

Fergus shrugged. 'I applied ages ago.'

'He'll breeze through it. He drives better than me these days,' Uncle Tally said.

'That's not saying a lot,' joked Da.

Mam flicked the suds off her fingers and let out the water. 'On you both go, then. Remember the L-plates, Fergus.'

Da extracted the car keys from his pocket. 'Mind out for the sheep,' he warned. It was what he always said. Fergus never knew if he meant actual sheep or

233

the sheep-like drivers who overtook just because the person in front overtook.

He and Uncle Tally left and got into the Austin Maxi. Fergus didn't bother getting the L-plates out of the glove compartment and Uncle Tally said nothing. Fergus reversed out of the drive.

'Mind the gate,' Uncle Tally warned.

He'd barely an inch on the passenger side. He was getting as bad as Mam. He straightened up and reversed again.

'That's better.'

Fergus drove to the top of the close.

'Where shall we go?' Uncle Tally said. 'The mountain road?'

'How about somewhere different?'

'Like where?'

'The sea. I haven't seen it in ages.'

'Have we time?'

'Mam and Da aren't wanting the car today, far as I know.'

'OK. The sea it is.'

Fergus drove around the lough. There were three handsome white sails out, veering into a brisk wind, and two brightly painted rowing boats. Of the swans there was no sign. They took the main road. The soldier on duty at the border barely glanced at them as they went through. They cut cross-country towards Bundoran.

'I don't fancy the crowds,' Fergus said as they approached signs for the resort.

'Keep going. There's a spit of land I know, with a fine strand. I haven't been there in years.'

'It's too chilly to swim.'

'It's always too chilly to swim in this godforsaken place.'

'Why don't you ever go on holiday, Unk? To Majorca or somewhere?'

'No mon, no fun,' Uncle Tally quipped. 'Turn right at the next junction.'

Fergus turned and followed a narrow road. Views of shining sea opened up. It was hard to tell where the water ended and the sky began. Fermanagh's shower-clouds had gone. Here the sun shone through a brilliant haze.

'Jesus, Unk. There's a permanent rain-cloud over Drumleash compared to this.'

'It's the mountain. Clouds always hang about over high ground.'

'So why do we live up there? We're all fools.'

'We are that. Every last one of us. Pull in here.'

Fergus drew up in a lay-by hard on the coastline. 'Why didn't you ever move away, Unk?'

'Dunno. Call me foolish, but I love Drumleash. It must be an acquired taste.'

'Yeah. And maybe it takes a lifetime to acquire it.' Fergus turned off the engine but kept his arms resting on the steering wheel. Uncle Tally wound down the window. Dry grasses hissed. Bright yellow flowers fluttered in the scrub. Beyond was a strip of bone-white sand and then the endless shimmer of sea. 'Wouldn't you prefer to live out here?'

Uncle Tally shook his head.

'Why not?'

'The ocean is vast, Fergus. You can see no end to it. It's like looking at eternity.'

'Isn't that what's great about it?'

'For you, perhaps. For me, Fergus, it's a reminder.'

'A reminder of what?'

'Death.'

Fergus stared out at the gentle void. He could see two lads' heads bobbing, a trail of their footprints across the sand, leading back to a mini-mound of clothing. 'I remember now, Unk.'

'What?'

'The last time you brought us here. Years ago. It was the time you saved Joey's life.'

'I didn't save him, Fergus. I just stopped him going out beyond his depth.'

'You did save him. He was caught in a current.'

Uncle Tally raised protesting hands.

'Afterwards you told us not to tell Mam about it.'

'Did I?'

'Yes. That's how I knew it was serious.'

Uncle Tally laughed. 'Well. It must have been serious, I s'pose, if I actually got in the water.'

'You ran in, shouting, then you got hold of Joe's neck and swam sideways. I was in the shallows, shaking with terror.'

'You've an elephant's memory.'

'He was nearly blue when you got out.'

Uncle Tally took out his fags and lit one. 'Never did like the sea.' He smoked without offering one to Fergus.

'Unk?'

'What?'

'I forgot to tell you what Joe said to me. The last time I visited him.'

'He mentioned me, did he?'

'Yes. He asked how you were. I said nothing about . . . you know what.'

'What?'

'Cindy.'

'Oh. Cindy.' Uncle Tally looked along the length of his cigarette as if it was lopsided. 'Did he say anything else?'

'Not much. Just to tell you it was "all for the best".'

' "All for the best"?'

'Those were the words.'

Uncle Tally took a last drag on the cigarette, then stubbed it out. '*What* was all for the best?'

'I dunno, Unk. That's all he said. I thought he meant Cindy.'

'Yeah, s'pose that was it. Cindy.'

'Unk?'

'What?'

'It's sad, isn't it? Your saving Joe all those years ago. And now this.' Fergus pointed through the windshield as if the view beyond constituted whatever lay at the end of starvation.

Uncle Tally grimaced. 'You have to wonder.'

'Wonder what, Unk?'

Uncle Tally didn't answer. Instead he lit another fag. The silence in the car grew. He exhaled. 'They say drowning's a pleasant death.'

Fergus stared at the boundless blue, numb.

'I'm glad you're getting out of the North, Fergus. Believe me. We'll miss you. But we'll breathe easier when you're gone.'

When I'm gone. Yes. You could say there's safety where I'm going.

'Unk. Let's head back.'

'You sure you don't want to get out and walk?'

Fergus shook his head. 'I've seen as much as I need to.'

'You sound tired. Shall I drive?'

'Would you?'

As they got out to swap seats, Fergus felt the wind in his hair. He'd not cut it since his exams and it was shoulder-length, like a girl's. He wet his finger to judge the wind direction. It felt as if it was coming from everywhere at once. He strained to hear the sea over the sound of the wind. He made out the softest of whispers, like a memory of a memory, an irregular heartbeat.

They drove back the way they'd come. In the wing mirror, Fergus could see the green hedges retreating, the final inlets, and then the sky behind, turning orange, then pink. Ahead, the evening thickened. After they passed back over the border, he broke a long silence. 'Unk, d'you know what Semtex looks like?'

Uncle Tally missed a gear change. The car nearly stalled. 'Semtex?'

'Yeah. You know. The explosive.'

'Why d'you ask?'

'Just curious. After that bomb last night up in Derry.'

'How d'you know that was Semtex?'

'Dunno. Just assumed.'

'I wouldn't assume anything. Could have been old-fashioned TNT.' Uncle Tally's hands briefly raised themselves off the steering wheel. 'I'd say that wasn't a Provo job.'

'That's what someone else told me. So, Unk, you don't know what Semtex looks like?'

'Haven't a clue. Isn't it in your science books?'

'No.'

'You'd have to ask a demolition expert. Or a soldier.'

Fergus smiled. *A soldier.* As they looped around the lough, the sun seemed to draw up close to them. It was bulging out of itself, a pulsating disc of crimson.

'Only look, Unk.'

The road was deserted, so Uncle Tally pulled up. They watched the sun as it sank below the mountain with a final flare of green. Colour drained away from the land. The lough turned grey and the trees black. Uncle Tally restarted the car. Fergus sat back and shut his eyes, listening to the hum of the tyres on the road and imagining the sound as the endless lapping of the sea. *An eternity, Fergus. A reminder.* In the quiet of the twilight, with the familiar presence of his uncle, something like peace came down on him.

Thirty-six

On my last night I sat like a queen on a throne of bound straw in one of the settlement's barns, receiving visitors. My heart pumped. My eyes stared into the dark. I could hear the low murmur of the guards talking to one another outside.

First Mam came, offering me her beautiful bangle. It had come from over the water years ago and was passed on from oldest daughter to oldest daughter in our family. Mam slipped it over my hand onto my wrist next to the rope they'd used to bind me. She kissed my cheeks. 'Oh, Mel,' she said. 'My first baby.' She knelt and threw her arms around me.

'Don't cry, Mam,' I said. 'It's the one way we all go.'

She stroked the bangle. 'They say if you wear this when the baby's seed is sown, the baby will come out perfect. And look what happened.'

'You got me,' I quipped.

'Yes. And you are perfect. My own Mel. Always busy, always cheerful. The house will fall to pieces without you.'

Then Da came and knelt beside Mam. 'Mel,' he said. 'You're not the child time forgot. Nothing or nobody could ever forget you.'

I smiled and combed out my fringe with the fingers of my

*bound hands, until Da reached over and took them in his.
'Go carefully, Mel. When you get to the other side, take
comfort. I'll be close on your heels.'*

*It was only then that I saw how pale and thin Da had
become in that endless winter and realized how he'd been
denying himself food on our behalf.*

'Oh, Da,' I murmured. 'You too?'

*'Me too,' he said, chafing my hands. He put a forefinger
to my cheek and wiped away a stream of sudden tears.*

When the alarm went off next morning, Fergus awoke,
rubbing his smarting eyes. He groaned and flattened
the alarm face-down on the bedside table. *Today is the
day. The last of the packets.*

He waited a few seconds and then got out of bed.
He changed and did some ritual stretching. On his
way down the hall, he stopped on an impulse and
opened the door to the girls' room. Theresa was flat
on her belly on the top bunk, with an arm dangling
down over the edge. Cath, in the lower bunk, was
tangled up in the Dalmatian dots of Joe's old coverlet.
She was chewing the corner of it in her sleep. The
sound of the two girls breathing was like the pulsing of
tiny bird-wings. As he moved to close the door, Cath's
eyelids fell open. She blinked and moaned, then
turned to the wall.

He stretched a hand out towards them, then
shrugged. Then he tiptoed away.

Outside, the day was cool and grey, the breeze
chilly. A curtain of haze hung over the hills. On the
grass verge of the close he stretched his hamstrings,

rocking on his heel. *You must be fit for the Olympics by now.* His calves were solid, his speed never better. But he'd only ever run on rough ground, not on a track. He'd no idea how close to the professional mark he was, but he'd been treasuring the idea of joining an athletics club at university. *It doesn't matter now. Nothing matters.*

He started down the close. Drumleash was quiet, but from down the street he heard the rasping sound of somebody opening an old-fashioned sash window. Only Finicule's Bar had windows like that. Maybe Uncle Tally was awake early too. He turned off up past the school and started the climb.

In the Forestry Commission, he got the last packet from the tyre. 'Don't even think of looking, Fergus,' Rafters had said. Despite that, he'd often been tempted to open them and see what was inside. But the gaffer tape was always secure. Re-closing it without it being obvious he'd been spying would have been impossible. *Unless,* he thought, *I brought another jiffy bag, my own gaffer and scissors. Why did I never think of that?*

It was too late now. He ran on up the mountain. He lifted his eyes to the white mist swirling overhead. *The ceilings, Fergus. They dripped with blood and gore and gold.* The memory of Cora's voice took him back into bed with her, lying like two question marks. *Kissus maximus resumus.* There was nobody to hear him, so he shouted her name. CO*R-R-R*A. Amazingly, the tip of his tongue vibrated on the roof of his mouth. The 'r' rolled. Perhaps she could hear him, somewhere in

Dublin, asleep in her bed. *In the middle of a dream, Cora. In the middle of a dream I call your name.*

He jumped over the stream but didn't stop to drink. The going got hard. His thoughts tuned out to the white noise of running. He was aware only of the anaerobic rhythm of his breath, the poundings of his trainers, the heat. Ahead loomed the sentry hut. He stopped and turned back to see the view.

'*You're not the child time forgot, Mel. Nothing or nobody could ever forget you.*'

I'm seeing the land, Mel, Fergus thought. *Through your eyes. Settlements, cattle, fields. It's cold. And the lough's down there somewhere. You can glimpse it only when the clouds shift. And it's beautiful, an acquired taste: a beauty that takes a lifetime to understand.*

He skirted the sentry hut and ran the last few furlongs to the dry-stone wall. This time he didn't swap the packets. He took the waiting packet out, added it to the one bulging in his waistband and ran back the way he'd come.

Joe's watch said 6:58, early yet. He paused, panting. The familiar sun rose, a pale disc behind a bank of cloud. The North spread out before him, sleeping in the mists, untroubled. Behind him was the green of Leitrim. His watch crawled to 7:05. Somewhere in Long Kesh, he pictured Joe as he was now, his arm dangling over the edge of his cot, like Theresa's had: but Joe's forearm was like that of a starving child. His body lay curled like a foetus. Even the remotest part of Joe's brain, the part that dreamed, was quiet. *In that quiet, guarded place, Fergus, I kept my final vigil.*

243

Fergus stood up, checked his packages and began his final run.

He didn't loop the long way round, but headed straight to the sentry hut. He listened for a trombone but could hear only the telegraphic calls of skylarks.

Perhaps nobody would be there. Perhaps if nobody was there, that would be a sign. A sign that he should just take the packets and post them through the door of the police station in Roscillin and wash his hands of it.

Perhaps . . .

He drew up to the hut, and in the doorway was a slender silhouette: half a rifle, half a cigarette, half a torso. For a moment the figure looked taller than Owain. Fergus froze. He'd never once considered the possibility that somebody other than Owain might be on duty.

The figure turned and peered, shading its eyes. 'Fergus. I'm glad it's you. It's a good cool day for running.'

Fergus's heart leaped, then fell again. He swallowed and walked forward. 'Owain.' He walked into Owain's sights and raised his hands.

Owain raised two eyes to heaven. 'Hello, Mr Terrorist.' He rattled the rifle on his shoulder. 'How's the insurrection going?'

Fergus scrunched up his eyes. 'I'm serious. I'm handing myself in.'

'Great. So what am I supposed to do? Frog-march you all the way to Roscillin?'

'Owain. Honest. I've two packages here.' Fergus

slowly drew a brown jiffy from his waistband. Owain made no move. He looked on with a wondering smile. Fergus put the packet on the ground at Owain's feet. He placed the second packet alongside it.

'There. All yours.'

Owain's cigarette burned down to the stub. He flicked it away. 'What's in them?'

'Dunno.'

'You're pulling my leg, Fergus. Like that rat and dog story. I figured out afterwards. It was an Irish tease.'

'No, it wasn't. A priest really did tell me that story.'

'Ha-ha.'

They both stood still, watching each other. Owain grinned. 'OK. So tell me more about these packets.'

Beads of sweat trickled down Fergus's back. 'Can I sit on that rock?'

'Feel free.'

Fergus sat down on the rock where he'd rested his twisted ankle in June. He stared at the mountainside without seeing it. 'You know the brother I told you about last time? The one I said was in Rome?'

'Yeah. The lucky bugger. What about him?'

'He's not in Rome.'

'No?'

'He's in Long Kesh.' The words were like a door slamming shut, the end of the chatting and the camaraderie.

Owain frowned as if puzzled. 'You mean the Maze?'

245

'Yes. Our Joey's in there and he's on hunger strike. Day fifty.'

'Day fifty?' Owain echoed.

Fergus nodded.

Owain's rifle stayed slung on his shoulder. His face muscles puckered. 'I'm sorry, Fergus.'

'Yeah. Me too.'

'Is he——?'

'Conscious? Kind of. We expect to hear he's gone into a coma any day.'

They said nothing. Fergus pressed his palm into a crevice in the rock, hard.

'So what's that got to do with these?' Owain tipped the rifle nozzle towards the packets on the ground. One bulged, the other was slim. Blank and gaffer-taped, they sat waiting. Grass blades poked up around them like miniature sentinels.

'The Provos approached me. Don't ask me who. I can't say.'

'The Provos?'

Fergus nodded. 'They asked me to ferry these back and forth over the border. And that's what I've been doing. All summer long.'

'So you haven't exactly been training for the Olympics?'

'No. I did run before the packets. But the Provos caught on to me. They saw their chance.' Fergus wrung his hands. 'Believe me, Owain, I didn't mean to get involved. But they said if I did this for them, they'd send in the word to Joey to order him off his strike.'

'And you believed them?'

Fergus's cheeks were on fire. 'Yes. At first.' He wiped the sweat off his forehead. 'Then nothing happened. Joe said the Provos were right behind him. So I stopped believing.'

'But you kept going with the packets?'

'Yes.'

'Why?' Owain's rifle had slipped from his shoulder down to his elbow crook.

Fergus was silent.

'Why, Fergus? Did they threaten you?'

'No.'

'Your family?'

'No.' He looked up.

Owain stared at him, his face pinched.

Fergus gulped. 'You. They threatened you.'

'Me?'

Fergus nodded. *Tatty-bread, dead.*

Owain whistled through his teeth. He heaved the rifle back onto his shoulder. 'You're not having me on?'

'Swear to God. They said it would be the easiest thing in the world to come up here one morning and shoot you through the head.'

'Christ Almighty. It would.' Owain looked around as if a marksman might be lurking in the gorse. 'But why pick on me?'

Fergus sighed, sick to his stomach. 'I told them about you. How we'd got talking. And your being from Wales. He said you'd have been better off staying down a mine.'

'He?'

'I can't say who. It's more than my life's worth.'

Owain shielded his eyes. 'God. This bloody place.'

'Telling me.'

They looked at each other, then eyed the brown packets.

'Owain?'

'Yes?'

'What's Semtex like?'

'Semtex? Is that what's in there?'

'I think so. Your man said it was for a target. A military target. He didn't say what.'

Owain prodded one of the packets with the end of the rifle. 'Hell.' He stooped over and picked up the one that bulged. 'Semtex comes in different forms. Often greyish, like plasticine. It smells like almonds.' He put the packet up to his nose. 'It would be well wrapped, of course.' He turned it over in his hand, feeling the weight. 'It's hard to combust. Safe to transport.' He ran his finger along the darker brown of the gaffer tape. 'You've been back and forth with these all summer?'

'Twelve times.'

Owain whistled. 'That's some Semtex. What are they planning on doing? Blowing up half Ulster?'

Fergus got off the rock and turned away to face the valley, the curl of the lough, the pale gleam of the North behind. 'It makes me sick. After that bomb on Saturday night.'

'The one in Londonderry?'

'Yeah.'

'It was nasty, that. Those women out celebrating.'

Fergus stared at the untroubled land below. 'Awful.'

'So what d'you want me to do, Fergus?'

'Shoot me. Arrest me. I don't care. I just want out.'

'Fergus?'

'What?'

'Do you really think I'd shoot you?'

Fergus angrily brushed the hem of his sweatshirt across his eyes. 'No. S'pose not.' He turned back again.

'Don't know what to do with you.' Owain leaned his rifle up against the hut. He stood with his hands in his pockets, biting his lip.

'Those packets, Owain. Somebody out there's received the ones I've already delivered. They're putting together a bomb, I know it. You have to turn me in. I can't stand the guilt. It's killing me. I'd rather go to prison. Serve time. Like I said, I want out.'

Owain picked up the packets from the ground and placed them on the rock where Fergus had been sitting. Together they stared at them. 'Tell you what, Fergus. We'll open them.' Owain got a Swiss army knife out of a pocket and opened up a narrow silver blade.

'Right.' Fergus winced as the blade went in. It was like seeing Da open the champagne last Christmas. He'd the bottle pointed straight at the glass cabinet and Fergus had found himself covering his ears, waiting for the pop. 'Christ. Be careful.'

Owain paused. 'You don't think it's booby-trapped?'

'They never meant it to get into your hands, did they?'

'No.' Owain took out the blade and stared through a tiny slit. 'There's no wires or anything.'

'Phew.'

'Fergus, I don't know if I am going to turn you in.'

Fergus stared at Owain, wide-eyed. '*What?*'

'You're in one trap, I'm in another.' As he spoke, Owain sliced the silver blade roughly through the tape. Grey fluff from the bag's padding floated out. 'You and me – we're like two rats in two cages looking across at one another.'

Owain held the bulging jiffy open. Together they peered inside. Fergus could see polythene, little more. He became aware of Owain's hand on his elbow, his breathing, shallow and fast.

'What is it?' Fergus whispered. 'What's in there?'

Owain put his hand in. Fergus gasped. He pulled on a strip of polythene. As Owain drew it out, dozens of small neat sachets erupted, silver, with perforated edges, spangling the light like square coins. Following them came green oblong sheaths with small dots going around in a ring – *Mon-Tue-Wed-Thur-Fri-Sat-Sun* chased around the edge.

Fergus swayed, gripping the rock. 'Christ alive.'

'Bloody Nora.'

'Condoms.'

'And the bleeding Pill,' Owain laughed. 'Microgynon.'

Fergus bent double, choking. Owain thumped him hard on the back. He spluttered, spat, groaned.

'You've been fucking teasing me,' Owain hooted. 'All along. You bloody bog-eyed Irish taig. I'll give you a bollocking.'

Fergus screeched, half squealing. He slid off the rock, sending the packets at his feet flying. 'Condoms!' He clutched his side. '*Selling condoms tuppence a pair.* Michael Rafters, I will kill you. You bastard. Condoms.'

Owain gave his shoulder a playful kick. 'You didn't know?'

'No.'

'You really thought it was Semtex?'

'Yes.' Fergus grabbed the stitch of relief in his side, hobbled up to his feet, then collapsed against the rock with sobs of laughter. Tears of relief rolled unchecked. He felt Owain's arm across his shoulders. The two of them swayed and squealed like two stuck pigs.

'You've been had, Fergus.'

'I know.'

'What's in the other?'

'Let's find out.'

Owain quickly opened the second packet. A typed list floated out, then a roll of punts. They fell about, laughing like clowns. A magpie cackled along with them. Sheep baaed as if affronted. Then the rumble of a distant truck brought them to their senses.

'Quick. It's the chaps relieving me. Put all this stuff back in the bag and go, Fergus.'

Together they scrabbled on the ground, pouring the contraceptives back into the ripped jiffy. Fergus stuffed them down his front, hoping they wouldn't spill. Owain slapped him on the back.

'Bye, Ferg.'

'Bye.' They grinned at each other. Fergus turned and ran, gripping his belly as if he'd a stitch. He turned round to see Owain wave his rifle. 'You bloody bog-eyed Irish taig,' he called. Then the truck came up. Fergus swerved into the verge, crouched, and after it had passed, jogged on.

Michael Rafters, he thought. *Am I going to pay you back for this. Am I going to thump you.* He got back to the Forestry Commission and stopped at the tyre. He poured out the condoms and pills and arranged them all around the rim. The bag with the inventory and punts he kept on him.

Then he crept among the pine needles to a dip in the ground. He crouched down, pulling some ferns over him for camouflage, and waited.

He watched the grubs and listened to the thrupping of finches. *You and me. We're like two rats in two cages looking across at one another.* His brother Joe was dying. Cora was on her way. His own future was restored, not by any virtue of his own, but by a trick. It didn't matter. He was free again, poised for sweet revenge. He listened out for the sound of Rafters' Triumph. The smell of pine cones intoxicated him. The shadows of the fir trees were alive with secrets.

Thirty-seven

After an hour by Joe's watch, there was an unexpected sound: the rusty squeak of bicycle brakes. *Rafters on a bike?* Then the crack of a twig. *Rafters on foot?* And then the man himself, less of a panther today, more of a hound on the scent. Fergus saw the glossy back of Michael Rafters' leather jacket, bending low, then a hand reaching down into the tyre.

He sprang out of the dip, sending the fern branches flying. Launching himself at Rafters' back, he sent the man sprawling over the tyre. He pounced on top of him. Rafters jerked and twisted. They rolled over. Fergus felt his forehead slap the tyre's rubber and an elbow dig into his Adam's apple. He grunted and swung himself back on top. He rammed his forearm over Rafters' throat. In the mayhem, the silver pouches of condoms skidded and hopped on the ground. Microgynons rattled in their packs. A grouse squawked out of a thicket.

'Bastard.'

'Fergus—'

'Lying toe-rag.'

Rafters struggled, but the summer of training had made Fergus wiry. He bunched a fist with his hand and brought it right up to Rafters' nose. Rafters tried to knee him in the groin, but Fergus jerked upwards, then slammed his side down so hard that Rafters was pinned fast.

'You and your bloody packets,' he yelled. 'I'll throttle you.'

Rafters' body flattened out with surrender. 'OK. I get the message. I'm sorry.'

'Sorry?'

'Yeah. What else am I supposed to say?'

Fergus shook out his clenched hand. 'OK. You're sorry.' He got to his feet. Rafters made a move to get up and speak again, but Fergus kicked earth and pine needles over his face. 'Sorry isn't enough.'

Rafters rolled onto his stomach and spluttered out the dirt. Fergus watched, arms folded. 'Got a cough, Mr Dung-heap?' Then he got the other packet out and flicked the edges of the punts between his fingertips. 'Condoms, Dafters. The Pill. Since when did the IRA make bombs out of contraceptives?'

'Yeah. Well. You and me, we've kept half the female population of Inchquin from being up the pole.' Rafters sniggered. 'Better than bombing the Brits out of the place, if you ask me.'

'*We three kings of buggered-up Eire, selling condoms, tuppence a pair* . . . I never could remember the next line.'

'I don't think there was any more.' Rafters brushed down his front and perched like a gnome

254

on the rubber rim of the tyre. 'D'you want a fag?'

'No. Just tell me why.'

'Why what?'

'Why you got me involved.'

'You want to know?'

'Yeah. Couldn't you have driven over the border with your condoms and pills and flogged them over there? Why ask me to do it?'

Rafters chuckled. 'I did. Until three months ago, back in May, I hit a problem.'

'What problem?'

'A bollard.'

'A bollard?'

'A bollard in Roscillin, near the roundabout, right outside the police station. I was driving home from the club.'

Fergus stared. 'Your TR7?'

Rafters looked pained. 'Smashed.'

'Jesus. Tragic.'

'Telling me. Then the police came out and breathalysed me. I got banned from driving for three months. The bastards.'

May, June, July. Fergus started giggling.

'Don't you laugh, Fergus McCann.'

'How's the Triumph? Not a write-off?'

'No. Thanks to this little bit of cross-border co-operation, it's now fixed. Hallelujah.'

'Cross-border cooperation?'

'My Inchquin contact, don't you know, says I'm the local hero. It's the Third World down there. The local doctor won't prescribe the Pill in a month of

Sundays. And the shops don't sell condoms for fear of the local priest.'

'Who's your Inchquin contact?'

'Shush. Can't say. But he refuses to drive over the border on account of having Form.'

'Form?'

'You know. History. With the Provos.'

'Oh.' Fergus took the elastic band from around the money and started counting. 'You're a mean tyke, Michael Rafters. You could have cut me in. There's nearly a hundred punts here.'

'Yeah. Well. Call it my revenge, not cutting you in.'

'Revenge? What for?'

'Throwing up over my shoe. Remember?'

'I didn't throw up over your shoe.'

'You did. The time we went carol-singing. You got drunk on the Bulmer's.'

'That was years ago.'

'Yeah. But the spew was spectacular. Besides, if I'd cut you in, I'd never have got my Triumph fixed. Or had my holiday.'

'Your holiday?' Fergus stared at Rafters' bronze complexion. So much for the notion that he'd been off doing military training.

'Marbella. Very nice.'

'Bastard. I've been up and down that mountain with those bloody packets, dodging the soldiers. And all along, you were having me on. About killing the soldier up there. Not to mention what you promised about Joe.'

Rafters winced. 'I'm sorry about that. But

256

just so you know, I really did speak to somebody.'

'You did? Who?'

'Somebody I know. In the high command.'

'What did they say?'

Rafters shook his head. 'Nothing doing.'

Fergus put the elastic band back around the money and tossed it over to Rafters.

Rafters caught it, grinning. 'Go on. Take twenty. Thirty.'

Fergus paused. Rafters held out the notes.

'Go on. Buy something to cheer yourself up.'

Fergus was about to say no, then he thought of the state-of-the-art running shoes he'd be able to buy. 'OK.' He pocketed the money.

Rafters started gathering up the strewn packets. 'You know, Fergus, you surprised me.'

'Why?'

'All that conscience stuff. Getting matey with a squaddie. That from a McCann? Wonders never cease.'

Fergus shrugged. 'We're not all die-hards like Joe.'

'So you aren't. Hey, Fergus?'

'What?'

'Can you keep my operation secret?'

Fergus snorted at the word 'operation'. 'It's not illegal, is it?'

Michael seesawed his hand. 'It's not exactly legal, either. Besides, I'm planning to expand. Into other areas.' He lowered his voice, his eyes scouring the pine trees. 'Sheep.'

'*Sheep?*'

'Shush! There's a packet to be made out of sheep. With the EU subsidies and all. Don't tell your family, will you? Or anyone else in Drumleash?'

'OK. But why not?' Fergus remembered the boxes of fags he'd seen in Uncle Tally's room. 'Everyone's at it, aren't they?'

'I don't want the Provos getting on to me. Otherwise they'll take half the profits.'

'God. This place. It's insane.'

'Telling me. When I've earned enough, I'm emigrating. Permanently.'

'Where to?'

'Spain, of course. I fancy the sunshine.'

Fergus bent down and picked up the last few condom packets.

'Keep them,' Rafters said. 'You never know.'

Fergus blushed, thinking of Cora. He shrugged, pocketing them along with the money.

'Fergus?'

'What?'

'I'm sorry. I didn't think you'd get so wound up. I nearly told you, that time on the bus. But the garage had just called that morning and said they needed another down payment for the spraying.' He reached over and touched Fergus's shoulder. 'I didn't think the strikes would last this long, Fergus. I thought Joe would be off it by now. I really did. I'm sorry.'

Fergus shrugged. 'So'm I.'

'You know what I call this place, when I'm being polite?'

'No. What?'

'A perforated Ulster.'

Fergus snorted.

'And you know what I call it when I'm being impolite?'

'What?'

'A pig's fuck. S'long.'

Rafters waved and strode off. Through the triangular edges of the trees, Fergus watched him retreat, his sleek figure gleaming as sunlight eked through. Fergus waited a minute, feeling the smooth mini-parcels in his pocket. *A man for the main chance is right*. Then he followed. At the Commission's boundary, he breathed in the morning's freshness and trotted downhill, composing the rest of the condom song as he went:

We three kings of buggered-up Eire,
Selling condoms tuppence a pair,
Ribbed or funky,
Thin or chunky,
They'll blow you to sweet Kildare.

Thirty-eight

Then Brennor came. He stood in the doorway, his face in shadow. 'How's my little sister?'

'Growing every day,' I snapped. 'How's my little brother?'

Brennor's glossy black hair was thicker than ever, his skin rosy. He was the only one in Inchquinoag that had so robust a look. He was only twelve but he had to stoop as he came through the door.

'Is it true what they say?' he said.

'What?'

'That you bring bad luck?'

I shivered. I looked at my bound hands. 'I don't know, Brennor. What do you think?'

'You've never brought bad luck to me. Only good luck.' He stood there, uncertain. 'I'd take your place if I could, only I don't think I'd like being hanged.'

'Hanged?'

'That's what they're going to do. Hang you.'

I felt cold fingers tightening at my throat. I shut my eyes but fear still stared me in the face. I imagined the fear as a stoat, hairs bristling. It snarled, then turned tail and left me. 'You mustn't worry, Brennor. I'm fine.'

'Mel? If you meet Boss Shaughn on the other side, will you tell him something from me?'

'What?'

Brennor tilted his head toward the rafters. I tried to see his expression but it was too dark. 'Nothing. Goodbye, Mel.'

He left me as suddenly as he'd come.

Now everyone I loved had come to visit me. All but Rur. As the night hours slid towards dawn, I waited for him. Down on the sward, the watchers of the settlement clanged the morning bell. But still Rur didn't come.

From somewhere the muffled peal of a bell woke Fergus up. He'd been waiting for something in his dream, he remembered, and the ringing meant time was up. He sat bolt upright. Daylight seeped through the curtains. The house was quiet. He worked out it was Tuesday.

Joe. Fifty-one days of starvation.

Cora. Today was the day.

Joe's watch said it was 9:30. He hugged a pillow to himself. *Soon, sooner, soonest.* Whatever had been eluding him in his dream was surely on its way.

'Fergus!' Mam called from the hall outside. 'Are you alive or dead?'

He dragged himself out of bed. 'Alive,' he replied. Then he muttered, 'Just.' He padded out into the hall, where Mam was at the other end, on her way out. She'd a bright scarf knotted around her chin and one foot out the door. Her face looked pinched, but there was something new stirring there, a sense of purpose. 'There's been an urgent call, Fergus.'

The bell in his dream must have been the phone ringing. Something tightened around his throat. 'Joe?'

'He's the same. It was the prison chaplain calling.'

'Oh. Him again.'

'He's got a proposal, Fergus.'

'What? Another round of prayer?'

'Shush.' But Mam's face fell into a smile. 'I think this time it's more than a prayer.'

'Mam, the Dublin ladies. They're coming today.'

Mam waved a dismissive hand. 'You'll have to see to them. I'm away. The Caseys have taken the girls off to the seaside. They won't be back till late.'

'Thank the Lord for small mercies.'

Mam smiled. It was her own phrase when minor domestic crises were averted. She nodded and closed the door after her.

Fergus ate three bowls of cornflakes. Then he aired the twin room, got the sheets from the press, and made up the beds with the hospital corners. He got the Windowlene out and rubbed the mirror. He dusted the surfaces down with a damp rag. As he worked he played Stiff Little Fingers at top volume. '*You gotta suss suss suss suss suss out, Suss suspect device,*' he crooned over the drone of the vacuum cleaner. The room done, he got out the Belleek vase again. This time, he snipped two scarlet dahlias in the front garden and arranged them. With the white and green of the fine bone china, they cut a dash. He hunted in the kitchen press for the castor sugar. His hand ranged through the mixed spice and almond essence and other baking things, but the castor sugar was nowhere. He put ordinary granulated sugar in instead.

The phone rang. He remembered how the last time he'd answered to Michael Rafters, hoping it might be Cora. Was it Cora this time? Or news regarding Joe? He whipped the receiver up to his ear.

'*Yes?*'

'Fergus? It's me. Padraig.'

He breathed out, relieved.

'You still there?'

'Yep. Yo-ho, Padraig.'

'Fergus, I've a panic coming on. The exams.'

'What about them?'

'The results are due out any day.'

'Christ. I'd forgotten.'

'How could you've forgotten?'

Fergus twisted the receiver wire around his fingers. *How?*

'Fergus?'

'What?'

'Forget I asked that. It was stupid.'

'OK.' Now Fergus came to think of it, the memory of the physics multiple-choice paper was like a vice clamping down on him. 'Hell.'

'Hell is right. I'm in a sweat.'

'Me too.'

'I thought up a joke. To keep us both cool.'

'Oh, no. What?'

'What d'you call a fella who used to be mad about tractors but isn't any more?'

Fergus stared at the mouthpiece. The man was certifiable. 'What old yoke of a joke is *that*?'

'Go on. Have a guess. Staying cool's a clue.'

'Dunno.'

'You're gonna love this.' A hee-haw came down the line. 'An extractor fan. Get it?'

Fergus felt queasy. 'Aw. Padraig.' He folded over, gripping the hall table. 'That's p-p-p—'

'What? Priceless?'

'Pitiful,' he screeched.

Padraig brayed like a demented donkey. 'Stay cool, Fergus.'

'Yeah. Will do.'

'Bye.'

'Bye.' Fergus put the phone down. With a madcap friend like that, who needed enemies? he thought. He hugged himself. Soon, sooner, soonest, he'd be telling Cora the joke.

Twenty minutes later, the Dublin ladies arrived. They stepped out of the familiar Renault, brown from their travels, smaller than he'd remembered, their clothes a bit crumpled. The summer months had taken them in one direction and his memory in another. They looked more like sisters than ever, with Cora the taller. In his imaginings, Cora always had on a flowing dress and Felicity a safari suit. But today it was the other way round. Felicity wore a light-patterned sun-dress and Cora khaki trousers with a skinny black T-shirt. Her hair, instead of being lightened by the southern sunshine, seemed darker. Her expression was hidden by enormous sunglasses. She appeared to be gazing up at the roof of the bungalow as if it was a relic of a former empire. Felicity was frowning slightly. There was a whiff of a quarrel about them.

'Hello there,' he called from the front door.

'H'lo, Fergus.' Felicity smiled. 'Your hair's grown.'

'S'pose.' Fergus felt the ends and grinned. 'You've brought the fine weather with you.'

He gave them a spare key and showed them to the twin room. Cora flopped on the bed, pushing the sunglasses up over her head.

'So, Fergus,' Felicity said. 'We're here to decide Mel's fate.'

'I thought she'd already met her fate,' Cora said.

'Her second fate, then. We've to decide what comes next.' Felicity smoothed the coverlet on her bed. 'How's your mam keeping? Cora said she was busy visiting relatives?'

Fergus nodded. 'She said to make yourselves at home.'

'How've you all been?'

'Fine. Thanks for the card.' He looked at Cora. Her eyelashes fluttered.

'It was nothing,' Felicity said. 'Come on, Cora. We've to dash into Roscillin straight away. Professor Taylor's organized the meeting there. Can you join us, Fergus?'

Fergus thought of the phone, ready to ring at any time with news of Joe. 'How long will it be?'

'A couple of hours. That's all.'

'Then yes. I'll come.'

Cora got in the back seat of the Renault, saying nothing. She sat to the side, propped up in the corner. She might as well have been on planet Pluto. Felicity chatted on as she drove. Fergus's mind wandered.

'What's your opinion, Fergus?'

'Sorry. What?'

'D'you think we'd be better off burying her?'

'Who?'

'Mel, of course.'

Fergus felt foolish. 'Maybe.'

'I think the idea of displaying her is despicable.' It was Cora's voice, almost the first thing she'd said since arriving.

Felicity's hands rose from the steering wheel. 'Professor Taylor wants her in a museum case, for all to see. I want her kept privately, not for public view. In a few years' time there'll be all sorts of new tests we can't do now. A burial would be a waste. Wouldn't it?'

A burial would be a waste. Fergus thought of cells breaking down, transforming themselves into other kinds of life. He thought of the plot under the great Scots pine. 'I'm not sure,' he said.

Nothing more was said. Sunlight streamed down as they drove around the lough. The water was clear and inviting.

'Don't people ever swim in it?' Cora asked.

'The lough?'

'Yes. The weather's warm enough.'

Fergus turned, smiling. 'The water's icy,' he said, 'in all weathers. It's deep. And full of monsters.'

'Ha-ha. I think I'll try it later.'

'You'd freeze,' Felicity said. 'I don't want you going down with another cold.'

'I won't get another cold. Besides—'

'Joe and I used to swim in it,' Fergus said to stop the mounting argument. 'But then we were nutters, the pair of us.'

'Joe?' Cora asked.

'My brother.'

'I didn't know you had a brother.'

'I have.' *But for how much longer?* Fergus stared out of the window, grimacing. Two white bombshells flew down and hit the water surface. The swans were back again.

'Where is he?'

Fergus nearly said Rome, then thought better of it. 'London.' He turned round to face Cora. 'The water gave us ice-cream headaches,' he said. 'You know. The kind where the top of your nose and temples hurt.'

'Ouch. Maybe I'll stick to the Mediterranean.'

The atmosphere in the car lightened, as if a fresh front had come in. They drove into Roscillin town.

'We're meeting in the main hotel,' Felicity said. 'Do you know it?'

'The Roscillin Arms?' It was a Protestant hangout if ever there was one. A Catholic wouldn't normally be seen dead in the place. 'It's on the high street. You can't miss it.'

'Professor Taylor and I have prepared a slideshow in the conference room. Today and tomorrow afternoon we're running over all the finds, discussing our theories. We've two government men coming up, one

267

from Dublin, the other from Belfast. Plus we'll be thrashing out where Mel should go now we've finished the investigations. North or south.'

'Or underground,' added Cora.

They got out in the hotel car park, round the back of the building. It gave onto a pretty garden that Fergus had never seen before. A well-kept lawn was dotted with young crab-apple trees. Around the edge ran a stream, over which two tiny wooden bridges beckoned.

'Mam?' Cora said. 'Can I come in in five minutes? I want to see the garden.'

'OK. There's time. What about you, Fergus?'

Fergus grinned foolishly. 'Maybe I'll show Cora around.'

Felicity raised an eyebrow. The garden was minute. She smiled. 'Fine. See you soon.' She strode away, a black briefcase with golden clip-locks under her arm.

'Anyone else walking into that hotel with that briefcase . . .' Fergus said.

'What?'

'They'd be strip-searched.'

Cora stared at him. 'You're not serious?'

'Yes. This hotel – it's strictly a Unionist affair.'

'*U*nionist?' Her eyebrows nudged up against her fringe.

The way Cora had dragged out the 'U' of 'Unionist' was worse than her rolled 'r's. Felicity's jaunty figure vanished around the corner.

'Christ, Cora.'

Her arms were folded across her waist, but her

268

eyes goaded him on. He made a grab, she dodged, feinted, then he caught her. Soon his mouth and arms and lungs and ribcage were full of her. A hard knot in his belly exploded. The old Cora was back, laughing and mocking him. He lifted her off the ground. She thumped his back and shook herself free. Next she'd scampered off over one of the little bridges. He chased after her, caught a handful of her T-shirt and pinned her to himself. 'Cora.'

'Fergus. Just the one.'

'One good one?'

'OK.'

The one good one over, Fergus fanned his face. 'H'lo there, Kissus Maximus.'

'H'lo there, Resumus. We'd better go in.'

'OK.' When they got round to the entrance, Fergus gripped her elbow. 'Cora,' he whispered, wiggling his eyebrows.

'What?'

'What d'you call a fellow who used to be mad-crazy for tractors and isn't any more?'

Thirty-nine

The hum of the hotel kitchen's extractor fan came in through the open window. Professor Taylor had closed the curtains to darken the room and they sat in two semicircle rows, watching a progression of slides. There were shots of the bog, a cross-section of the soil, a view of the cut, then of Mel's body, first as Fergus had found it, then after it had been transported to the abattoir.

Then came the close-ups: the bangle, the spools of the fingertips, the tiny slit on Mel's back, the bonnet with its strings, a close-up sample of her shift. The weft of the fabric was subtle, clearly a thing made by hand.

'The bangle alone,' Felicity said, 'would have constituted a major discovery. It is beautifully made, slender, and of a style the expert has recognized as similar to another find, from France. Or, as it was then called, Gaul.'

There was a collective intake of breath. 'It's not Irish?' the man from Dublin said, sounding put-out.

Felicity tilted her head. 'Celtic, rather than Irish, perhaps.'

'Celtic is an umbrella term,' Professor Taylor interjected. 'But in reality the swirls and spirals and crosses we think of as quintessentially Celtic reappear in designs all around the world.'

Quintessentially? The man was on his academic high-horse. All pretence of collaboration was gone. The room bristled with archaeological rivalry. Felicity and the Belfast professor, the best of friends normally, were each trying to outdo the other and emerge as the legitimate authority on Mel.

'The bangle is older than Mel,' Felicity said. 'It was a precious thing, handed down perhaps from mother to daughter. Who knows? Perhaps Mel's own mother gave it to her just prior to her execution.'

'You mean sacrifice,' Professor Taylor countered. 'And the idea of her mother giving it to her is just romantic speculation.'

'Where do *you* think the bangle came from?'

'I don't make any assumptions. But I'd say it was a precious object belonging to the tribe or clan as a whole. Their putting it on the victim's wrist was part of the ritual of sacrifice.'

'If it was a sacrifice,' Felicity said.

'The stomach contents! The place where she was found. It fits the Iron-Age pattern.'

'Maybe. But in my opinion, we'll never know for sure. We know *how* Mel met her death. We may never know *why.*'

The next picture was of the love knot Mel had held in her hand. 'It's hard to resist seeing this as a token from somebody Mel loved,' Felicity said. 'For me, this was almost the most exciting find of all. It's an instance, surely, of a continuity of sensibility over the centuries. Love knots such as these were popular until Victorian times. Maybe soon they'll have another vogue.'

There was spellbound silence. The next picture on the screen was of Mel's face. Fergus was struck again by its serenity.

'She's a beauty,' Professor Taylor said, as if talking of a pet pony.

Felicity pointed a ruler to where a strand of hair had escaped the bonnet. 'We can't be sure of her hair colour. A quality of the bog has reddened it. But from a dissection of the hair strands, we think she may have been fair-haired.'

'Pale-skinned, blue-eyed, fair-haired,' Professor Taylor rhapsodized.

'An artist colleague of mine,' Felicity interrupted, 'has drawn a picture of Mel, an impression of how she looked when alive.'

She shifted on to the next slide. You could have heard a pin drop. Fergus leaned forward, gripping the edge of his chair. A charcoal drawing appeared on the screen, showing a young, merry girl, bonnet half on, half off. Something of her dwarfism was apparent in the round vitality of her expression, or maybe in the way her arms and shoulders made the head seem a little larger than life. The artist had captured the essence of the dead girl's visage.

'Oh my God,' he whispered. 'That's her. Mel.'

Cora's hand briefly found his and squeezed

it. She leaned over and whispered, 'D'you like it?'

'Yes.'

'I did it.' The words were just loud enough for the silent room to overhear.

Felicity chuckled. 'I should say the artist in question was Cora O'Brien. My daughter.'

There was a round of enthused clapping.

Professor Taylor cleared his throat. 'To cut to the chase,' he said, 'our various radiocarbon-dating procedures gave us the year that Mel was killed as AD eighty. Early Roman times, as far as Britain was concerned.'

'But not for Ireland,' Felicity said. 'Tacitus reports his father-in-law, Agricola, as saying that "Hibernia" could be conquered easily, but that the collective Roman will was not there. Ireland, although a trading partner of the empire from early times, was never colonized. The borderland between our current counties of Leitrim and Fermanagh was largely unaffected by the changes underway in Britain.'

'How accurate is the date?' someone asked.

'There's a margin of error, always,' Professor Taylor said. 'But we did two separate tests. We dendrodated a wooden stump found nearby, which we think may have been part of the gallows from which the girl was hanged. Remarkably, they both came out at the same year. The Iron-Age date, the noose, the burial in the bog all point to a pattern of human sacrifice, prevalent at this time.'

'But why?' The government man from Belfast spoke. 'Was it some primitive religious thing?'

273

There was silence.

'I don't think so,' Felicity said. 'I think religion was just the façade. As it sometimes is today.' There was a tense silence. Professor Taylor clicked the slideshow on to a final artist's impression done in charcoal. Cora had drawn an Iron-Age village: round huts, a fire, dogs, penned animals, people walking around in simple robes and skins. He snorted as if it was the Hollywood version of the time, a far cry from reality.

'There is probably more to Mel's story than we'll ever know,' Felicity continued. 'My guess is that some crime within the clan was committed at a time of terrible hunger and want. And Mel, by virtue of her dwarfism, was scapegoated.'

The quiet man from the North cleared his throat. 'Interesting. But is there evidence?'

Felicity nodded. 'Some. I looked up several ancient sources and discovered that there are reports of a severe winter in AD eighty or thereabouts – a protracted winter, one commentator said, with "fogs and red rain" across much of Europe. And Mel's stomach revealed a poor-quality last meal. And there is other evidence of malnourishment. I am sure that her death was related to an ancient famine.'

Two sparks collided in Fergus's mind. 'I have it!' he exclaimed from the back.

People whispered, turning round.

'I should have introduced Fergus McCann,' Felicity said. 'He is the lad who discovered Mel and stopped the JCB from going in and destroying her. We are all in his debt.'

There was another round of clapping.

'What were you going to say, Fergus?' Felicity said.

Fergus's ears burned. But he got the word out. 'Pompeii.'

Professor Taylor flipped to the next slide, which was blank. A rectangle of plain yellow light brightened the white screen.

'Pompeii?' Felicity said, puzzled.

'AD seventy-nine, the year before. Don't you see?'

There was silence. Something dawned on Felicity's face.

'You mean—'

'Volcanoes are famous for producing severe winters afterwards.' Fergus's voice stumbled over itself with eagerness. 'The high content of sulphur in the atmosphere blocks the sun. If the prevailing winds brought the volcanic ash northwards, it might have been the cause of the bad winter you spoke about. The one in which Mel died.'

Felicity whistled through her teeth. 'You mean, indirectly, Mel might have been another victim of Vesuvius?'

'Poppycock! Mere speculation!' exploded Professor Taylor. The room erupted, almost as if it was a volcano itself, with loud exclamations, chatterings, chair-scrapings.

Cora's elbow nudged Fergus's, making every little hair on his arm stand upright. 'Now you've done it,' she chortled. 'They're all at loggerheads.'

Arguments were breaking out everywhere. The government representatives, Professor Taylor, and the teams of student collaborators seemed to be beside themselves. Somebody turned the lights on, another person opened the curtains. Cora tugged his arm. He thought of the neat little bridges over the stream where they had kissed, then of the long, hard winter that had ended in Mel's death, the ash spewed from the faraway volcano, wreaking havoc directly and indirectly. 'The meeting will resume tomorrow,' Professor Taylor bellowed over the rising din. People shifted from their chairs. Felicity sorted out her papers and put them back into her briefcase. Across the room, her eyes met Fergus's. Her lips twitched. She winked. Then she mouthed three words. *We did it.*

'Let's go,' whispered Cora. 'Before the stampede.'

Forty

There was time for a hurried kiss out by the crab-apple trees, then Cora pushed him away. 'Mam will catch us,' she hissed.

'Would it matter?' asked Fergus.

'Dunno. Maybe. Maybe not.'

Then Felicity appeared, beaming. She invited Fergus to the archaeologists' evening meal. He pictured the phone in the hall at home, ready to ring any time with news of Joe and nobody there to hear it. He was suddenly exhausted.

'I've things I have to do,' he lied. 'I'll catch the bus back to Drumleash.'

'You're sure?'

'Certain.'

Cora's face was impervious, as if the kissing in the hotel garden had never been. 'See you later,' she said. They exchanged glances. Something unsaid flashed in her eyes, but what it was he could not decipher.

On the bus home, the road had never seemed twistier nor his fellow passengers more raucous. Three girls were taking off Abba songs with bad Swedish accents. A gang of lads shoved each other in the aisles. He'd a sense of the whole planet teetering, seesawing, nobody knowing or caring where they'd end up. The slideshow flickered in his head, image after image of Mel – her wounds, her clothes, the remnants of her forgotten life. *Click.* The spools on her fingertips. *Click.* Her love knot. *Click.* Her laughing, living face. *Click.* Joe swimming in the lough, squealing with the cold. *Click.* Joe in his prison cot, an emaciated hand hanging down. And at last the shining blank, the empty rectangle of light.

Joe, he thought. *Don't go.*

But in a terrible moment he felt Joe slipping from him, beyond the reach of pleas or arguments, prayers or priests. Nothing could bring him back. The bus took a tight corner. The passengers clung to the rails. There was laughter, exclamations. A grapefruit from someone's shopping rolled down the gangway. The mountain crumbled to earth, inch by inch.

It's only a matter of time, Fergus thought. *For everything, everywhere.*

The lough surface shivered, as if in fear of its final evaporation. He imagined Joe's emaciated arm rising from the water, like the hand that caught Excalibur when King Arthur died. The gleaming limb held the sword by the hilt and waved a last farewell. Then metal and flesh sank into the deep, never more to be seen in this world.

'Oh, Joe,' he whispered. 'Joe.'

Forty-one

The phone call from the prison came at seven o'clock. Tea had been cleared away. Da sat with the *Roscillin Star* in his chair, tapping his foot on the lino. Mam was drying the last glass. She put it down on the draining board.

'You get it, Fergus,' she whispered.

Fergus went to the hall and picked up the phone. His teeth were clenched. His heart shrank into itself like a frightened animal.

'H'lo?' he managed.

'Is that Mr McCann?'

'It's Fergus McCann.'

'It's the prison doctor here.'

Fergus grimaced, winding the receiver wire in and out of his fingers.

'It's about Joe.'

'Is he alive?'

'He is. But there's been a change.'

A change of heart. A change of plan. What change?

'He's passed into a coma.'

279

'A coma?'

Suddenly Mam's fingers were biting into his shoulder. 'Give it here, Fergus. Give me.'

'Just a minute,' he told the caller. He unwound the wire from his fingers and pressed the receiver into Mam's hand. 'He's alive,' he whispered.

'What news do you have of my son?' she rasped.

Fergus watched as Mam listened. Her forehead furrowed, her mouth became an impregnable line of defence.

'Can I see him?'

The faint buzz of a reply seemed to satisfy her. 'I'll be there tonight.'

A further buzz seemed to be arguing.

'I understand.' She met Fergus's eye, holding the receiver away from her ear. 'It's only the beginning, he says, Fergus. The beginning of the end.'

She turned back to the receiver. 'I'll come anyway.'

She set down the phone and crossed herself. 'Fergus. You and me and Da. This is the moment. Now. We've got to talk.'

'Talk?'

'About Joe.'

'What's there to say, Mam? Haven't we said it all?'

'No. We haven't.'

She went back into the kitchen. 'Malachy,' she said.

Da looked up from the paper, his eyes stricken. 'It's over, isn't it?'

Mam shook her head. 'No. He's in a coma.'

'A coma?'

'The doctor says it's the beginning of the end. He won't wake up again.'

Da folded the paper up into neat quarters. He put it on the table and smoothed it down. 'Then it is over.'

'It's never over until it's over, Malachy.'

Da put his forehead onto his palms, shaking his head. 'Should we drive over? Would they let us see him? Would he even know we were there?'

Mam sat down by Da's side. 'Fergus,' she said, 'make another pot of tea.'

Fergus put the kettle on and got the teapot down. He put three spoonfuls in and poured hot water in with great concentration.

'I've a proposal to make,' Mam said when tea was on the table.

Da looked up, raising his empty hands.

'The prison chaplain called us together today,' she said. 'He'd spoken to everyone. Prison people. The doctors. Sinn Fein, even.'

'So?'

'They want the strike to end. Everyone.'

'Sinn Fein? I don't believe it,' Da said.

'The man's a priest. He wouldn't lie.'

'Priests are the best bloody liars of the lot.'

Fergus poured out three cups of tea. It was strong and black. He poured in the milk, with two spoons of sugar for himself and Da, none for Mam.

'Fergus, put a spoon in for me,' she said.

'But I thought—'

'Never you mind.'

Da took a sip, then snorted. 'What does it matter

what other people want or don't want? Our Joe's an inch from death. He's in his final coma. It's over.'

Mam took her tea and stirred it again. She lifted the cup to her lips and drank. The motion was deliberate, as if the tea was a magic potion. 'We are Joe's family. We can say it's not over. That's what the prison chaplain brought us together today to say. We have the right.'

'What do you mean?' Fergus said.

'We only have to say the word and Joey will be saved.'

'Saved?'

'He'll have a drip put up. A drip to feed him.'

For a fleeting moment Fergus thought of Lazarus, coming out of the tomb in his swathing bands. The thought made him shudder. Da pushed his teacup away.

'Pat, that's nonsense.'

'It's not.'

'Joe wouldn't thank you.'

'Maybe not. But I'm his mother.'

'You are. But Joe's life is his own.' Da said the words slowly, as if to a five-year-old. 'His own to take.'

Mam's face crumpled.

'Pat, listen to me. We can't play God.'

Mam put the teacup down crooked, so that liquid slopped into the saucer.

'It's not playing God. And I don't care if Joe wakes up and never talks to us again. At least he'd be alive. He'd be alive with his life before him. I could live with that. I could.'

'Pat, I'm telling you, Joe's life is his own. Not yours.'

'If he'd taken an overdose – if he was on top of a building, about to jump – we'd save him, wouldn't we?'

Da shrugged. 'You said yourself – or that chaplain of yours said so a few weeks back – what Joe's doing isn't suicide.'

The anguished workings of Mam's mind worked across her face. Fergus could see she'd been out-manoeuvred.

'Da. Mam—'

'What difference does it make if it's suicide or something else?'

'Every difference.'

A terrible thing happened. Mam stood up and made as if to strike Da across the face. Da didn't wince or move. He caught at her hand at the last second, trapping it in his. Fergus froze, terrified he was going to strike her back. But he didn't. Instead he held Mam's hand close to his face and stifled a sob. Then he stroked her fingers and gave her palm a kiss.

'Pat, love, let it go. Just let it go.'

She pulled her hand away. Grabbing a tea-towel, she pressed her face into it, sobbing.

'I can't. It's Joey. How can I let go of him?' Then, 'Fergus? Haven't you an argument for Da? Haven't you?'

They waited while she cried. At last they heard her breathing calmly. She folded the tea-towel over the bar on the cooker.

'Sit down, Pat,' Da coaxed.

Mam sat down, her face ravaged.

'Mam?' Fergus whispered.

'What?'

'If they did feed Joe, could they really save his life?'

She folded her hands together. 'That's what the doctor says. But he said something else.'

'What?'

'The longer we leave it, the more likely it is Joe will be . . . damaged.'

'Damaged? What kind of damage?'

'I don't know. They don't know.'

'Physical? Mental?'

Mam put her face in her hands. 'He might be all right,' she whispered. 'God willing.'

Da thumped the tabletop. 'This is sickening,' he said. 'You'd interfere with everything Joe's done, everything he's done for his country, everything he's tried to achieve by this amazing, courageous sacrifice. You'd interfere, just so he'd end up a cabbage?'

Mam looked up, white. 'It's only a risk. And if we gave the go-ahead, here and now, the risk would be lower. Please, Malachy. We've only to pick up the phone. We've only to say the word.'

And Joe will be saved, but not healed?

'No,' Da said. The word came out low and soft but had the finality of a commander's order to his troops.

'I say yes, Malachy. Doesn't my word count as much as yours?'

Da bit his lip and turned away. 'If Joe was here, you know what he'd say, don't you?'

284

There was no denying it. Mam raised two protesting hands.

'So that's two to one.'

Fergus swilled the last of his tea-leaves round in his cup. 'Two to two,' he said.

'What?'

'I'm with Mam. Sorry, Da.'

Da glared. 'I cannot believe my ears.' His face went purple. 'You're just a kid.'

'I'm not. I'm eighteen. I voted, didn't I?'

'Yes, you did. For Sands. And now look at you. Turncoat.'

'Da, I've wanted to be a doctor for as long as I can remember. I've no choice but to vote for life. Please. My vote counts.'

Da's face was rigid. Fergus put his cup down. The sword had fallen from Joe's grasp and his arm in the water was sinking until only the wrist, shorn of its watch, was visible. 'Theresa and Cath, Da,' he pleaded. 'They'd want Joe back alive too. At all costs.'

'They're too young to understand. Leave them out of it.'

'What about Uncle Tally, Da? What would he say?'

'Leave Uncle Tally out of it,' Mam snapped. 'He's not immediate family.'

Da thumped the table. 'He *is* immediate family. And Uncle Tally would agree with me. You know it.'

Fergus stared. 'I'm not so sure, Da.'

Da waved a dismissive hand. 'He'd either agree with me or say nothing.'

Say nothing? Yes. That was Uncle Tally. He never

wanted to get involved. But in this case, doing nothing was the same as letting Joe die. Fergus pressed his fists into his eyes.

'But anyway,' Da was saying, 'it's not a voting matter.'

'No, it isn't,' Mam said. 'It's a matter of you, Malachy. Laying down the law.' She got up, pushing the table away from her. 'This house, it's not a republic. It's a bloody dictatorship.' She seized the cups off the table and threw them into the sink. The hot tap gushed, teaspoons rattled. 'I will never forgive you for this, Malachy. Not so long as I ever live. So help me God.'

Forty-two

Mam left the house soon after and drove off to see Joe. Da went to bed without a word. Fergus put away the tea things. Soon Theresa and Cath came in, worn out after a day at the seaside. He made them hot chocolates and they went off to bed without protest.

The house grew quiet. He took a kitchen chair out into the garden and sat in the middle of the lawn, staring into the half-dark. *Fergus*, Mam kept whispering in his head. *Can you think of some more arguments?* A breeze stirred. Heavy flowers nodded on their stems. He could smell Drumleash and feel its slow, steady pulse. He looked up towards the silhouette of the mountain, imagining the huts Cora had drawn and the life it had once supported. A feeling of all time running concurrently came over him. Was it AD 1981 or AD 80? Could both times exist at once? Could the last kiss with Cora by the crab-apples be happening for ever, in a universe where every moment was eternally present?

After the morning bell, Fergus, the door opened. And there was Rur.

'*Mel*,' he said. '*Oh, Mel.*'

He remembered Cora's drawing of the living Mel, her jauntiness, her bonnet half on, half off. Then her laughing face melded into Joe's, as it had been the time they'd gone dipping in the lough. 'Get in, Fergus.' 'I won't.' 'It'll freeze the bollocks off you, Fergus. It's like being baptized.'

'Fergus?'

The voice came to him across the garden from the kitchen door. *Cora?* But the 'r' wasn't right. He turned. It was Felicity, hovering in the kitchen light.

'Can I join you?'

He waved a hand as if to say, *Feel free.*

She came out and stood at his side, staring up at the shadowy rise of the mountain and the fine dots of stars beyond. 'It's a fine evening.'

'Yes.'

'And mild.'

'Yes.'

'Fergus?'

She put a hand on his shoulder. 'What?'

'I know.'

He stared up at her. 'You know?' *About Joe? How could she know?*

She nodded. 'About how you feel. For Cora.'

'Oh. Cora.' He sat forward clasping his hands, eyeing the ground. 'Is it that obvious?'

Felicity smiled. 'Cora told me. This evening.'

Fergus shifted on his chair. 'Where is she? Is she all right?'

'In bed. She's a bit under the weather. Nothing serious. Tired.'

Fergus nodded. 'Tired.'

'I'm not putting this very well. After the meeting closes tomorrow, Fergus, we're straight back to Dublin. Then, on Friday, Cora's flying off to America.'

'America?'

'Michigan. Her father lives there.'

He remembered what Cora had told him. *My dad lives in Michigan, with a new woman and kids. Good luck to him. I haven't seen him in years.* 'For how long?'

'I don't know. As long as she chooses.' Felicity walked over to a dahlia, lifting a drooping head. She bent to smell it.

'They don't have much fragrance,' Fergus said.

'No. So they don't.' Felicity let the head drop back. 'For years, Cora's struggled with what happened between her father and me. After he left, she refused to discuss him. And she got faddish.'

'Faddish?'

'About school. Eating. Everything. She got wild, angry. Sometimes she'd take it out on me, but most times on herself.' Felicity's face looked pale and strained. 'I had to get her seen by doctors, Fergus. Doctors and psychologists.'

Fergus peered at Felicity's face through the darkness. 'I'd no idea.'

'She's been a tearaway. Boyfriends, late nights, diets.'

Fergus dug his fingers into his knees. 'I see.'

'She's getting better, Fergus. Maybe it's partly

289

down to you. She's definitely calmed down since we started coming here.'

'Really?' He twisted his sweatshirt around his fingers.

'Yes. She likes you. I can tell.'

'Then why does she have to go away?'

Felicity sighed. 'It's her anger with Kevin, her father. Kevin and myself, we've persuaded her to take a year out. She'd given up on her studies anyway. So she's off out to Michigan to see her dad. And maybe that will help.'

'Is it what she wants?'

Felicity didn't answer. Instead she sat down on the grass beside him, cross-legged, plucking at the grass.

'It isn't what she wants, is it?'

'It's what she needs. Trust me. I'm her mother. I only want what's right for her. This trip will do her good. Kevin and me, we weren't right for each other. But he's not the demon she makes out.'

'And I'm not right for her?'

'You may be. Who knows? But you're not the only lad who's fallen for her. And her boyfriends never last long. Like I said, she has fads.' Felicity shrugged. 'I'd rather she met a good person like you and settled into something real. But she thrives, Cora does, on change.'

Kissus continuus. Perhaps he'd always had a suspicion that whatever it was she felt for him was different from what he felt for her. He saw her eyes, always mocking and laughing, as if everything that

290

had happened was a jaunty spin of a Ferris wheel.

'Life is like that,' Felicity said. 'Meetings. Partings.' She rested her chin on her knees. 'For me, there was someone before Kevin. We were drawn to each other. But he was young and shy. Nothing happened. Sometimes, today, I wonder what my life would've been like if I'd taken things into my own hands.'

Fergus watched Felicity brushing away the invisible visions of what might have been. They sat together in the dark, saying nothing. Time went backwards. The door that Rur opened, closed again. Mel was in her dark hut, waiting. In Long Kesh, Mam sat at Joe's bed-side, waiting. Cora turned in her sleep, pushing the covers from her.

'Fergus?'

'What?'

'If you find time passes and you can't forget Cora, then remember one thing, won't you? It's what my father told me years ago and I've never forgotten.'

'What?'

'He said that we suffer more from the sins of omission than the sins of commission.' Felicity shuffled to her feet.

'What does that mean?'

'I suppose that often more harm is done by what we fail to do than by what we do.'

Fergus felt her hand again on his shoulder. 'And what you said today about Pompeii, Fergus, was amazing.'

She left him then, and went indoors. Soon the light from the twin room was out. The garden plunged into deeper darkness. A large swath of cloud shifted eastward, covering the moon. A planet flickered in the lower sky, bright and hard, like a jewel.

Forty-three

The door opened, Fergus. It did. And Rur came in and said,
'Mel, I've brought you some food.'

Fergus got up from the chair in the garden and
went inside the silent house. He padded down the
bungalow hall to his parents' room. He knocked softly
and called, 'Da?'

'What is it?' came Da's voice, anxious.

Fergus went in, closing the door behind him. 'Da,
can we talk?'

'What do you want?' Da switched on the bedside
lamp. His eyes were red. It was obvious he'd been
weeping.

'Da, it's a known fact.' He sat down on Mam's side
of the bed.

'What?'

'We do more harm by the sins of omission than by
the sins of commission.' Fergus shut his eyes tight,
forcing back his own tears. He grabbed the edge of
the bedside table, then picked up the telephone
extension's receiver. The dial tone hummed. Anxiety
waited at the other end.

'God. Son. What's all this baloney?' But Da had his arms cradled around him.

'It may be a sin to intervene with Joe, Da. But it's a worse sin if we don't.' He swallowed, his heart thumping. 'If we do nothing, there'll be no forgiveness. Never. The future will go wrong. Everything will go wrong. I know it, Da. Believe me.'

He didn't need to say the rest. *Mam will leave you. Theresa and Cath will grow up wrong. I'll go wrong. Joe will be the lucky one, oblivious, his body breaking up underground, mindlessly. And the British will still own the North. The bombs will still go off. For years to come, the misery of it. The mourning and the weeping. The vale of tears.*

'Jesus. Is there no peace left, anywhere?' Da raved. He grabbed the phone from Fergus. 'God forgive me. What else can a man do with a family like mine?' He dialled the series of numbers Mam had printed in large figures on the notepad by the phone. 'Hello,' Da bellowed when someone replied. 'Is that the doctor treating my son? My son, Joe McCann?'

Only say the word, Fergus. The one redeeming word.

Forty-four

Rur stood before me in the hut. In his hand was a bowl of steaming porridge.

'Eat this, Mel.'

He placed the bowl in my bound hands. I felt the warmth seep into my skin, my nerves, my bloodstream. I shut my eyes to stop the tears of relief that Rur had come. The coldness of death retreated with the warmth of the gruel.

'Thank you, Rur,' I said. He spooned the food into my mouth and I swallowed.

'Mel?' he said, on the last spoonful.

'What?'

'Did you kill my father?'

My jaw hung open. 'No. Of course not,' I whispered. 'I thought—'

The spoon of gruel hung motionless. Rur peered at me.

'You thought I killed my father?'

I nodded over the steaming mess. 'Didn't you?'

Rur stared beyond me, bewildered. 'You're doing this for me, aren't you?'

'This place, Rur. It needs you. It doesn't need me.' I declined the last spoonful. 'It's over.'

'This is wrong, Mel, all wrong.' He put the spoon back in the bowl. 'I didn't kill him, Mel. I left him that night by the lough, flat out, drunk. But later I went back. Somebody had smashed a rock on his head. And I saw footprints, Mel. Footprints in the sand. Little ones. Like yours. That's when I pushed Da's body into the lough, hoping people would call it an accident.'

Then the truth dawned. 'Brennor,' I gasped. If you see Boss Shaughn on the other side, Mel. Tell him not to put a curse on me, his murderer.

'Brennor?' said Rur. 'Then he should pay, not you.'

He got up as if to call out for the guards. The bowl fell to the ground. I put my bound hands to his knees to stop him.

'No, Rur. I beg you. Leave things as they are.'

'How can I? How can I let you die, Mel?'

'If Brennor dies, my mother will too. And the people who hate me will not be assuaged. My time has come, Rur.'

Rur knelt down again, shaking his head. He got out his knife from his belt and cut through the rope around my wrists. 'There, Mel. Now you are free. I can distract the guards while you run away from here, away from all this hate.'

I chafed my wrists and pushed Mam's bangle further up my arm. I smiled and shook my head. 'No, Rur. If I escape, somebody else will be made to pay the price.'

Rur stood still, then moaned. 'What can we do, Mel?' he whispered, kneeling beside my throne of straw.

'Don't let them hang me alive. I can't stand the thought of the rope tightening around my neck.'

Rur touched my neck, his eyes large with pity. 'Oh, Mel.'

'Stab me first, Rur, with your knife. As the sun comes up, in the back, fast and clean.'

296

Then Rur lifted me off my straw throne and held me hard to his heart. I put a hand to his strong, stout neck and stroked the place where the hairline ended. This is the best that life can bring, I thought. The best that life can bring, and the worst.

'Rur,' I said, tugging on a strand of his fine brown hair. 'Let me go to my grave with a part of you.'

He put me down and cut off a lock, and twisted it into a knot. He put it into my freed hand and my fingers curled fast around it.

The front door slammed. Fergus could hear the sounds of Felicity and Cora chatting in the twin room next door. He leaped out of bed, confused. The world tilted. He'd to steady himself by gripping the bedpost. *Joe, on a drip-feed. Mam gone to see him. Da gone out to work. And Cora, flying away to Michigan.*

He got out of bed, flung off his pyjamas and put on his jeans. The running sweatshirt with the puma had holes under the arms. It hadn't been washed in a week. He kicked it under the bed and found a white T-shirt in a drawer with a faded picture of Che Guevara on it. He put that on instead and padded out to the kitchen.

In the fridge, he found the bacon, sausages and eggs. What did Mam do? Did she start with the sausages or the bacon? In a lifetime of fries, he'd never noticed. He lined the food up on the chopping board.

Theresa appeared at the door in her nightie. 'You're supposed to prick 'em.'

'What?'

'The sausages, stupid.'

'Oh.' He got a fork and stabbed at them. Then he looked up.

'You put them in first,' Theresa said, yawning. 'Then the bacon. Then the eggs.'

'Lay up the table for the guests, will you?'

The sausages hissed and spat as he cooked. Felicity put her head round the kitchen door. 'Anything I can do to help?'

'Everything's under control.'

'Great. Call if you need me.'

Felicity disappeared. A sausage made a sound like a hiccup. He put the bacon in. Immediately it turned a paler pink. The rind crinkled. Theresa came in from laying the table. 'You're supposed to turn them, dummy. With this.' She got out the fish slice.

'I know. Stop bossing me around.' He shook the pan. Cath came in and watched as if the best programme ever was on TV.

'I'm starved,' she said.

'Have some cornflakes.'

'The packet's nearly empty.'

He remembered the three bowls he'd had yesterday. 'Have a cut of bread.' He flipped the bacon over. 'I've got news for you two.'

'What?' asked Theresa.

'Joe. He's on the mend.'

Cath grinned. 'Told you, Theresa.' She stuck her tongue out at her sister. 'Theresa said he'd be

298

dead in a week. I said he wouldn't. I did a novena like Mam told me and it worked.'

Fergus grinned, turning the sausages. Fat spat.

'What d'you mean, he's on the mend?' Theresa said. 'He's starving to death, isn't he?'

'The doctors are feeding him, T. On a drip.'

'D'you mean like they did the suffragettes?'

Fergus stared over the frying pan. 'The suffragettes?'

'Yeah. Mrs Tracey at school says these posh English ladies chained themselves to railings to get the vote for women. Then they got arrested. Then in prison they went on hunger strike. Then the mean guards force-fed them so they couldn't die, however much they wanted to, and become holy martyrs. Is it like that with Joe?'

'Kind of. Only Joe's asleep while they're doing it. He doesn't know he's being fed.'

Theresa's eyes screwed up as she thought about it. 'That's good, isn't it? If he doesn't know, then he hasn't given in?'

'Yes. Pass me the eggs, Cath.'

He cracked first one egg, then another on the edge of the pan like he'd seen Mam do countless times. The eggs plopped into the hot fat and sizzled up. By some intervention of the patron saint of cooking, the yolks didn't break. 'Now scoot,' he said. 'While I serve the guests.'

He got up the fries using plates from Mam's best dinner service, the one that was only ever used on Christmas Day. He brought them through to the dining room to where the Dublin ladies were waiting.

'A man of many talents,' Felicity said.

Cora sniffed her plate. 'Not bad, Fergus,' she approved, picking up her fork. She pronounced Fergus in the old way, with the 'r' rolling out to him across the room. Her face was pale and sleepy, her hair rumpled, her eyes dusky. Her cutlery swooped down on the food. She yawned. 'I could eat a pony.'

Fergus sat down opposite. 'Can I come in with you again today?'

'Of course,' Felicity said. 'If you don't mind making your own way home again?'

'No.'

On the final ride in the green Renault, Cora again sat in the back, exclaiming at everything they saw: the swans, the boats, the flatness of the mountain top, now that it was visible. Felicity was silent. When they drew up at the Roscillin Arms Hotel, she switched off the engine.

'I'm nervous,' she said.

Fergus stared. 'Nervous? You?'

Felicity shrugged. 'A lot rides on this. It's like the final sprint in a kind of archaeology Olympics.'

'You'll be fine.' He turned and nodded at Cora. 'You won your case when you showed us Cora's picture of Mel.'

In the meeting room, however, the arguments about the fate of the bog child meandered for two hours before her final destination started to veer southwards. Professor Taylor's nostrils flared and twitched. Felicity sat poised and quiet, a Dubliner with a mission. Fergus stared out of the peaceful open window, forearm-to-forearm with Cora, drifting. Sometimes he was with Mam next to Joe, watching the lines on the hospital monitoring machine. Then he was back in AD 80, imagining Mel's last hours. *The best that life can bring, Fergus, and the worst.* Then Cora nudged him and the thought of parting was like being told to tear off his skin.

'Let's have a last walk in the park,' she whispered to him.

They left the hotel and wandered down the high street. They passed the second-hand TV shop, where all twelve screens showed Margaret Thatcher giving a speech somewhere, and went down the alleyway. The graffiti'd slogans – BRITS OUT and the joke about Bobby Sands's phone number in the afterlife – had been removed. The wall was empty and white, waiting for the next can of spray.

In the park, a lunch-time brass band played jaunty airs in the stand. Women with prams and buggies lingered under the shade of the withered plane trees. Young people lolled on the grass. The players had a quick-step going, with a toe-tapping pulse. The volume surged to a triumphant conclusion, followed by scattered applause. Next, the band played that same stately tune Owain had rendered on his trombone, the one that reminded Fergus of the sliced-bread advert. He scoured the players, remembering that Owain had said he'd agreed to play that day. But Owain's pale, intent face wasn't there. The uniforms of the Ulster Defence Regiment glittered in the afternoon sunshine. Cymbals clashed, trumpets shone, but there was no trombone. They finished the piece differently than Owain had.

'They're sitting ducks,' he muttered to Cora.

'Sitting ducks? Who?'

'The band players. They're all UDR fellows. An IRA target.'

'I don't get all these initials,' Cora said.

'Can't say I blame you.' He'd a sudden vision of the bandstand blowing up in their faces. Linking her arm with his, he propelled her towards the café where they'd sat before. They bought drinks and made for a sweep of late hydrangeas over on the far side of the park, where nobody was about. The grass was fresh-mown. They sat down.

'Felicity told me you're off to Michigan,' Fergus said.

Cora nodded. 'Yes. They're making me go.' She drank her Tango off and lay down on the grass. 'Let's not talk about it.'

'OK. What shall we talk about?'

Cora scrunched up her face, thinking. 'D'you remember the giggling game?'

'What?'

'You know. Everyone lies with a head on somebody else's stomach. It makes a staircase of people all over the lawn. And somebody starts giggling and it spreads up and down, all over.'

'Yeah, I remember. Kids' stuff. Anyway, you can't play it with two.'

'Who says?' Cora patted her stomach. 'Go on.'

He lay down with his head on her stomach. A snatch of the Radetzky March drifted over to him. '*Didi-dum, didi-dum, didi-dum-dum-dum,*' he crooned. Cora's belly became a restless ocean as he hummed. His head was a listing boat. He started giggling.

'You're out of key,' Cora laughed. He felt her fingers in his long hair. 'You know who you look like with your hair like that?'

'Something out of *Planet of the Apes?*'

'No. Georgie Best.'

He rolled over and kissed her. Bits of grass were everywhere, on their clothes, in their hair, between their lips.

'Hey. It's my turn,' she said.

'Your turn?'

'To lie on *your* stomach.'

He let her head lie on his belly, and through the hydrangea blooms he watched a cumulus cloud growing overhead. 'Did you know we can make clouds rain?' he murmured.

'Hey?'

'We can fly through them on aeroplanes, trailing silver nitrate. And hey presto, raindrops start falling.'

'I never knew that.'

'It's called cloud-seeding.'

'It doesn't sound right, interfering with nature like that.'

Fergus drummed his fingers on her scalp, like rain.

'Is that supposed to make me laugh, Fergus?'

'No.' Fergus thought of the plane carrying Cora

303

away from him. He saw the boundless Atlantic, the sky arching over it, the trail of the jet, the storm systems growing and dissipating. Then he saw the bloated heads of the hydrangeas, their colour going to brown. He pinched the tops of Cora's ears. 'OK. What d'you call a tractor that isn't really a tractor?' he said.

Cora groaned, but started giggling. 'Dunno. What?'

Fergus's own belly started shifting. 'A contractor.' Suddenly a handful of loose grass was flung on his face and Cora's head was butting his ribs like a goat. 'Ouch. Christ, Cora. What am I going to do without you?'

Cora sat up and brushed off the grass. Then she stood, absently plucking at the withered petals on the hydrangeas. He rose too, a numbness growing inside him at her silence.

Just as he started to say, *Forget I said that*, she said, 'Write maybe?'

She strolled back across the park and out onto the road, smoothing down her jeans as she went. Smiling, he followed her, oblivious to the band's raucous finale, the merry *rum-pa-pas* of the trumpets and the first spots of rain. Michael Rafters' sparkling blue Triumph zoomed down the high street but he did not notice. Nor did he take in the television screens in the TV shop, flickering with pictures of a blown-up army vehicle. All Fergus could see were a thousand airmail letters, flying west and east, leaving trails of silver nitrate across the sky.

When they got back to the hotel car park, Felicity

was waiting for them with a stiff brown folder in her hand.

'We won,' she said. 'Mel is coming down to Dublin.' She handed the folder to Cora. Cora peeped inside briefly, then handed it on to Fergus, with her old mocking smile. 'It's for you.'

'For me? What's in it?'

'Open it and see.'

He opened the folder and there before him was Cora's charcoaled original of the living, laughing Mel.

'For me?' he whispered, ghosting a fingertip over the tresses of her hair. 'Really for me?'

Forty-five

Fergus waved the green Renault on its way down the high street. He saw it circle the mini-roundabout by the police station and gave a last salute as it went up over the brow of the hill. Then it vanished.

For a long time he stood on one of the wooden bridges behind the hotel, staring at the waving weeds in the little stream. When it started to rain, he put the folder inside his Che Guevara T-shirt and made a dash for the nearby chip shop. He found a fifty-pence piece in his pocket and bought some chips, dowsed them with vinegar, wolfed them down. His lips stung and his fingers tasted of salt. The shower passed.

The bus came right away, and when it set him down in Drumleash, he walked up the main street towards home. He passed Finicule's and smelled its familiar scent of wood-grain and beer. He popped in to find Uncle Tally sprawled on a chair, reading the paper. The ancient wireless over the fag machine blared out the local Republican show. Irish words merged with Irish reels.

'Hi there, Unk.'

'Hi, Fergus. Will I pour you a Guinness?'

'OK. A glass, only.'

Tally poured them both a half-pint. Fergus drained the beer nearly in one go. 'Unk?'

'What?'

'The bog child's going south. To Dublin. And as for Joe, we're bringing him back from the grave.'

'What on earth d'you mean?'

'The doctors are feeding him while he's unconscious. Through a drip. It's our decision.'

There was a long silence.

'Aren't you glad? He won't die, Unk. He'll live.'

Uncle Tally's face was inscrutable. He looked at a spot over Fergus's shoulder, at something that lay beyond. 'Glad,' he said tonelessly. Then, 'No wonder your da didn't call in as he promised. I thought maybe something had happened to Joe. But I didn't expect this.'

Fergus frowned, puzzled. 'But—'

'Fergus?'

'What?'

'Don't forget the driving test. Tomorrow afternoon.'

Fergus slapped his forehead. 'Christ. I *had* forgotten.'

'I'll be round tomorrow afternoon, two sharp?'

'OK.'

'Don't be nervous. After the A levels, it's nothing. We'll go over the manoeuvres beforehand, the three-point turns.'

'Right.'

'It'll be a breeze.'

The voices on the radio were laughing, the afternoon light in the bar grew golden. Fergus yawned.

'Want another, Fergus?'

'No. I'd better get back to see if there's news of Joe.'

'Mind how you go, Fergus.'

'Goodbye, Unk.'

Uncle Tally began pouring another glass for himself from behind the old wooden bar. 'Goodbye.'

Walking up the close, Fergus saw the family Austin back in the driveway: Mam was home. The dahlias in the front were brilliant after the rain shower. He let himself in, noticing some mail on the doormat. Mam hadn't seen it: she must have come in round the back. He picked up the envelopes and walked through the kitchen into the garden beyond, and there she was, drinking tea in her flowery dressing gown and suede slippers, looking quietly out towards the mountain. He felt as if he was made of a thousand and one beads in a kaleidoscope, tilting round, dropping into a brand-new pattern every five minutes with every encounter.

'How's Joey doing, Mam?' he asked.

'Oh, Fergus. There you are. He's turned a corner. A definite corner,' she said. Her voice wobbled. He saw what she saw – the anaemic hospital light, the white of the sheets, the wires and tubes and little bleeps.

He stood beside her, a hand on her shoulder. 'Will he be all right? Will he recover?'

Mam's hand found his. 'It's too early to say. We've to wait and see. That's what the doctors say.'

Fifty-two days of fasting. He remembered what he'd read back at the start, courtesy of a gleeful Republican commentator in the *Roscillin Star*:

For the first three days, the body uses up the glucose in the body. Then it uses up the body-fat. After three weeks, it runs out of body-fat. After that the body literally starts to eat itself.

Joe. Is there no end to the consequences?

'We've to hope for the best, Mam.'

She nodded. 'I'm away to bed, Fergus. I'm wrecked.'

'OK, Mam.'

'What are you doing?'

He looked down at the envelope topmost in his hand and saw it was addressed to him. 'Dunno.'

'Don't go running up that mountain, Fergus.'

'Why not?'

'According to the news on the radio, there was an army vehicle blown up near the sentry hut earlier today. Four soldiers died.'

She tilted the rest of her tea onto the lawn and drifted through the kitchen door, waving a weary hand.

The thousand and one beads that made up Fergus McCann swirled red and black. No pattern formed, just chaos. He was back at the bandstand, with the stately air playing. He was scouring the faces and this time Owain was there. His intent, pale face shone down on him. The silver of his trombone was liquid, like mercury. And his lips were speaking and playing at the same time. *'It's a question posed by the music, Fergus,'* he said. *'Being answered, but not as you expected. A feminine ending.'*

'Owain?' he whispered. He peered up at the mountain as if by some miracle of prayer he might make out Owain up there, in the little sentry hut, waving his SLR, but the mountainside stared back, relentless in its emptiness. *This place, Owain. It's the beginning and end of all sorrow.* He opened the topmost envelope without thinking, and his future fell out of it, a B and a B and a B.

Forty-six

It was the first and the last time that I walked at the head of the clan's procession. The rope was ready around my neck. I had on a white shift the women had made especially. Mam's bangle sparkled on my wrist. Hidden in my hand was Rur's knot of hair.

Rur walked behind me, with my family. I could hear Mam's moans. I could hear the footsteps of the townspeople. In Inchquinoag forest I could hear every last leaf, trembling.

Padum, padum, padum, went my heart. It would surely explode and kill me before they did. Padum, padum, it said. I live. I work. I pump. This cannot be. I've a lifetime of beating still to do.

As we came to the place where the view opens up to the head of the lough, they let me stop. My home stretched before me in the dawn shadow. The hills cascaded downwards, embracing their descent. A skylark rose up, brown and small. It climbed its invisible staircase, crooning.

Death is not a reaper, like they say, nor even a friend. It is dark, fierce water, an inundation.

The person holding the rope gave the line between my neck and his hand a flick. I walked up the final stretch of

311

hill. We came to the ordained place. A gallows, hardly higher than myself, had been erected. A block of wood was placed beneath in readiness.

'Do you want a blindfold?' the executioner asked.

'No,' I replied.

The prayer was said, the old prayer. Forgive us for what we have done, and for what we have failed to do. Brennor's voice was loudest. I stepped up onto the block and turned towards them.

The faces were cruel, solemn, pitying, triumphant, sad, anguished. Brennor's face and Rur's face were side by side. One was ashen, the other broken. I foresaw the coming years of violence, the old grudges leapfrogging over generations, re-appearing in different forms.

I smiled down a last time and turned away to the east. Rur, I prayed in my head. Have a care. I felt his breath on my neck. I smelled his smell. The merest rim of the sun nudged up over the mountain.

The metal slid home, fast and free. I took my last breath and let it go, jumping into the next day. Silver light fizzed and shot apart. Love fell in particles, like snow.

Fergus screamed in the darkness, then woke up. He'd a pain in his shoulder blade.

'Mel?' he gasped. The curtains billowed, as if possessed. He doubled up, groaning.

'Owain,' he whispered.

The news he'd seen before coming to bed had revealed the names of the killed, with one Private Owain Jenkins amongst them. He saw the Land Rover coming up the hill, then down, the awful sound of the explosion, and now the cells of Owain's body, scattered over the mountain, breaking down and changing into something else. *The bog claimed a life for a life, so they say,* he remembered Felicity saying when they'd raised Mel from her resting place.

He got out of bed and looked out of the window. Outside was the half-light before dawn. The pebbledash of the wall over the way was grey.

Almost without thinking, he groped for his running shorts and trainers. He'd a need for air, action: anything but the nightmarish pictures in his head.

Out on the close, all was hushed. The only noise was of a streetlamp that blinked crazily, humming. Its bulb was ready to blow, its light pink-tinged. He shivered, picking up pace. His trainers tapped softly along the pavement.

Again he heard the noise of the old-fashioned sash window down at Finicule's being opened. He paused, listening.

The sound wasn't repeated. Uncle Tally, up early again. Or maybe unable to go to sleep.

Softly he ran past the school, up to the end of the tarmacadam. His head was like a slideshow again. Mel's fingertips, with their beautiful spools. Cora's hand, plucking the petals off the withered hydrangea. The little wound in Mel's back. Owain setting his sights on something invisible in the air. The love knot Mel had carried in her hand. Joe's palm pressed to the glass divider. Uncle Tally in the car, looking out to sea. *A reminder of death, Fergus.*

He ran into the Forestry Commission, darting among the trees. He stumbled and fell among the pine cones, picked himself up and broke cover as the crescent moon dangled low in the sky, and the grey in the east turned blue.

When he came to the place where the lough opened up, he stopped. He turned back to look at the view. Ghostly curves cascaded down. The lough was a mere darkness. He deviated off towards the place where Mel was found and at last came to the cut where he'd waited that first day, the day of her discovery, when Uncle Tally had driven off to get the Gardai. He panted. Blood pumped. Then quiet came. Voices from that happy, distant morning wafted over to him on the breeze. *'You could make your own distillery, Unk.'* *'But what would you distil?'* *'The prayers, Unk. What else?'* He sat down on the springy turf, gulping for air. As his breathing slowed, the hum of insects and the small conversations of early birds were audible. There was no sign of the creamy white kid or the sparrowhawk he'd seen that day.

He looked down towards the plain, the place he'd lived all his life. The past rolled out before him. The family trips, the laughs, the squabbles, the afternoons with Uncle Tally. He saw the recent weeks: the packets, exam papers, the counting-off of days as Joe fasted. The condoms and pills, himself and Cora lying like two question marks, and Mel, the laughing, living Mel of his imaginings. And he saw the funeral party around the Sheehans' family plot, the men in balaclavas.

The Provos with the Drumleash slope to their shoulders. The man at the end, who'd reminded him of Joe. And then he knew.

The local bomb-maker, Deus. Thaddeus.

Part of him had known it all along. The smell of Christmas in Uncle Tally's room had been of marzipan, almond-flavoured: the smell of Semtex.

'Don't tell your family, Fergus,' he heard Michael Rafters pleading. 'I don't want the Provos getting on to me.'

At the time he'd thought Rafters meant Joe. But Joe had been unreachable, hardly conscious. He'd meant someone else. Then there was Mam, forever down on Uncle Tally. Now he knew why. Uncle Tally led, and Joe followed. 'Tell Uncle Tally it was all for the best,' Joe had said. It had been a message from comrade to comrade, not rivals in love. He recalled that visitors to Long Kesh were sometimes finger-printed: not a risk Uncle Tally would want to run, and Joe would have understood. There was no Cindy in the case at all.

Uncle Tally, a bomb-maker, in it up to his neck, despite protesting his detachment.

The bottom fell out of Fergus's world. Nothing seemed the way it had been before. He watched the sun rise without seeing. Skylarks began their song without his hearing. Then a cold, weary fury hardened in him.

We sin, Fergus, more by the sin of omission than of commission. It was Felicity again, smiling in the darkness of the back garden with the stars spangled

315

overhead. Then she was standing by the white screen of the slideshow, next to Mel's merry, living face.

The image faded into an empty rectangle of light.

He groaned, picking himself up. He knew he had to speak out, no matter how remote the chances were that he would be listened to. Slowly he ran down the hill, through the Forestry, and back to Drumleash. Every step of the way he worked on the arguments. Uncle Tally, you could have killed an innocent bystander. Uncle Tally, Owain had a life to live, same as you or me. Uncle Tally, violence begets more violence. *Old grudges leapfrog over generations.* The sentences came and went, but all he could see was Uncle Tally's face, implacable.

But when he reached Drumleash, all need for argument was over. At Finicule's, the police had stolen a march on the day. An ambulance flashed, sirens wailed, walkie-talkies crackled. He blinked, breathless, a sharp stitch in his side. The side door to Uncle Tally's bed-sit was wide open. Two constables were posted on either side. He craned his neck, trying to look up the narrow staircase, but saw only darkness.

He spotted an RUC officer he recognized from Roscillin.

'What's going on?' he asked.

'Stand back, stand back. We're taking out the body.'

He heard a kerfuffle on the stairs. 'Mind. It's steep.' 'Keep him steady.' 'Lift at your end.' 'Christ. McCann was heavier than he looked.'

A stretcher appeared, covered over with the

purple blanket Fergus recognized from Uncle Tally's bed. The men bearing the stretcher slid it into the waiting ambulance without delay.

'Jesus. What is this?' Fergus whispered.

The RUC officer said, 'Nothing you won't hear about later.'

'I need to know now,' Fergus pleaded. 'I knew this man.'

Finally the officer told him what had happened. The bomb-disposal experts had found a fingerprint on the device that had killed the soldiers yesterday. The match fitted the print that an undercover agent had taken off a glass a few weeks ago, from a pint of beer poured by one Thaddeus McCann. And that same Thaddeus McCann, would you believe it, had been shot dead while resisting arrest.

Forty-seven

The funeral under the great Scots pine was a quiet affair. Even the Provos' final salute seemed muted. After it was over, the people of Drumleash dispersed in silence. Mam and the girls put on a spread back at the bungalow, but only the Sheehans and the Caseys came. They just had the one sandwich and went home. Of Harry, the publican of Finicule's, where Uncle Tally had lived and worked down the years, there was no sign. People said he'd gone to ground, others that he'd fled the country under a new identity.

Three weeks later, Fergus loaded his rucksack into the boot of the Austin Maxi. Mam gave Theresa instructions for getting the tea. Da looked up from the *Roscillin Star* and smiled sadly.

'Fergus,' he said. 'So you're leaving us?'

'Yes.'

'It's what your Uncle Tally always wanted for you. We'd two boys, a soldier and a student. He promised us never to say a word to you. And he kept that promise.' Da's eyes filmed up. 'Tally never kept a gun in his room at Finicule's. I want you to remember that, Fergus.'

'I know, Da. You keep saying. And I'll remember.'

Da put a twenty-pound note in his hand and turned away. Theresa and Cath stood waiting to say goodbye at the front door. Cath gave him a collage she'd made on a page of A4. Dalmatian dog spots danced all over it. She'd cut them out from Joe's old coverlet that Mam said was worn out and only good for dusters. She'd glued scrunched-up bubblegum wrappers amongst them.

'What's it supposed to be?' Fergus said.

'It's the skin of a patient. Somebody with the plague *and* chicken pox.'

'God help them. And God help me.'

Theresa said she'd no card, only some advice.

'What's that?'

'Be prepared.'

'Be prepared for what?'

Theresa leaned forward and whispered in his ear, 'I saw the condoms. In your bedroom.'

'You little snoop—'

'I know all about it.'

Fergus stared, then laughed and put a finger to his lips. 'You're wise beyond your years, Theresa McCann.'

'I know. Good luck, Dr McCann.'

Fergus got behind the wheel of the Maxi while Mam put the learner plates up. He groaned. Uncle Tally's death had meant he'd missed the chance to take his test and now he'd to wait until the Christmas holidays. He backed out of the drive as the girls waved frantically, hooted the horn and drove off down the close. Mam and he said little as they crossed the rolling plains and hills of the North. They came at last to Antrim and to Larne and descended into the brightly lit harbour. Fergus pulled up on the dockside, close to where the ferry boat was moored. He hefted the rucksack onto his back and together they walked over to the departure point.

'Have you everything?' Mam fretted. 'The cake, the papers, the directions?'

'Yes. Everything.'

'Because all I can see from here are those.' Mam shook the new trainers that dangled down, knotted to the drawstring at the top of the rucksack. He'd bought them with the money from Rafters' 'operation'. 'Watch they don't come loose.' They were top-of-the-range, springy, with pumas racing off the edges.

Fergus smiled. 'They're safe enough.'

They came to the barrier where he had to go through and she couldn't. She'd her lips between her teeth. Her eyes glistened. Her sunglasses sat on her head and he'd never seen her look so happy or so sad. 'Oh, Fergus. They'll make a fine doctor of you.'

She pulled him into a rough hug. Eighteen years of scoldings, nudgings, goadings, praisings and teasings were in it. 'What will I do without you?'

'You've Theresa trained up now, Mam,' he said.

'Get along with you.' She released him from her arms.

He was about to go when he thought of something. 'Mam?'

'What?'

He rolled up his sleeve and took off Joe's watch. 'Take this.'

'Why give that to me? Didn't Joe give it to you to mind?'

'I don't want to risk losing it, Mam. It said in the brochure to keep valuables to a minimum in the halls of residence. Besides . . .'

'Besides what?'

'I reckon they'll let Joe out soon. Early.'

'D'you really think so?'

'Yes.'

Mam took the watch and put it on her own wrist, smiling. 'He's coming along grand, the doctors say. Maybe he'll even be right as rain.'

Fergus suppressed a shrug. What he'd seen of Joe was hardly grand. 'He's definitely improved,' he said. He gave Mam a final hug. 'You've one son going and another returning.' He quickly went through the gate, showing his ticket.

'I'll be waving from the car,' Mam called.

Fergus turned. 'See you at Christmas,' he called back.

He was down the ramp and up the steps to the top deck in a few minutes. He went to the boat's starboard and found a space by the railing. There was the old Maxi, and Mam beside it, her trouser suit a neat navy and her hair let loose. She waved the giant pot of Marmite she'd bought for him at the last minute but forgot to add to his rucksack, where there was no room anyway. He opened his two hands, grinning, and the funnel gave its boom of departure. Imperceptibly, the boat moved. He grabbed the rail and waved. Mam leaned on the bonnet, waving, smiling, and although he couldn't see from so far away, he knew that she was crying. She was saying something that he couldn't make out. Perhaps it was *Study hard*, or *Write often*, or maybe, *Don't forget to go to mass*. He nodded and the boat pulled away. A rope unspooled. The gap between the boat's flank and the massive rubber tyres of the dockside turned from a foot to a man's length, then a tennis court. Still Mam waved. He threw his arms wide as if sending a last hug over the water, and the boat began turning. Mam stood up and opened the car door, blowing a kiss. He watched the coast slip away. Larne retreated, as he'd imagined it the day of Lennie Sheehan's funeral, then Antrim, then the five other counties in all their throes. The summer of the bog child was over. Mel's living, laughing face, as drawn by Cora, now framed and in his rucksack, would go with him wherever he went. But the old Fergus of that time would never return. Cells would die and be born. New places and faces would jostle with the old. Letters would go back and forth bringing news and conversation. The Fergus who'd return at Christmas would already be different. He'd years of the changing to come. The studying, the books, exams, arguments, theories. The jokes and pints, laughter, kisses and songs. Life was like running, ninety per cent sweat and toil, ten per cent joy. The small figure of his mam got back into the car. Soon, the Maxi flashed silver and brown as it climbed back up the hill. He turned away and walked across the deck to the other side.

Author's note

In 1981, several members of the Provisional IRA and of the Irish National Liberation Army in prison in Long Kesh, also known as HMP Maze, went on a hunger strike in an effort to persuade the British authorities that they should be accorded Special Category status as political prisoners. Ten men actually starved themselves to death. By the summer of 1981, partly as a result of an intervention by Prison Chaplain Father Faul, some of the families gave permission for their sons to be removed while unconscious to hospital beds, where they could be drip-fed. Others decided not to intervene. The strike finally ended in October 1981. Some of the demands of the hunger strikers were subsequently met.

In my story, the hunger strikers Joe McCann and Lennie Sheehan are entirely fictional, as are all the other characters.

Acknowledgements

I would like to thank my beloved friend Helen Graves, who sifted through the final MS with deftness and aplomb. Dr Conor Carville lent me his acute Northern Ireland ear. I would also like to thank my publisher David Fickling for his inspirational belief from the outset in this story and, as ever, Bella Pearson, Annie Eaton, Kelly Hurst and Sophie Nelson for their invaluable input. The story's first reader was Hilary Delamere, my agent, and as ever she held the ball of wool steady while I walked into the labyrinth.

I also owe a massive debt to BBC/Open University's *Timewatch* for its inspirational programme on recent discoveries of bog people in Ireland and to the classic *The Bog People: Iron-Age Man Preserved* (Faber and Faber Ltd, 1969) by P. V. Glob. Maximum thanks are also due to Yoko Ono and the estate of John Lennon for the use of Lennon's song lyrics from *Imagine:* indeed, all the songs from this album provided a mesmerizing soundtrack while I worked.

Finally, I would like to thank my husband Geoff Morgan for lending me his old physics A-level exercise book and cheering me along every step of the way.

Copyright Acknowledgements